For Shelley

I0642615

Copyright © 2024 by M. C. Harwell
Published by arrangement with
Advanced Concept Design
ACD Books
ISBN13   978-1-965535-00-4

For Information, address
markcharwell@gmail.com

Printed in the United States of America
First E-print 8/18/24
First Paperback printing September 2024

Foul Pray

by M.C. Harwell

Chapter I

Eutychus's scream echoed among the tall Scots pines, piercing the morning fog's shroud.

My jittery nerves raised gooseflesh, my gaze skittering left and right in search of my wicked friend. Abbot Mutter had forbidden us to venture into the ancient woods a mile beyond the walls of our cloistered monastery. "Full of thieves and cutthroats, Picts and Scots," he had told us. And now I trembled, sure that God's scolding finger had found me, his wrath at hand.

The lichen-covered trees stood silent, a deep palisade of wooden sentinels harboring the ghosts and woodland devils of my forefathers. I crouched among the ferns, frightened that wraiths on white chargers might plow through the hanging mists and impale me.

"Clodius …" Eutychus moaned, his voice weak and loaded with pain.

Eutychus had raced me to the shadowy woods where a placid lake awaited. Though we worked the same fields dawn-to-dusk and ate the same meager rations, my shorter legs and heavier bones slowed me. I could never catch him in a sprint.

"Clodius … help me … a snake bit me."

My gaze shot to my sandals. Every desiccated oak leaf's tip piercing the mat of tangled pine straw became a viper's pointed snout. I genuflected. God forgive me! I just wanted to swim!

"Here … I'm over here."

Feathery stalks rustled thirty paces to my left. Curled fingers and pale skin feebly pushed above the green foliage. I caught my breath, arresting my frightened panting, rebuking my shameless quivering. Eutychus needed my help. I tromped a path through the groundcover, scanning every leaf

1

and shadow for any sign of the serpent.

Eutychus lay on his back, the sleeves of his undyed woolen habit had fallen back to his elbows, his tousled black hair was tangled with pine needles and dead leaves. His eyelids fluttered open, his blue eyes pleading. "My left calf. It's on fire."

I knelt beside him. "I'm here." I gasped. A crimson trail trickled down the contours of his lower leg. Blood oozed from two bright red pinpricks just beneath his left shin bone. I crossed my chest a second time to ward off evil spirits that lingered near the wound. "Can you walk?"

My friend shifted his leg. His face contorted with pain. "I don't know."

"Brother Finnian will know what to do. We must get to the infirmary. I'll help you up." I dug my hands beneath his arms, pulled him into a sitting position, then wrapped his left arm around my neck and shoulders. "Lean on me. Try not to push with your left leg. Come on. Up with you."

Eutychus gritted his teeth. "I can't walk. We'll never make it. Maybe you should run for help."

If I ran there and back precious time would expire. The route crossed more than a mile of Northern Britannia's hills and dales, low pasture walls, and a shallow brook before reaching the rutted trail leading to St. Antony's. Every heartbeat drew the venom deeper within Eutychus's flesh. "Get on my back." I said and bent at my waist. I lifted his feet from the earth and wrapped my arms around his thighs. He leaned upon my shoulders, locking his hands about my chest. My knees buckled under his weight. I drew a sharp breath and steadied my legs. I stepped forward, right foot first to ward away bad luck, and silently asked God to strengthen my muscles. My next step froze mid-stride.

Beneath the withered fronds of a fountain-like fern, shiny basilisk eyes peered from the darkness. Fangs glimmered. A muscular coil of camouflaged armor poised ready to spring.

Lightning shot through my arteries. My brain said scream, my legs said run, but my body turned to stone. I held

2

my breath, afraid to even blink. My eyes began to burn. My chest heaved; my lungs starved for air. Only my innards stirred, wrenching and squirming, a fetid slurry streaming down my thighs, stinging my skin.

The big snake lifted its head higher, rising nearer to my legs. A forked tongue flitted from its mouth, in and out, in and out. The beast sensed me.

A panicked prayer escaped my lips. A lifetime of sins flashed through my mind—disgust of my mother, thieving, lying, my yearnings for her, the girl in the market—a sordid heap of evil bound for damnation. God have mercy!

Eutychus whispered, "Set me down."

A force beyond my will seized me. A spasm released my grip. Eutychus slid from my back, his feet softly touching the earth. He slowly squatted, reaching with one hand to the ground. Then swift as the flap of a bird's wing, his arm blurred. A round stone smashed into the serpent. Its head and two coiled loops flopped backward into the fern's stalks. The remainder of its body followed, rapidly unwinding, slithering into the underbrush.

I sucked air into my burning lungs. Slowly, my mind cleared, realizing I would not die. My breathing returned to normal. A warm wetness made my thighs clammy. My grungy, yellowed linen tunic beneath my habit clung to my rear. My nose twitched, catching a putrid odor.

Eutychus's nose crinkled. He pinched his nostrils. "Eyew! What's that smell?"

I lowered my left foot to the turf, spreading my legs wide. The stinging in my rectum had drooled to my knees.

Eutychus shirked away, hopping on his one good leg. "I always thought it was just a vulgar figure of speech."

I had escaped a deadly horror only to land into a stinking pit of shame. Eutychus would never let me forget this humiliation. My body shuddered, cold sweat dripping down my face. I feared snakes more than the devil. Now the whole world would know of my fearfulness.

My cheeks burned, but I set aside my embarrassment and

bent lower, keeping my knees far apart. "Come on. Climb on my back. Before the venom takes hold."

"Not me! I'll gag to death before we reach home. Go wash in the lake."

I'd been so flustered the obvious answer had not dawned on me. I jerked a nod and shambled to the water's edge. I hesitated, remembering that a slimy creature remained hidden. I scanned the water. My thick red hair and green eyes reflected in the calm pool. My cheeks' freckles looked like tears, my pale skin the jaundiced tint of cowardice.

Eutychus guffawed. "Don't worry. Snakes don't swim." He shrugged. "At least I've never actually seen one swimming."

His words did little to calm my trepidation, but the wetness clinging to my buttocks had cooled. My legs shivered. Snake or not, I plunged forward, plowing waist deep into the frigid water, washing the evidence of my fears clean. I swam deeper with broad, sweeping strokes, relishing the currents swirling through my body's creases, the drenched wool of my robe flapping against my goose-pimpled skin. I arched my back and kicked. My head splashed above the surface.

My companion smiled, watching me from the water's edge. My pride partially restored, I kicked forward, reaching with an overhead stroke when my dripping eyes glimpsed a hairy form floating upon the surface, trapped beneath a grayed tree trunk that had tilted into the lake, its gnarled roots ripped from the shoreline. Blinking hard, trying to clear my sight, with water choking me, I splashed back to the shore. My feet touched mud. I clambered out of the water and fell face first to dry earth, gasping for breath.

Eutychus laughed. "What'd you see this time, a sea monster?"

I stabbed my finger at the fallen tree. "There's a body!"

His laughter stopped. His face turned pale. He hopped to the shoreline and peered over the side of the fallen gray trunk.

I threw off my habit. I shivered uncontrollably. Wearing only my linen tunic, I climbed over the tree and dropped back into the lake. Water swallowed me to my neck. The body, covered with a russet monk's habit, floated face down, wedged beneath a limb. I hesitated, prayed to God to shield me from death's evil spirits, then pried the corpse's shoulder free of the dead wood. I lifted beneath the armpits. Eutychus grabbed the collar and tugged, lifting the deadweight over the trunk to the muddy bank.

I splashed back to the shore.

Eutychus stood motionless, still favoring his wounded leg, staring at the corpse's back.

I knelt, grabbed two handfuls of soaked wool and rolled the body over.

Brother Adalbert's wide dead eyes stared blankly into space; his jaw locked open in a silent, terrified scream.

Chapter II

Eutychus and I stood rigid, like the old Roman statues. My shock cleared before my companion's, our forgotten crisis bursting through my paralysis. We must act quickly, or else the monks would be digging two new graves.

I wrung the water from my drenched habit, pulled it over my head, and turned my back to Eutychus. "Climb on. There's nothing we can do for Adalbert. Hurry!"

Eutychus's eyes glistened, his gaze focused on Adalbert's corpse. I pulled at his limp arm. His head jerked, eyelids narrowed, teeth bared. Would he lunge at me? Confusion joined my emotional morass; but his features softened just as swiftly, calming my alarm. He wiped his cheeks with the back of his hand, lowered his gaze, and hobbled to my rear. I bent lower, and he hopped to my back. My hands secured to his legs, I drew a deep breath and stepped right foot first, hoping for a happier result this time.

We exited the woods to a gently sloping green pasture, the tall grass sprinkled with yellow daffodils, their sweet scent suspended in the mist. The clear water of a shallow stream, splashing over rounded stones, babbled at the foot of the hillock. The spring-fed pool at the stream's source had tempted Eutychus to disregard Abbot Mutter's warning. Spring's warming winds made the frigid water tolerable. He'd goaded me until I had once again agreed to join him, perhaps explaining why the viper had selected him for punishment, his temptation being the greater sin, though I, like Adam, could hardly claim innocence.

I sloshed through the fast-running water. Almost falling upon a slimy stone, I stutter-stepped, restoring my balance without dropping my charge, who had grown ominously quiet. His arms remained firmly wrapped across my chest, a reassurance that he had not died. Quickening my pace, reaching dry ground, my breathing labored but steady, I hustled up the opposing hillside, ignoring the burning in my thighs.

6

All the while that I ran, my head churned with dreadful images. Abbot Mutter's piercing gray eyes glared down his crooked nose, his wrinkled lips arched high. Prior Tomas's angry, dark stare joined the vision, his accusing finger trembling with rage. Shame flooded into my spirit. The ominous specters loomed, judging me, pitying me, and promising retribution. In just a few heartbeats my life had changed from a naughty swim with my best friend to utter calamity. Eutychus dying, Adalbert's corpse rotting, no lie I could spin would hide the truth.

At the top of the hill, the monks' compound came into view, at least a half mile farther, bordered on its eastern edge by rectangular fields of green barley, hops, and wheat and the straight rows of an apple orchard.

"We're close," I said, huffing and puffing.

Eutychus did not respond, though he tightened his forearm muscles.

I continued down the hill, gaining speed to the point I feared tumbling. The turf leveled at the base, saving me from falling, but the weight on my back suddenly doubled. I stopped at the edge of a crumbling pasture wall, hefted Eutychus higher on my back with a bounce, and side-stepped over the lowest point to the Roman road on its other side. Weeds and bramble bushes sprouted from great divots left by the locals who had pilfered the paving to build their walls and houses. The treacherous footing slowed me to a cautious walk. My lungs welcomed the breather. My confidence buoyed as my feet landed on the dirt trail leading to the monastery's front gate. Though scarred with deep ruts trenched by carts, the center of the trail remained level, except for the occasional stone outcropping revealed by wind and rain.

As I neared the gate, tonsured heads popped above the green stalks of grain; sunburned faces turned. Shouts followed the beat of wooden sandals stomping packed earth. Before my arrival at the gate, two monks reached me, their hands lifting the burden from my shoulders.

"What happened?" Brother Michael stammered, wiping away the sweat dripping from his forehead into his only good eye.

I bent double, clutching my knees. "Snake … bit by … a snake."

Brother Silvanius, a strong, skinny man nearer my nineteen years than the other monks, cradled Eutychus at his chest. "Michael, run ahead to find Brother Finnian. I'll take Eutychus to the infirmary."

Michael sprinted through the open main gate and disappeared behind the wall. Silvanius trailed him, hustling with long, urgent strides. I stumbled along behind. More monks ran to join us. By the time we reached the infirmary, a dozen shaved heads crowded around. Silvanius gently lay Eutychus on a straw-stuffed mattress.

Brother Finnian, the infirmarian, pushed through the crowd, his head the shape of a blunt-edged rectangle, as much chin as forehead. He made the sign of the cross at his chest, then knelt to examine Eutychus's calf. He pulled the habit above his patient's knee, revealing burning red flesh, swollen to more than double its normal size.

"Lord help us," he said.

"It was an adder," I said.

Finnian squinted and stroked his broad chin. "Where did this happen?"

My throat constricted. I thought to lie but resisted Satan's urge. My sweaty face must have flushed a darker red, because Finnian's eyelids narrowed, his blue eyes fixed on me with a well-earned suspicion.

My head sank into my shoulders. "In the woods. Near the lake."

Finnian's lips twisted into a frown. His gaze shifted back to Eutychus's leg. "Then most likely poisonous." He extended his hand to Eutychus's face, clamping his fingers on my friend's jaw, then shaking gently. "Can you hear me, boy?"

Eutychus's eyes remained shut. He groaned in an

incomprehensible delirium.

Finnian's thick lips stretched tight. He jerked his hand away from Eutychus's chin. His fingers spread wide and froze. "There's more than just poison at work here."

I swallowed hard and stammered. "B-brother Adalbert. We found his body."

A muffled, collective gasp rippled through the other monks. Finnian's blue eyes shot wide. "Adalbert? Dead? How?"

"I found him floating when I swam. After the snake bit Eutychus. We didn't have time to examine—"

Finnian's eyebrows cocked high. "Eutychus wounded, and you went for a swim!"

I dropped my gaze to the stone floor. I couldn't escape the heat of his stare. A hush swept across the gathering, the judgment in the other men's faces so palpable my shoulders sagged like a massive millstone had lowered upon my neck. But the odoriferous truth embarrassed me more than their accusation. My lips clamped tightly.

Finnian scowled and turned his attention back to Eutychus. "Madness—the both of you. Let's hope some nefarious spirit hasn't entered his wound as you dallied. We must cut the skin to drain the poison and balance the humors." He turned to the faces staring at him. "Michael, fetch Malthius and the abbot. Tell Malthius to bring his razor."

Michael ran off without a word.

The invisible weight bending my back doubled. So far, I had avoided Abbot Mutter. I dreaded the inevitable confrontation. My gaze shifted to Eutychus, still delirious, his body shivering despite the warmth of the room. I envied his distress. He might be spared punishment if he lived. I, on the other hand, was both healthy and guilty.

As I contemplated my bleak future, Brother Malthius arrived, blade in hand. He had a beaked nose and large, round, brown eyes that looked ready to pop from their sockets. The brothers parted to give him access to the bed.

9

He bent to scrutinize the wound, then spat on the blade and wiped both edges clean on the left sleeve of his garment. He used the same knife to shave faces. "This won't take long," he said. He lowered the razor to Eutychus's calf. His hand moved sharply with a practiced stroke, slicing through the puncture wounds. New blood dripped down the patient's leg. Finnian placed a wooden bowl beneath the wound to catch the flow.

"Brothers, your prayers would be of more use than your gawking," Abbot Mutter said.

Heads bowed and feet shuffled as the onlookers sheepishly vacated the infirmary. I slunk among them, hoping to join their retreat and avoid the abbot's gaze.

"Not you, Clodius," he said.

I gulped, my bowels wanting to empty sluicing worms.

Abbot Mutter calmly stepped to the edge of the bed. The ring of gray hair about his head matched the color of his probing eyes. "Are you certain it's an adder's bite?" he asked Finnian.

The infirmarian nodded. "It explains the swelling. We may need to remove the infected limb."

Eutychus's leg jerked with a spasm. He released a half-conscious, protesting groan.

"That should not be necessary," the abbot said. "Ah, here is Brother Michael now."

Michael crossed the threshold of the stone-walled infirmary, clutching a thick, leather-bound volume at his chest. He rushed to the abbot and handed him the book. Mutter opened the cover and lifted the book's bottom edge to his eye level. He turned through several pages, inspecting each, not appearing to read the words but rather inspecting the surface of each sheet.

"Humph," he grunted and tapped his finger on a selected page. He turned back to Michael. "Hold it open for me." He handed the volume to Michael, then extended his hand to Brother Malthius, who like me, gazed wide-eyed at the abbot. "Your razor, please."

Malthius wiped the bloody blade on his sleeve and offered the knife. Mutter gripped the top edge of the blade with his right hand, then lightly scraped across the top of the dense handwriting covering the page. "This is Bishop Patrick's Psalter, copied with his own hand while teaching in Armagh."

My jaw dropped. I knew the power of holy relics but had never witnessed a miracle. I leaned closer, eager to see the supernatural unfold, briefly forgetting my transgressions.

Abbot Mutter collected the almost invisible shavings in his cupped left hand. "There are no snakes in Hibernia. The grass and weeds are poisonous to them." He handed the blade back to the barber. "A cup of water," he said.

Malthius nodded and stepped away. He returned with a wooden cup. The abbot brushed the contents of his palm into the water, then stirred with his right forefinger. He handed the mixture to Brother Finnian. His gaze fell upon me. His lips screwed tightly, his left eyebrow arching. He shook his head, and his lips spread with a wry smile. "It's not a miracle," he said. "It's simple science. The pollen collects on pages written in Hibernia, adhering to the wet ink. It retains its potency. It not only kills serpents, but it is also an antidote against their venom. Give the boy the potion twice a day until the swelling stops. He'll recover."

My excitement faded, but the abbot's profound grasp of nature awed me. Facts and circumstances that seemed random and unrelated had been harnessed by his divine insight into a life-saving tonic. Ah, to someday command such blessed wisdom.

Finnian lifted Eutychus's head and held the cup to his lips. My friend swallowed it with difficulty. My anxiety diminished with each of his gulps.

"Brother Michael tells me you went to the forest." The dim light filtering through the infirmary's small windows etched deep shadows across the abbot's forehead.

My shame returned. "Yes, Father."

"You found Brother Adalbert dead?"

"Yes, Father."

He wagged his bony finger at me. "Snakes are not the worst that can happen to you, Clodius. The woods are filled with far greater dangers. You and Eutychus might have easily shared Brother Adalbert's fate."

I lowered my chin to my chest. He was wrong of course. Snakes were the very worst thing that could happen. "Yes, Father."

"God has punished Eutychus and spared you only so that he should not perish. Don't think you will escape God's wrath." He turned to Michael. "Brother Michael, after you return the book to my library gather a helper. Clodius will tell you where to find Brother Adalbert's body. If the snake is still there, kill it. We mustn't leave vipers to terrorize our flock. But if you see any signs of trouble, come back immediately and return before dusk in any event."

The abbot laid a heavy hand on my shoulder. "Your robe is damp. Change your clothes then report to Prior Tomas. He'll decide what corporal punishment is warranted. When he's done, come to my office. I'll determine the appropriate penance."

Chapter III

My feet seemed leaden as I trudged toward the storeroom in the main house. The infirmary opened to a peristyle, a rectangular colonnade surrounding the inner garden, the largest open area within the villa. The garden had two rows of rose bushes and a dry, broken fountain in the center.

I crossed the garden and walked to the west end of the house, passing through a double archway and into the atrium located at the house's front entrance. The atrium had an open tiled roof through which rain fell and collected in a stone basin surrounding a six-foot limestone cross. Doors to the right led to the kitchen and to the left to storage rooms where we kept robes produced on our looms, egg-sized blue balls of woad, red madder, and yellow welk, which we used for dyes and paint, and sealed ceramic bottles with wicker bases containing our precious sacramental wine.

I shuffled into the storage room and found a clean and dry undyed habit folded and stacked on a shelf. Novices wore undyed cloth. If the brotherhood accepted me, I would receive a new russet habit at consecration.

A shiver coursed up my back. I pulled the damp cloth of my robe and tunic over my head and tossed them to the floor. Pushing my head through the top of the new robe, the fresh smell cheered my spirit, and the dry cloth warmed my body. My nose awakened to the sour odor of my old clothes. Gathering them from the floor, I carried them to the kitchen door and tossed them to the pile of dirty linens that would be washed and cleaned by the novices on laundry duty.

When I turned around, Michael and Gunther, a hulking blond, faced me. Michael explained he had recruited Gunther for their snake hunt and to retrieve Adalbert's corpse. They presented a well-armed host. Michael carried a hoe and Gunther a sickle. If they encountered a hole needing digging or a field requiring harvesting, they were well prepared. Even a snake might give a second thought before attacking them. If they found trouble of a different sort, however, they would be almost defenseless.

I explained where Eutychus and I had left Adalbert. I couldn't tell if Michael understood my directions. He had lost vision in his left eye to a ram's horn as a child. The injury left him with a milky white glaze over his pupil. The same animal had punctured his right cheek, leaving a dimpled scar. His disfigurement and sporadic tics made it difficult to read his thoughts.

Gunther slapped his palm to his shaved bald spot and shook his head. "What in God's good name was Brother Adalbert doing out there?"

I sheepishly rolled my shoulders. "Eutychus and I went to swim."

Michael grimaced. "Adalbert wasn't much of a swimmer. Was he clothed?"

I nodded. "Robe, tunic, and sandals."

Gunther grunted. "Then he wasn't swimming."

Michael cocked his head. His tanned cheek twitched. "Did you see any wound?"

I shook my head. "We didn't have time to look. I assumed he'd run afoul of another snake."

Michael scratched the back of his brown hair. "That doesn't make sense. Even if he fell into the lake, the venom does not act quickly. He would have had the time and strength to climb ashore and seek help."

"No use speculating," Gunther said. He swatted a fly biting his muscular arm. "Come on. We'll know soon enough."

The men exited the villa, Gunther taking the lead though Michael outranked him by several years. I pivoted to look for the prior in his office at the rear of the villa when his deep voice stopped me dead.

"Clodius."

I turned to the voice. Prior Tomas's tall, lean figure blocked the afternoon light at the atrium's entrance, throwing a shadow over me.

"Clodius, Clodius, Clodius, what mischievous spirit has

possessed you, my son?" He stepped through the doorway, his shadow yielding to the sun's orange glow filling the room.

I bowed my head, looking at his sandals. "I'm sorry, Prior. I've disobeyed the abbot."

Tomas smiled and brushed his jet-black hair from his forehead. "Sorrier that you were caught than that you were disobedient, I'll wager."

His jest confused me. I held my bow and my silence. Tomas was second-in-command of the monastery, responsible for managing our day-to-day operations. Abbot Mutter provided our spiritual guidance. The prior organized labor and enforced regulations. He'd never struck me as a man with a sense of humor.

Tomas's curled knuckle touched the bottom of my chin. He lifted my gaze to his. "The winter was long and cold. Spring's warmth is inviting. I understand. But it's not an excuse to disregard the rules."

"I know, Father."

"Do you, Clodius? Really?"

"Yes, Father."

"Then explain why the abbot has forbidden the novices to go to the woods and the lake."

I paused, carefully considering the best answer. "Because it is dangerous, Father."

"Dangerous? How so? Don't you know how to swim?"

I bit my lower lip. "The abbot doesn't fear our drowning. The woods are full of brigands. He fears we will be assaulted, or worse."

Tomas grinned. "Just so, Clodius. And it's not all about you. We've dispatched two men to bring Brother Adalbert's body home. What happens if they encounter the same misfortune that befell Adalbert?"

My heavy head retreated farther into my shoulders.

"That's right, Clodius. If you disobey and are harmed, you place others in jeopardy. We'd come for you no matter the hazard."

"I'm sorry, Prior. I never considered that."

"That's why we have rules. It's why we follow orders. Discipline and obedience are critical to our survival. How long do you think an army would last if a soldier could not count on the man beside him?"

"Not very long," I said.

"And we are no different. Do you understand?"

"Yes, Father."

"Good." Tomas stepped backward and folded his soft hands behind him. He turned to leave.

Had I escaped with mere castigation? No caning? No stocks? No extra labor? I couldn't believe my good fortune.

Tomas spun back. "But we must ensure this lesson is well-learned."

I gulped.

"For starters, you will dig Brother Adalbert's grave. I don't suppose Eutychus is fit enough to be of any use, so find Fritigern and Olaf to help you. It won't hurt for the other novices to share in these lessons. I'll meet you in the cemetery to lay out the site."

"Yes, Prior."

"For the next week you will have kitchen duty for every meal, laundry and latrine duty every day, and except for when your chores require otherwise, you are confined to the monastery and the fields."

"Yes, Prior."

"Don't disappoint me again, Clodius. Next time I won't be as lenient."

Mustering my utmost contrition, I responded, "Yes, Father," but the emotions of my heart did not match the words from my lips for I saw the punishment as the cost of my disobedience, not a remedy. While the abbot and prior could be placated by my pretended penitence, God could not be so easily deceived. A nervous tingle flowed down my neck. *What form would His retribution take?*

Chapter IV

I left the house in search of Olaf and Fritigern, relieved that I'd dodged a beating. The week would pass soon enough. The extra chores were a nuisance, but truth told, normal life differed little from confinement. Anyway, Eutychus and I wouldn't be sneaking away for a swim anytime soon; after finding a snake and a corpse, I'd resolved that unaided by Prior Tomas's tongue-lashing. I still must face whatever penance the abbot would mete out, but despite my best efforts to show remorse, I could not suppress the grin creeping to the corners of my mouth.

The complex retained its original Roman layout with a walled villa, a caldarium, a stable, and a slaves' compound. A graveyard, church, and brewery had been added by the first monks to inhabit St. Antony's and the slave quarters had been converted to a dormitory. They had also removed all vestiges of the prior owners' pagan worship.

Fritigern slouched on a wooden bench at the center of the herb garden near the church's front entrance. Brother Lucius, our corpulent cantor, sat closely beside him, their eyes shut, heads bowed, Lucius's pudgy fingers folded over Fritigern's brawny hands. The cantor mouthed words, but my distance prevented me from hearing their prayer.

Piety and reverence were, of course, admirable traits, but I rolled my eyes and frowned. Fritigern's bootlicking never ceased to make my skin crawl. Among the four novices, only Fritigern had voluntarily joined the monastery. His constant eagerness to please the monks, especially those with rank, made him a shining gem among our paltry assembly. Eutychus called him Doeskin, though we kept the cognomen our secret. A thick black hair covered his body, so coarse and tough that Brother Malthius had to shave him daily and griped that the novice's black whiskers chipped the sharp edge of his razor. But the nickname mocked his constant fawning more than his plentiful fur. He was bucking to someday replace the prior, then the abbot, and he even spoke of bishops as if he shared some common birthright.

The flap of my wooden sandals alerted them to my approach. They turned, their eyes bleary and red. Fritigern wiped his tears away, and his furry lids narrowed. "What do you want? Can't you see we're praying?" His burly chest puffed, and his thick arms reared like a plumed cockerel readying to fight.

Brother Lucius patted Fritigern's knee. "There, there, my child. Love thy neighbor. Clodius has had a difficult day. The Lord calls us to forgiveness and mercy." He smiled, creasing his roseate cheeks. "You look a man on a mission, my son. How can we help you?"

"Prior Tomas ordered me to fetch Fritigern and Olaf. We must dig a grave."

Lucius's wispy eyebrows arched, and he grimaced as if he felt an instant of pain. "Of course … for Brother Adalbert. Fritigern, you must help Clodius."

"It's … it's an honor," Fritigern said. He stood straight.

I shrugged. "Don't get too excited. Gravedigging is part of my punishment. Eutychus would be sharing the job except that he's on his back in the infirmary. The prior drafted you and Olaf instead."

Fritigern glared at me, his blue eyes challenging. "How typical. Every time you two are up to no good the rest of us get stuck with the dirty work. But this once I won't complain. Adalbert deserves much better than your sinful hands to prepare his final resting place."

I returned his stare. "Don't think I look forward to being shoulder-to-shoulder with you digging a six-foot hole."

Brother Lucius jumped to his feet. "Boys, you mustn't quarrel. This is a time for mourning. Everyone is hurting in their own way. What one counts as suffering is to another reckoned a blessing. We each do our part in the service of the Lord. Now away, both of you. Holes don't dig themselves. I saw Olaf near the stables. You should find him there."

We sauntered to the dilapidated barn. The former Roman occupants of the estate would have kept their chariot horses there, with a team of slaves to clean the barn and groom the animals. We had only one ox who pulled a plow for planting and drew a wagon on market days. Novices substituted for the slaves.

Skinny Olaf handled a pitchfork, spreading clean hay in an empty stall. His fair skin and blond hair betrayed his northern barbarian lineage. He stopped his work, his bright blue eyes filled with angst. "How's Eutychus?"

My head still boiled with resentment for the obnoxious, hairy novice walking beside me. Olaf's question caught me off-balance. I'd been so wrapped in self-pity and anger I'd all but forgotten that my best friend lay near death. A pulse of guilt soured my mouth. "He—he's still in the infirmary. His leg looks pretty bad."

Olaf's pink lips sagged and quivered. He'd yet to sprout whiskers, and his voice retained a prepubescent pitch. "Oh …"

I forced a smile. "The abbot's given him a tonic. He says Eutychus will heal quickly."

Olaf's narrow face cheered. "Is it okay if I visit him?"

"Sure, though you might wait until tomorrow. He's feverish right now. I doubt he'd know you're there."

Fritigern huffed loudly. "It's not Eutychus who needs your attention. Prior Tomas orders us to dig Brother Adalbert's grave. If you don't like it, you can thank your sinful, convalescing friend for the extra chore."

Olaf leaned the pitchfork against the stall's wooden wall. "I don't mind. Not if it helps Eutychus."

I led our group to the toolshed. My companions grabbed shovels. I lifted a pickax in addition to a shovel knowing that we'd be certain to hit stones in our digging. We trudged to the east side of our compound, finding Prior Tomas with half-mad Brother Lazarus waiting for us in the small, grass-covered graveyard outside the wall. Tomas faced Lazarus with his hands on his shoulders. Lazarus's head bobbed in obedience to whatever the prior told him. Their faces turned to us at our approach. Tomas squeezed, then released

19

Lazarus's upper arm. The slouching monk showed a crooked leer with missing teeth, then turned away from us and hustled with an awkward gait back toward the church.

Two stone crosses marked the graves of the previous abbots. The remainder of the dozen wooden crosses in the small cemetery displayed the names of the departed, painted or shallowly etched. Our chores included maintaining the cemetery and replacing the wooden monuments from time to time as they decayed.

The prior asked for my shovel and jabbed the ground, marking the corners of the gravesite. He handed the tool back and retreated to a stone bench to watch us dig.

Sweating profusely, we vigorously set about the task. Olaf, the youngest, though no one knew his age for sure, struggled the most. He had small hands and a slight frame. Fritigern made up the difference, spading big chunks of dirt with each thrust of his burly arms. Only a few inches into our excavation, we groaned as iron clanged against a large, buried rock. Olaf and Fritigern dug around its edges while I hammered the point of my pickax at one end, hoping to lever the stone loose.

"My hands are already blistered," Olaf said.

"Too much soft living is your problem," Fritigern said.

"Remember, you're doing God's work, boys," Tomas said. "Hard work disciplines the body and frees the mind of sinful distractions. Count your blessings as you dig."

Fritigern grunted. "Count my blessings," he muttered. "I'd count two more if we dug graves for you and Eutychus."

I stopped tugging on the handle of the pickax. "Adalbert's death wasn't our fault."

Fritigern straightened, wiped his broad forehead, and snarled at me. "Says you."

Olaf cringed. He glanced over his narrow shoulder at the prior. "Keep your voices down. You'll get us into trouble."

My blood boiled, but I restrained my anger. Grasping the pickax handle, giving a vicious tug, I pried the stone free of the black soil.

"Besides," Olaf said, his voice consoling. "Clodius and Eutychus had nothing to do with Adalbert's death. You can't blame them."

Fritigern sneered. "Maybe. Maybe not. Who knows what they were up to in the forest. Maybe Adalbert happened upon them where they weren't supposed to be, and they drowned him to keep his mouth shut."

I leaped across our shallow hole and clasped my hands around Fritigern's thick neck. He tumbled backward with me on his chest. A strong hand yanked the rear collar of my habit, jerking me off white-eyed Fritigern before my choking grip could do serious damage.

"Stop your fighting!" Prior Tomas yelled. He tossed me to the ground.

The fire raging in my head quieted. I glared at Fritigern but knew better than to challenge the prior.

"What madness is this? You're defiling holy ground!" Tomas said.

"It's Fritigern's fault," Olaf said. "He accused Clodius of murdering Brother Adalbert."

Prior Tomas's oval face flushed red. He looked aghast at Fritigern. "You said *what*? How dare you? Apologize this instant!"

Fritigern raised his head, pushing on his elbows. He rubbed his sore neck with his left hand. He glowered at me with unrepentant eyes. "I'm sorry," he murmured.

"What did you say?" Tomas asked.

Fritigern pushed to his feet. "I'm sorry," he said louder.

"As you should be."

Fritigern scowled. "But Adalbert's death wasn't an accident. Somebody murdered him, and it wasn't any robber, Scot, or Pict."

Tomas snapped, "Don't be impudent. How could you possibly know what happened?"

"Because snakes don't throw you into water, and no robber would kill a monk. Adalbert didn't own anything except for the habit he wore. The killer didn't even take that."

"And the Scots and Picts? Do you suppose they are so selective?"

"If raiders were in the area, we'd know. They travel in packs and leave a trail of destruction. They don't just kill a wandering holy man and disappear."

The prior's anger faded. His eyes rolled upward to his left. He stroked his clean-shaven chin. He glanced at me and frowned. "And you, are you so thin-skinned you must resort to violence? You should know better!"

I bit my lip and lowered my gaze to my dirty toes.

"The abbot will hear of this, Clodius." Tomas pointed at the gravesite. "Now get back to work. All of you."

I scrambled to my feet, grabbed my shovel, and returned to my labors. Fritigern and Olaf joined me. We dug without speaking. My furry co-laborer's grunts, huffs, and nasty glances signaled our row lived on. I regretted having lost my temper but refused to offer Fritigern peace. Yet, as I mulled over his words, a begrudging respect took root within me. The hairy oaf had unjustly accused me, but to my amazement, he was right about one thing.

Adalbert had been murdered, and not by thieves or barbarian invaders.

Chapter V

After digging Adalbert's grave, we returned the tools to the shed. Olaf and Fritigern left for the dormitory, and I plodded back to the estate house dreading my next audience with the abbot. I passed through the atrium and walked to the back of the garden.

The abbot always kept his office door open. His weathered scalp and gray hair reflected the light of a candle, his eyes lowered to a massive book on his desk. We weren't supposed to have vices, and I wasn't sure that reading could count as a sin, but if it could, that would be the abbot's downfall. King Midas's greed for gold could hardly match the abbot's obsession for the 108 volumes stacked on his library shelves. Not even Bishop Bonifatius in Coria had so many.

The library stood on the left side of the abbot's office. Rows of thick, heavy, leather-bound volumes lined the shelves. Each book's page was vellum, made from calfskin. The finest sheets came from the skins of calf fetuses, cut from the bellies of their butchered mothers. A single volume might require two hundred hides from the poor creatures. Some books were said to be worth their weight in gold. That might have explained the abbot's fascination for them. As for me, I had trouble getting past the image of all those slaughtered animals.

Through the windows of the scriptorium, next to the library, Mutter's pets, Brother Cassius and Brother Fabian, worked by candlelight, meticulously copying texts and illuminating pages with intricate scripts and beautiful paintings. Both men looked in their thirties. Cassius had strong, slender fingers half again longer than my own, with which he gracefully directed his stylus. Fabian's thick, black brow stretched across his forehead with no break above his nose, making a furry canopy for his squinting eyes.

I straightened my shoulders, drew a deep breath, and marched into the abbot's office. It had the musty smell of old books laced with an acrid odor of the vinegar we used to clean the scribes' brushes.

The abbot lifted his gray head as I stepped through his doorway and scrutinized me. His lower lip thrust upward. "You've had quite a day, young Clodius. I can't remember its equal."

I folded my hands at my waist, lowered my chin, and tried to look contrite. The pain from the blisters on my hands helped.

Though seventy, Mutter sat straight and steady. Weather and age had wrinkled his skin, but he never showed difficulty in pulling the heavy volumes from his library's shelves. "I was almost ready to forgive your disobedient jaunt to the forest," he said. "Finding Adalbert's body seemed penance enough. But fighting in the cemetery … dear Lord, what were you thinking?"

My head shrank into the folds of my hood gathered about my neck. "I'm sorry, Father. I lost my temper."

"Lost your wits is more like it. What kind of example do you make? You're a senior novice. The other boys look up to you. I shudder to think the damage you've done to poor gentle Olaf. As for Fritigern, whatever could have set you off against him?"

"He accused me of killing Adalbert." My blood boiled with the memory.

Mutter shook his head. "Dear me. Whatever gave him such a notion?"

"He says robbers don't target monks, and if barbarians lurked in the woods, we'd know about it. I agree with him. Someone local killed Adalbert, but it wasn't Eutychus or me." My enthusiasm broke the illusion of my half-hearted contrition. I abruptly shut my mouth and re-planted my chin into my breast.

Mutter's chest sank with a rumbling sigh. "You have keen powers of observation, Clodius, and an inquisitive mind. I'm sure that God has some special purpose for you." He leaned back in his chair. His gaze softened, but his lips screwed tightly like he'd bitten a lemon. "Brother Adalbert was a troubled man. I don't suppose you knew that. Most didn't. He tended to keep to himself. He had a hard life before he came to the brotherhood. He never told me all the details … just pieces he confessed over the years … his past may have found him at last."

"Who?"

"I don't think we'll ever know. Whoever killed him will be long gone by now. The foul deed accomplished, there'd be no reason for him to stay." Mutter studied my face. I must not have been good at disguising my dissatisfaction. "Speak up if you have something to say, Clodius."

"Is there nothing we can do?"

"What have you in mind?"

I shook my head. "Is there no justice?"

The abbot grinned. He leaned forward, resting his forearms on the edge of his table. "I've sent word to Prefect Linus. Coria's watchmen will keep a lookout for any suspicious strangers. But there's little hope they'll find the man. As for your interest in justice, I'm heartened to know we are of one mind. What does justice require of those who disobey their abbot and fight on hallowed ground?"

My gaze fell back to my feet to avoid his stare. Of course, I knew the answer he wanted though I would have liked to remind him of Christ's forgiveness. Let him without sin throw the first stone. That sort of thing. The scriptures contained many useful defenses to turn the tables on your accusers. Eutychus had taught me that much. But Abbot Mutter did not look to be in a forgiving mood. I replied in a subdued, contrite voice, "That I be punished, Father."

"A thousand lashes are a waste on an unrepentant heart. What I have in mind will not harm your body but might be every bit as painful."

I really liked the part about not harming my body. I lifted my head to receive my sentence.

"There's so much good in you, Clodius. It's in every man. Our problem is that we become lazy, too willing to lie rather than to pay the price for our mistakes, too ready to steal the fruits of one man's labor rather than struggle to grow our own. Sin is an easy habit to acquire, son, but a tough one to quit. It requires fortitude and perseverance, but foremost it requires humility. Do you understand what it means to have a humble heart?"

I shrugged. "Yes, Father … I think so."

"Maybe this will clarify the meaning. You will apologize to Prior Tomas, Fritigern, and Olaf. And I don't mean you'll just say you're sorry. You will bend on your knees and ask for their forgiveness."

The red hairs on my neck bristled. I'd rather take the lashes.

"More importantly, before you apologize to your brothers, you will spend all night at the altar asking for God's forgiveness. I expect to find you there from bedtime until the monks assemble for morning prayers."

Bedtime followed total darkness. The monks assembled for prayers three hours after midnight. I'd be kneeling in the church for at least six hours. Reciting the Pater Noster consumed only a few breaths. Six hours seemed an excessively long duration to request forgiveness for two sins. I kept my thoughts to myself and my lips sealed. The abbot wasn't inviting a debate as to prayer's efficacy.

"Prayer will cleanse your mind and focus your thoughts. It's in the stillness and silence of our meditations that God speaks to us. Listen for his words, Clodius. He can teach you to tame whatever beast resides inside your heart."

"Yes, Father."

Mutter's gaze remained fixed on mine. His chin dipped an inch. His lids narrowed. The shadows from his brows darkened his eye sockets almost black. "One more thing," he said, his tone deeper, his voice stern. "You and Eutychus are on trial. No more nonsense. Is that clear?"

I tried to swallow, but my mouth had gone dry. "Yes, Father."

"The next time you go to the forest or the lake without

26

my permission you will be confined to your cell. If that doesn't work, then you will be expelled. I simply cannot tolerate willful disobedience."

I couldn't bear his scorn. If only I could somehow vanish.

"Self-denial. Meditation. Prayer. Obedience. Those are the foundation of our brotherhood. Pleasure. Excitement. Adventure. Insubordination. They are the works of the flesh, Clodius. If you pursue them, then there's no place for you here."

"Yes, Father," I said without looking up.

Mutter laid his hands on the massive volume opened on his desk. He softly tapped a page with his right forefinger, his gaze focused on me. I held to my supplicant's pose, pressing with the balls of my feet to keep my body from swaying.

Tap-tap. Tap-tap. Tap-tap.

I longed to escape, but he had not dismissed me. I feared he might plumb my heart and find the shameful heap of transgressions squeezed into my fleshy bag of skin and bones. At least he had not asked how many times Eutychus and I had sneaked away to swim.

Tap-tap. Tap.

Mutter closed his hand and spoke in a gentle tone. "I haven't forgotten what it is to be a young man, Clodius. The whole world seems like its blossoming anew, opening with a delicious fragrance, beckoning to caress its supple petals, to taste its sweet nectar. It's a trying time for any man, especially the young." He paused and stretched his fingers. "But we are not called to be just any man, Clodius. For us, it is not the flesh, not the world that molds our character. It is our spirit and God's divine Holy Spirit that abides in us. Just as a flower will die without sun and water and be strangled by weeds, our spirit grows when we feed our minds with God's holiness, and we shun the sins that stunt and choke our maturity. We are set apart. Set apart to be holy so our minds and souls may share in God's blessed glory. You cannot have both. You cannot possess this world and God's glory among us. Your novitiate is nearing the end. You will have to make

27

a choice, my son."

I didn't know how long I'd been standing there. My body rocked from my toes to my heels. I focused on holding rigid, fighting the fatigue in my knees. My palms sweated. Something tickled inside my nose. I yearned to scratch it. The abbot kept droning on, something about the world, my soul, a choice. What choice did I have? I could leave St. Antony's, but where would I live? What would I eat? I had no family—no real family—to help me. Abbot Mutter and Prior Tomas were the closest thing to parents I'd ever known. Leave and starve. Stay and survive. Not much of a choice.

"Do you understand, Clodius?"

My head jerked alert. "Yes, Father."

"Don't disappoint me again. You may go now."

Chapter VI

Michael and Gunther arrived just before dusk. The western sky burned with a blood red haze, the moon rising in the east with a crimson glow. The monks carried a makeshift litter between them, an old blanket stretched over gnarled oak branches. Brother Adalbert's feet and hands dangled beyond the blanket and jostled with their steps. His head and ghastly white face protruded from the top of the grungy habit covering his body.

I gathered with the other monks who rushed to gawk at the awful scene. Hands flew across faces and chests, making the sign of the cross while lips murmured prayers and incantations to chase off evil spirits. We formed a solemn procession led by the litter bearers to the front steps of the church. Michael and Gunther ascended while the rest of us hung back at the base. They lay down the litter, made the sign of the cross, then stepped away.

Abbot Mutter and Prior Tomas emerged from the church's front door. The abbot calmly folded his wrinkled hands at his breast and bowed his head in an attitude of prayer.

Prior Tomas threw his lean arms skyward, his gaze jumping from face to face. "Where's Brother Malthius? You there, Olaf. Run to fetch him!"

Olaf bounded toward the dormitory.

Tomas pointed into the crowd. His bony finger rested on me. "Clodius, come here. The rest of you, it's not dark yet; there's still work to be done."

I climbed the steps.

Rapid, heavy footsteps signaled Brother Malthius's arrival with Olaf. Malthius pushed through the scattering crowd. "Let me by!" He hustled up the steps to join us.

Tomas pointed at Adalbert's face. "Clodius, is this as you found him?"

Adalbert's bulging eyes stared into oblivion. Purple and blue splotches marred his swollen flesh. His turgid tongue, too big for his mouth, protruded from his locked jaw. A tiny snail fell from his left nostril into the folds of his bunched hood.

The contents of my stomach rumbled and surged to my throat. My palm clamped to my mouth, and I averted my eyes to keep from vomiting. I breathed heavily, regaining my composure, then glanced up at Prior Tomas's sympathetic dark eyes. "Yes, Father. He's the same."

Brother Malthius knelt beside the corpse. The ripped fabric of Adalbert's habit, stretched by water, hung loosely like made for someone twice his size.

"Do you think it was the snakes?" I asked.

"Seems likely," Malthius said, nodding his big square head. "Though it doesn't explain how he ended in the water."

"Maybe he fell in after one bit him," Tomas said.

Brother Michael flinched and said, "What was he doing there?"

Gunther winked. "We've determined he didn't go for a swim, eh, Clodius."

Michael grunted. His neck jerked with his tic. "Maybe he just liked to watch boys swimming."

"Why would he want to do that?" I asked.

Michael did not answer.

Mutter stirred from his meditation. His gray eyes flared open. "Enough talk! If you must jabber, lift your words to the Lord for the guidance of Poor Adalbert's soul to heaven."

Malthius's busy hands rolled up the hem of Adalbert's torn habit. He stopped when a bloated purple tube flopped from beneath the robe covering Adalbert's scrotum. "Sweet Mother of God protect us," Malthius blurted.

"What is it?" Mutter said.

Malthius lifted the edge of the rolled robe and peered at Adalbert's stomach. "Those are his intestines. He has a deep gash across his abdomen." He lowered the robe and stared up at the abbot. "This wasn't any serpent, Father. Someone split him open with a blade. Can't say for sure but my guess is he's been dead for days."

Mutter's placid expression did not change. His eyes shifted; his gaze fixed on me. His chin jerked a curt nod, confirmation of his theory that someone from Adalbert's shady past may have at last gotten even.

Tomas's cheeks rippled. "Eutychus attacked by a snake, Adalbert murdered by barbarians, when will you men learn to heed our warnings? The forest is not safe. This is what happens when you don't follow the rules."

I fixed my gaze on a crack in the stone floor's mortar to avoid Tomas's accusing eyes.

"Take his body inside the church," Mutter said. "Brother Malthius, clean him as best you can, we will have a funeral service after dinner."

Dinner consisted of a slice of barley bread with pottage, a soup the kitchener kept constantly cooking in the kitchen hearth, tossing in additional ingredients and scraps from time to time as the spirit and leftovers inspired him. Its flavor tended to change with the days. Tonight, it tasted strongly of yesterday's boiled onions. Though unappetizing, the hot meal filled me and buoyed my spirit. After finishing, I collected the emptied bowls and cups and carried them to the kitchen for cleaning.

The kitchen had a brick hearth with iron grating across the top for cooking and a separate wood-fired oven for baking. I dumped the dirty dishes into a plastered basin, the large sink was split into halves and filled with water for washing and rinsing the dishes.

Brother Haman stood at the kitchen's back door, one hand scratching his large belly, the other holding a dead rat by its tail. Nero, our floppy-eared foxhound, waited attentively a few feet outside, his big brown eyes focused on the dead rodent, his white tail thumping the packed dirt of the compound.

"Here's a toy, boy. Sorry I don't have any bones for you." Haman tossed the furry corpse underhanded, and Nero shot after it.

31

Praise the Lord that Nero, not the pottage, got the rats. There had been rumors.

Haman turned away from the door and caught me staring at him. His permanently moody eyes narrowed. "What are you looking at?"

I shifted my gaze to the water basin. "Nothing, Brother. I'm just cleaning the dishes."

"Lying is a sin, boy." He walked toward me; his black eyebrows cocked high. The kitchener's paunch stretched the fabric of his habit at his waist as he waddled. "Meat's a rare commodity, but I won't stoop to cooking vermin."

"Forgive me, Brother, there's some who joke and grumble. It's wrong for me to listen."

He lifted his pudgy hands. "I hear the complaints! I do the best I can! How many ways can you cook turnips and cabbage? I eat the same as I serve. Don't you think I would like to have a grilled rack of lamb or a—" He rubbed the back of his neck. His fat lips twisted with a sad frown. His harsh tone softened. "Just remembered that my last conversation with Adalbert had been about meat. I'd quite forgotten."

His rapid change in demeanor made me curious. "Pardon me. I don't mean to intrude but what did Adalbert have to say about meat?"

Haman stepped to the kitchen hearth and bent to inspect the fire. "He asked me if I knew how to cook a whole hog."

"A hog? We don't have any pigs."

"A fact I pointed out, but he wasn't put off."

"So, do you?"

"Do I what?"

"Know how to cook a hog?"

The kitchener slapped the hearth's metal door shut. "I've seen it done. When I was a boy, my village would roast a hog for Saturnalia. We'd have to build a spit, gut and splay the hog open. Yeah, I could do it."

"Did you tell Adalbert that."

"Sure."

"What did he say?"

"Nothing except maybe thanks." The kitchener paused. He tweaked his big nose with his thumb and forefinger. "All I remember is he scratched his chin and wandered off in one those thoughtful poses he was so good at. Seemed like his head was always somewhere else, that one. It was the last time I saw him ... three days ago." He released a wistful sigh.

"I wonder where he thought he could find a hog?"

Haman leaned against the wash basin. "Buy one in Coria if you have the money, but that wasn't possible. Maybe he thought he could barter with one of the pig farmers. All kind of pointless though. The abbot would never permit such extravagance. He'd insist we sell the meat and give the money to the almoner."

I shut my eyes but could not conjure an image of Abbot Mutter chewing on a juicy pork chop. Even harder to imagine one in my hands, though it set my mouth to salivating, nonetheless. The rich, not monks, feasted on meat. Even when God sent ravens carrying food to our blessed desert forefathers who fasted in Egypt's wilderness, the birds brought bread, olives, and honeycombs. If God didn't think that the hermit monks of Alexandria merited meat, what chance did we have?

My stomach gurgled with unsatisfied desires as I scrubbed and cleaned dishes. Haman wiped his hands on his apron, tossed the cloth to a table, and gestured for me to come with him. I dried my hands with a towel and followed him to the door overlooking the garden where the other monks assembled, making ready to form a single-file procession to the church.

"Forgive me, Brother," I said to Haman. "Do I have time to check on Eutychus?"

Haman frowned and scanned the monks congregating. "Be quick about it. Don't keep us waiting."

I left the refectory and crossed the peristyle garden in darkness to the infirmary. My motives were not fully charitable—not at all, actually. I breathlessly anticipated sharing the news of Adalbert's murder with my best friend. For the first time in our years together, I had the juicy story to share.

In the final year of our training before we could take the holy vows, have our heads tonsured, and become monks, neither of us had really chosen this career, at least not in a manner that would make the Lord proud. My oldest brother, Rubicus, had pushed me into the monastery. He had become the head of the family when my father, a wheelwright, dropped dead securing a new wheel to a wagon. Rubicus and Pilatus, my middle brother, had learned the craft, but they showed no inkling to teach me, a seven-year-old stripling, after my father's passing. Instead, Rubicus had deposited me at the monastery's front gate after my sixteenth birthday.

Eutychus came to the monastery willingly, though I suspected with mixed motives. His family had scratched out a meager living working a small farm just south of the great Roman wall that protected us from the northern barbarians. Eutychus had been captured by naked, blue-bodied Picts who killed his parents and burned down their farmhouse. He escaped after several months of enslavement and wandered, filthy and starving, into the monks' compound. The monks welcomed him, but honestly, Eutychus never showed much interest in our principal pastimes, prayers, hymns, or fasting. He showed more enthusiasm in learning to read, write, and do math, which the monks taught us.

Eutychus reclined alone in the infirmary, awake, his head on stacked pillows, his wounded leg raised in a sling, white bandages wrapped around his calf.

"How are you feeling?"

His body jerked. His eyes popped white.

"Sorry, I didn't mean to surprise you."

His blue eyes glistened in the candlelight. He wiped his eyelids with his fingers. "You didn't scare me."

"Are you still in pain?"

"My leg is throbbing, but I'll survive."

"Did you hear about Adalbert?"

Eutychus drew a deep breath and exhaled. "Yeah. Finnian told me."

Disappointment cooled my enthusiasm. "He may have been dead for days. He probably floated nearby when—"

Eutychus closed his lids and pinched the bridge of his straight nose. "Before ... when we went swimming ... you can say it."

An image of the crystal clear water filled my head. Four fluted columns stood on white paving atop a ten-foot-long stone embankment built by some rich Roman for his recreation decades earlier. Steps descending into the water shimmered darkly, covered with years of mud and algae, and almost invisible beneath the water's surface. Eutychus dunked my head. Water filled my mouth. Adalbert's corpse floated nearby, fouling the pool. I shuddered. "Don't you want to know what happened?"

Eutychus remained uncharacteristically solemn, continuing to squeeze between his eyes. He lowered his hand to his side, his eyes remaining closed. "I'm tired, Clodius. Later ... maybe. I need to sleep."

His indifference surprised me. I'd imagined him wide-eyed and breathless as I unfurled my gossip. "I'm sorry. It's just I thought you'd want to know."

"Later ... maybe in the morning."

To be blatantly honest, my feelings were indecent. I felt cheated. "Okay. Tomorrow maybe. The monks are assembling for the funeral. I must run. Goodnight, Eutychus."

Chapter VII

Brother Adalbert's corpse lay upon the church altar, but the former look of terror that had marred his features had been replaced with a smile of serene contentment. Malthius doubled as a mortician on the infrequent occasions we buried a brother. He'd learned a trick or two, bringing the deceased back to some semblance of life, and erasing the ghastly masks of death.

The entire complement of monks had assembled for the memorial service, twenty monks and three novices, excusing Eutychus who still recovered in the infirmary. I stood with my back to the east wall of the austere church, at the end of a row of nine men, looking across the nave to the nine monks and two novices lined opposite. Abbot Mutter and Prior Tomas stood at the head of the nave, above the altar table and the plain wooden rail that separated the altar dais from the narthex's walkway. The abbot's melodious voice led us in reciting the Pater Noster, our prayer echoing against the stone walls and rising into the heavy oak beams and pine rafters supporting the slate-tiled roof. The chant calmed me but did not quiet Brother Lucius's weeping.

A new habit, freshly dyed with 'madder, covered Adalbert's body. It retained a vibrant red shade, brighter than the faded, ruddy brown of the other monks' robes. A wooden cross garnished with white primrose blossoms lay atop his chest and his pallid, folded hands. Above his head, a leather-bound volume of John's gospel split open to the passage, *"dixit ei Iesus ego sum resurrectio et vita qui credit in me et si mortuus fuerit vivet."*

The discovery of Adalbert's body had hit everyone hard, but especially Lucius. Our forty-year-old cantor began crying when the service began and did not stop. His usually kind face contorted with grief and his beautiful voice uncharacteristically quavered. No one could carry a harmony like him, except maybe Brother Adalbert. The rest of us sang no better than a barnyard of pigs and goats at suppertime.

Without Adalbert's powerful harmony to drown out our squawks, our daily hymns became an ungodly assault upon unplugged ears.

The abbot concluded his prayer. Prior Tomas stepped forward. He lifted a silver goblet over the corpse's head and sprinkled water upon the frozen face with his fingers, dipping his hands repeatedly into the chalice, then flicking his digits while murmuring a blessing. The sharp features of his jaw, square chin, and high cheekbones contrasted with the homely and mostly downright ugly faces of the other men in the room. Tomas looked like a prince who had mistakenly arrived at a festival for trolls. Even his tonsured head looked distinguished, his jet-black hair, flecked with silver strands, appeared more like a crown than a ring of modesty.

After Prior Tomas concluded his blessings, Lucius stepped forward from my row, centering himself at the foot of the altar. He faced us, sniffed back a tear, then raised his pudgy hands above his shoulders. His lips opened to an oval. "*Domini est terra,*" he began with a pitch-perfect monotone chant. He dipped his hands, and we mimicked his words, sounding more like a herd of cattle storming up the narthex. We continued in this fashion, following his lead, thoroughly dismembering the twenty third psalm. Near the conclusion, Nero, who waited outside, joined in the chorus. His howling bellowed through the church's windows. If King David listened in heaven, surely he pleaded for God to unleash a thunderstorm to drown out the travesty. We completed the responsive hymn without divine retribution. Nero continued his sonorous serenade solo.

I felt a pang of guilt at my absence of any sincere remorse for Adalbert's death, but I had barely known the man. A reclusive fellow even by the monks' standard, and at least double my age, he often disappeared into the hills or forest for days at a time, presumably to seek solitude. I'd seen him at prayers, and in the refectory for meals, but searching my memory, I could not remember a single word we'd ever exchanged.

Nero's howling continued through the remainder of the funeral service. Abbot Mutter raised his voice unnaturally to counter the canine drone as he spoke the final prayer. The church echoed with "Amen."

Gunther and Michael broke from our ranks, climbed the dais to the altar, and hoisted Adalbert's litter to their shoulders. They descended the steps and led the senior monks at the head of each row toward the front door. The men formed straight lines, all the monks passing before me, as I waited with the other novices to join at the end.

Half-mad Brother Lazarus winked as he passed. He walked with an unbalanced cock in his shoulders. The vacant glaze to his unorthodox stare, his right eye gray, his left eye brown, worried me an empty attic substituted for a brain. How he had ever become a monk, I did not know. Most of the time, he spoke incoherently. He seldom did chores and disappeared more often any other monk. Prior Tomas allowed him greater latitude probably because of his disabilities. None of the monks appeared to resent his special treatment. Instead, most treated Lazarus with a mixture of reverence and caution. He occasionally would spout with mystical pronouncements or garbled messages that the monks debated were prophecies, glossolalia, or pure nonsense. Other times he could speak as clearly and cogently as the prior directing a work detail.

Cassius and Fabian, inseparable as Castor and Pollux, walked after Lazarus. Their bloodshot eyes and pale complexions contrasted brightly with the dark ink spots smudged on their pallid skin. The abbot's favorites, they seldom ventured outside the scriptorium where they spent long hours copying and illuminating texts. They taught the novices to write and paint, but I never showed much talent for it. So, after the first year of instruction, my lessons focused more on reading, which meant I had spent longer hours under the abbot's scrutiny.

Cassius curtly nodded his slender head as he passed me. It confused me. He'd never paid me much attention before.

Maybe he thought I merited special condolences like some mourning relative, tying me to the deceased because I had found the body. Whatever the reason, Fabian caught the gesture and brusquely mimicked the nod while simultaneously scratching the corner of his furry unbroken brow.

Haman waddled behind the scribes. The kitchener seemed to enjoy his cooking duties, though based on our menu he showed little acumen for it. He displayed greater skill as an eater. Haman and Lucius were the only chubby members of the brotherhood. I never begrudged them their hearty appetites. God bless them if they could fill up and keep it all down. They had stronger stomachs than I did.

Sandals clacked upon stone, everyone heading to the cemetery to bury poor Adalbert. I stepped forward to join the end of the procession.

"Clodius!"

Abbot Mutter's call paralyzed me.

"Aren't you forgetting something?"

"Father?"

"We've hands enough to bury our brother. Yours will serve best clasped at your chest, beseeching God's mercy."

I wistfully watched the monks and novices as they exited. I bowed to Mutter and turned back to the altar. A dreadfully long night of penance lay before me. In no hurry to begin, I slogged up the narthex. Prior Tomas remained behind to ensure my compliance. The abbot followed the others to the cemetery.

I fell to my knees before the railing and murmured the Pater Noster. Before the church's front door closed, I had prayed it twice. The prior's footsteps padded softly as he exited. I kept repeating the Lord's Prayer while the mumbled tones of the monk's final prayers filtered from the graveyard through the windows. The hiss and thump of dirt being shoveled to fill the grave competed for my attention as I changed my prayers to the psalms I could remember. That did not take long. I returned to the Pater Noster.

The shoveling stopped. The night became silent. A solemn loneliness engulfed me.

A penitent's long hours of prayer, kneeling before the cross, head bowed, hands clasped, face aglow with flickering candlelight, a wavering shadow cast upon the floor; it's a beautiful image of piety and humility. For me, however, reality proved less saintly. My twentieth time into the Lord's Prayer, my thoughts jumbled as my mind wandered. "Forgive me my trespasses as I forgive ..." Fritigern was a jackass. Yes, forgive him for being a jackass, but he was still a jackass. If he'd stop being a jackass, he wouldn't need my forgiveness. So, maybe someone should teach him to stop being a jackass. Maybe me. An image surfaced of Fritigern lying prostrate, whining for mercy, my right foot planted firmly against the back of his neck.

My sagging chin drooped to my chest.

My head jerked, jarring me awake. Correcting the wilting slump of my kneeling posture, I fidgeted, rocking from side to side. The pressure on my knees hurt. It had started with a mild discomfort focused just beneath my kneecaps and gradually increased to an awkward pinching sensation, then expanded to a painful tension in the ligaments behind my knees. If I could stand, for just a moment. Stretch my legs. Rub my knees. No one would know. No one would see.

My guilt-ridden conscience castigated me. God would know. God would see. Forgive me, God. I had much the Lord needed to forgive.

My mother's face filled my head, her eyeballs big as saucers, her gray hair wiry and disheveled, her mouth wide open, wrinkles creasing her chin and cheeks, rotted teeth gnashing, spittle spewing, her incoherent screams scorching my ears. In my lifetime, she'd always been unbalanced. My first memory of her involved a shrieking glee when she decapitated a rodent with a meat cleaver. A good shot, she nailed the vermin behind its gray ears half-way across our wattle and daub hut. Nothing impaired Mater's aim. But one question always worried me. Who would she aim at next?

When my father died, whatever little remained of mother's sanity disintegrated. She became a hunched, brooding thing, squatting in the darkest corner, not eating, not drinking, but exploding one night, a human maelstrom, flailing her arms, screaming at the top of her lungs, scaring me beyond any terror I'd ever known.

Then she collapsed. Dead as a wasted blackbird dropped from a tree.

"Demon possessed." The village priest's words still haunted me. My brothers paid the prelate most of what little silver our father had saved to placate the holy man's disdain and allow Mater's body to be buried next to Pater in the tiny church cemetery.

"God, forgive me for not loving her," I murmured.

The front of my knees grew numb. My ligaments burned with a locked, immobilized agony. My thoughts shifted from my mother's mortifying screech to the horror sealed across Adalbert's face. If, as the abbot suggested, Adalbert had been murdered by an ancient foe, the fatal blow must have been delivered by surprise from the look on his face. I could believe that Adalbert had a dark and secret history and that some avenging enemy from his past had murdered him, but I could not fathom why his body ended in the lake. A stranger wouldn't have known about the lake, or that Adalbert could be found there. If he had been murdered somewhere else, it made no sense to dump his corpse in the water without weights to sink it. And surprisingly, the abbot seemed eager to move on. Forgive and forget? Justice? Murder? Sin? The Fall? Falling …

My body jerked violently. For one heartbeat, my mind cleared of its drowsiness. I was supposed to be praying. Let me stand. Just for one second. Stretch my legs. Release the strain. Falling …

I shook my head, then slapped my face. The crack of my hand upon my cheek echoed, bouncing back from the ceiling. The sting helped to focus my thoughts. Deep, awesome silence surrounded me. A gentle night breeze whistled through the high windows. A scratching pitter-pat sounded above my head, the tiny feet of the night's scavengers scurrying across oak beams. Sleep tugged at my drowsy head, my eyelids heavy, my breathing slow and relaxed.

"Find the murderer."

My head jerked alert. I opened my eyes, glancing to my right and left, searching for the owner of the words. No one moved except the rats, and rats didn't talk. It had seemed so real, a quiet whisper in my ear. "Find the murderer … find the murderer … find the murderer." The words lingered in my head. Was this what Abbot Mutter had meant by God's voice?

Water splashed. A whimper followed. I squeezed my hands at my chest, pressing my fingertips against my knuckles, the pain reassuring me that I was not dreaming. Water stirred, the sound made by someone walking waist high in a pool, arms swishing, fingers extended, enjoying the refreshing embrace of a chilling lake. What sinful memory had my drowsiness uncorked? Stay awake. Lord, forgive my weakness. I dug my fingertips harder into my skin.

Another whimper. It was no memory or dream. The sound drifted to my ears upon the night's breeze. It had to come from the balneary, the decaying, former caldarium just behind the church where the monks bathed once a week, weather permitting. The bronze cauldron and lead piping that once carried heated water to the bath had long ago disappeared. Now the temperature of the tiny pool varied from refreshing to excruciating with the seasons.

A groan whispered, but not like the three words I had heard. Nor was it a groan of pain—more like a release of pain. Like someone standing, stretching their aching knees, rubbing their tortured ligaments. Dear Lord, I wanted to rise.

The groan repeated. My gaze fixed on the church's rear wall as if staring at stone would somehow sharpen my hearing. No, this groan didn't sound like someone standing or stretching. This groan arose from pleasure, a gutty, grinding, fully engrossed masculine ecstasy.

42

A third groan, this one louder, more urgent, a blast from a human bellows.

Silence.

The tinkle of dripping water chimed. My imagination? The wind whistled through the windows. Tiny claws scratched upon wood.

"Clodius."

My soul jumped halfway to Hades.

"I did not mean to frighten you," Abbot Mutter said.

I grabbed the altar railing to steady my shaking hands.

The abbot stood beside me, his arms folded at his chest, covered by the drooping sleeves of his robe. "It's just past midnight. Have you made peace with God?"

I didn't know what I'd been doing. My legs felt permanently crippled. Peace? God? Find the murderer … find the murderer. The whisper echoed in my ears. I told the abbot what he wanted to hear. "Yes, Father."

"Then I think you've been adequately punished. Go to bed. You can get a few hours of sleep before morning prayers."

"Thank you, Father." I pushed against the railing to stand, but my knees locked unresponsive. The abbot's hand gripped under my armpit. He lifted, helping me up. Heavenly relief coursed through my tortured joints and ligaments.

Mutter released me, and I hobbled to the side door, heading for the dormitory. Before crossing the threshold, I turned my head to find him. He knelt, head bowed, hands clasped, his face aglow, the picture of humility and piety.

Chapter VIII

I awoke much too early for my liking, Olaf's high-pitched voice piercing the darkness of my dormitory cell, calling the monks to morning prayers. I strapped my sandals to my feet, rose from my straw pallet, pulled on my woolen habit over my linen tunic, and shuffled outside.

Shadows hunched in the dark corridor ahead of me, silently trudging out of the dormitory and toward the church. A waning moon provided our only light across the compound. A few steps beyond the door, the moon ducked behind a cloud.

A monk in front of me stumbled. "Blessed Mother of God!"

"Watch your mouth, Brother," Prior Tomas said.

"Sorry," Michael said.

"Better to watch your feet," someone grumbled.

"Keep the silence!" Tomas snapped.

Except during worship, regulations required us to hold our tongues from wake-up until after our morning meal. The brothers often ignored the silence, even more frequently than Eutychus and I disobeyed the order to keep away from the lake.

Three candles lit the sanctuary, one at the altar and one on both sides of the narthex in the shallow alcoves sculpted into the plastered walls. We divided and formed into straight lines on each side. Prior Tomas silently counted heads. When he finished, he whispered into the abbot's ear. Our service began.

Fortunately for my sore knees, we stood as we chanted our prayers and hymns. My lips mechanically recited each word as my thoughts churned with the confusing sounds of my previous hours at the altar. I'd never experienced a divine call. Mutter had told me to listen for God's voice. The whisper seemed consistent with the story of Samuel and Eli, but I was no prophet. God would never use me, an unworthy cesspool of sin. Yet, a curiosity burned in me to know how Adalbert had died. Perhaps the Holy Spirit moved inside me. On the other hand, my jumbled memories had been blurred by unrelenting drowsiness. I might have been delusional.

After our morning prayers had concluded, we swayed and lumbered in silence back through the darkness to the refectory to break our fast with a bowl of wheat porridge. I spooned the tasteless gruel into my mouth while glancing at the other sleepy faces in the room. Aside from Eutychus's absence and Lucius's red, puffy eyes, all had returned to normal as if Adalbert had never existed.

The first silver band of dawn hung above the horizon as we exited the refectory, each man heading to his assigned chores. Today was market day in Coria. The local farmers and craftsmen would assemble to sell their produce and wares in the town forum. For me, it meant loading barrels of Brother Bremen's latest brew onto an ox-drawn wagon for delivery to the city's taverns. Eutychus's and my chores included accompanying Bremen. We had strong backs, yet to suffer from the joint and spinal injuries that afflicted so many of the monks from their years of working the fields, shouldering heavy loads of grain, and spending countless hours hunched on their knees before the altar.

Since Eutychus convalesced in the infirmary, Fritigern took his place. I did not welcome his company, but my hairy antagonist did not weigh foremost in my thoughts. I couldn't stop thinking about her, the fuller's daughter. I fantasized her wandering about the square. Unaccompanied. Looking for me. I shivered with a delicious chill.

Though I had been to the town many times and seen the girl frequently, propriety, decorum, but mostly cowardice had stopped me from approaching her. I only knew her auburn curls bouncing about her shoulders, her luminous green eyes, her narrow waist, the contour of her hips, her blossomed chest. Perspiration beaded on my forehead. I wiped my brow and glanced skyward, pretending the warmth of the rising sun and the weight of a barrel of beer on my shoulder caused my skin to flush.

I handed the last barrel up to Fritigern. He lashed it securely in the wagon. Bremen climbed to the center of the driver's bench. I stepped on the front wheel's rim to join him when Abbot Mutter's strong voice called out, "Clodius." I stopped in mid-climb and turned to face him.

Arms crossed, chin raised, the abbot peered down the ridge of his crooked nose. "Haven't you forgotten something?"

The image of the fuller's daughter still fogged my head. The abbot's imperious gaze returned me to reality. My stomach knotted. My final act of penance awaited.

The abbot waved both hands, signaling the men in the compound to gather. "Come, brothers. Clodius has something to say to Prior Tomas, Fritigern, and Olaf."

Tomas walked toward me. Fritigern hopped from the wagon and stood beside the prior. Olaf hustled from across the compound and slouched next to Fritigern. The other monks gathered around them. The cold stares of scores of judging eyes bore down upon me.

"Well, Clodius," the abbot said.

Dropping to my sore knees, drawing a deep breath, and hiding my resentment by forcing a penitent's dour frown on my mouth, I spoke "Prior Tomas, Brother Fritigern, Brother Olaf, I apologize for my rude conduct yesterday and beg your forgiveness."

Tomas smiled, his eyes warm and merciful. He stepped forward and placed his hand on my left shoulder. He gave it a pat. "I forgive you. With all my heart. I did not mean to be so rough when I grabbed you and tossed you to the dirt. Please forgive me for being so cross with you. I trust I did not injure you."

The moment felt awkward. The prior had out-humbled me. Even worse, he really meant it. Embarrassed at my insincerity, I became tongue-tied. I stammered a reply. "No, Prior. I mean yes, Prior. I mean the fault is mine. There is nothing to forgive."

Olaf looked down at the ground, his right foot idly scratching at the dusty surface. His mouth twisted. He shrugged, then nodded his head. He shyly glimpsed at me, then stepped back into the circle of men and hid behind their russet robes.

Fritigern smirked. He lifted his palms and rolled his shoulders. "Yeah, all right." He abruptly turned away and stepped back to the rear of the wagon where he would ride with the lashed barrels.

The abbot nodded at me, a satisfied grin creasing his mouth. "Very well, Clodius, your sins are forgotten. Now go and sin no more."

I rose and headed to the wagon, not feeling much like a man absolved. I felt humiliated. But at least the ordeal had ended.

"Clodius."

This time Tomas, not the abbot, called me. Instead of Mutter's judgmental tone, the prior spoke discreetly, so softly no one else could have heard.

I glanced at him. He cupped his hand and curled his fingers, beckoning for me to join him in the shady corner of the villa's wall removed from the dispersing brothers. What now? He must have remembered another filthy chore to give me.

Brown mud brick peeked through the many gaps where the exterior wall's saffron-stained plaster had cracked and crumbled. The original yellow hue had faded to the tint of soured milk, matching the noxious feeling of my innards as I dragged my feet to the prior.

"I'm proud of you, son."

My head recoiled. My dread vanished. "F-F-Father?"

"I'm afraid I may have misjudged you. Your quick wits and bravery saved Eutychus, and you found Brother Adalbert's body. You showed great courage."

I squinted and cocked my head. The version someone had told him of yesterday's adventure varied considerably from my memory. I did not count bravery and acuity among the attributes I had demonstrated, but I felt no need to correct the prior. After the morning's humiliation, my ego needed a boost, even if built upon skewed talk. My back stiffened, my chest rising. "Thank you, Prior."

"You're smart. You learn quickly. I'm sure you understand why I cannot abide your quarreling with the other boys. And don't worry yourself about the abbot's harshness. All will soon be forgotten. We have great hopes for you, Clodius. You have great promise."

My head swelled with the praise. "I'll do my best, Prior."

"I don't doubt it." He clapped his hand on my back. He glanced toward the abbot, and his lips drew taut. "I'm still worried that Adalbert's killer is lurking about. Did you notice anything, any clue as to who might have done this?"

I shook my head. "No, Father. Nothing. Just his body jammed beneath a tree trunk." I hated to disappoint him.

Tomas frowned and squeezed my shoulder. "Well, no matter. The abbot seems to think the murderer has escaped and will not return. I'm sure he's right. We'll trust God to see justice done."

"Yes, Father."

"Off you go. Bremen's waiting for you."

I hesitated. "Yes, Father." I gazed directly into his dark brown eyes. A warm sensation tingled in my heart. "And-and thank you."

He smiled, saluted with a tap of his finger to his brow, then strode in the direction of the church.

Chapter IX

The morning sun had risen above the compound's walls. Feathery clouds streaked the blue sky. I joined the hefty brewer and Fritigern waiting for me on the wagon.

Bremen reached down with one arm and lifted me to his right side on the driver's bench. The yeasty smell of fermented hops stung my nostrils. Brother Bremen supervised our brewery, producing a stout wheat ale we shared on special holidays and sold to Coria's taverns. I'd seen him carry two beer barrels on his shoulders. Rumors said he could just as easily drink them. Big, strong, and jovial, he sprouted a belly that bounced when he laughed. My favorite among the monks, he possessed a sly wit that kept me on my toes.

Bremen snapped the reins. "On with you, Castratus."

The ox bellowed a protest. The wagon jerked forward with a hard, creaking bounce.

Bremen leaned into my left ear. "Don't let the penance bother you, boy. We've all been down on our knees seeking forgiveness. Me more than most." Despite his cheerful nature, Bremen sometimes became moody and withdrawn. He never offered, and I didn't ask, but I sensed that he shouldered some cross from his past.

The prior's talk and Bremen's sympathy lifted my gloom. Thankfully, Eutychus had not witnessed my humiliation. There would have been no end to his laughter. My heart also cheered that the girl had not seen my groveling. Her face kept springing into my head. What an awful thought, to be branded by shame before she even knew my name.

The wagon bounced along the winding, rutted dirt track until we reached the old Roman road. For the next six miles, Bremen guided the ox either on or beside the pitted highway depending on how badly scarred the road had become. Along the route, other wagons carrying goods and herders with their flocks joined us, all making their way to the market. The road became especially hazardous as we crested a low ridge. The green water of the River Tyne stretched before us, spanned by Coria's wooden bridge, and the city's limestone walls beyond. Years of vandalism and the lack of any organized or regular maintenance had left fissures in the road's paving as large as sheep in some places. Most of the traffic abandoned the highway for the cleared pastures beyond its shoulders. The holes were not always obvious, some pits had filled with mud and thick weeds obscuring the hazard.

One poor soul had driven his wagon loaded with baskets of cabbages, turnips, and carrots into such a trap. The muck-filled hole swallowed a front wheel up to the axle. The man had only one arm, a shriveled stump jutting from his tunic's right sleeve. The mare drawing his wagon looked in no better shape. Scattered gray patches spoiled her chestnut coat, which variously sagged and stretched, exposing her rib cage. The man pushed with his good arm against the sunken wheel, and the horse strained, but their combined strength would never free the wheel without unloading the cargo. The other travelers seemed too busy to lend him aid.

Bremen nudged my arm. "There's a kindness that needs doing."

I nodded and hopped from my seat to the ground.

"Fritigern, give Clodius a hand," Bremen said.

My hairy companion looked over his shoulder. He jumped from our wagon's tail and came hurtling toward me, his face eager with the prospect of performing a good deed. In contrast to Fritigern, I felt oddly conflicted. This scene brought back many shameful memories. For most of my youth before coming to the monastery, my nefarious real brothers had preyed upon people in dire circumstances, extorting huge sums for assistance and coaching me to steal from their cargo. One good deed would hardly tilt the scales in my favor.

"I'll wait for you on the other side of the bridge if you don't catch up with me before then," Bremen said. He gave Castratus another sharp snap of the reins.

50

The one-armed man released his grip on the wheel, turned, and sneered as he heard us approach. He had wrinkled, weathered skin with a shaggy white beard. A grayish scar crossed his left brow, descending across his lids, a cloudy white film covering his iris. "Did I ask for your help?"

The other travelers might have ignored the man's predicament for a good reason. Fritigern ignored the rebuke. "When we find someone in need of help, we don't require an invitation."

The man hawked and spat. "I can't pay you."

I shrugged. "We wouldn't accept payment if you offered it."

The man frowned and slapped the mired wheel with frustration. He backed off a step. "If you insist, but I won't change my mind."

The man's rudeness stunned me. I hadn't come with any expectation of reward but expected the man to be appreciative. If his pride choked his gratitude, he could at least thank the Lord for sending us. So why did I feel abused? We had freely offered our assistance. Insisting on his praise would have been hypocritical.

The man avoided looking at us, keeping his gaze on his wagon, his horse, and the pitted road. He busied his hand, aimlessly fidgeting with his animal's harness and all but ignoring our presence. He needed more help than just rescuing his wagon.

I studied the depth of the hole. "We may need to lighten your load a little. But we can try to push it out first. How's your horse?"

The old man patted his mare's haunches, then stroked her tail. "Astor's barely a shadow of the warhorse she once was. But she can still pull a full wagon if she must."

As disagreeable as the old man acted, his display of affection for his mare moved me. "Good. How about if you go to the front and pull on her harness. Fritigern, you push at the wagon's rear. I'll push on the wheel."

51

The man nodded without looking up from the ground. He shuffled to the mare's nose while Fritigern stepped to the wagon's rear.

I bent low, anchoring my feet against the exposed edges of paving stones. I gripped the wooden wheel at its rim, bending into it as low as possible and drew a deep breath. "Ready! Go!"

The air exploded with our grunts and Astor's protesting snorts.

The man shouted, "Come on, ol' girl! Pull, darling!"

My legs and arms strained. My face heated. My feet dug into the stones. Just as I thought my strength would fail, the wheel rolled up and out of the hole.

"Whoa, girl," the man said.

The horse settled. I released the wheel and sank to my knees, gasping for air. Fritigern stepped from the rear of the wagon, his breathing deep and rapid. He surprised me by offering his hand to pull me to my feet. I had not asked for his help, resented his offer, and did not want to show him gratitude. Yes, I saw the symmetry. I accepted his hand, and he lifted me.

"Thanks," I said, feeling awkward and insincere.

"Come on. We'll have to run to catch up with Bremen."

I brushed the dirt from my robe where my knees had hit the road. "Go ahead. I'll be right behind you."

Fritigern glanced at the old man, who petted his horse's neck. "You're wasting your time with him."

"Probably."

Fritigern turned about and jogged along the side of the road toward the town.

I stepped to the front of the wagon. The mare's left leg had a long, jagged scar reaching from her forearm to her knee. "You both look like you've seen a few battles."

The man's eyelids narrowed. He wagged his stump. "You mean this? I served in a cavalry vexillation for sixteen years if you must know. Lost my arm to Danish raiders."

"I'm sure the emperor appreciated your sacrifice."

"Humph! The army discharged me as soon as I could walk. All they gave me was Astor and her only because she'd been made lame by a spear."

I furrowed my brow in what I hoped showed sympathy. "That must have been hard for you."

"What's it to me? That's life, boy. The world doesn't ask for mercy and doesn't give any. The army tossed me and Astor aside just like the Romans abandoned our island to save their own hides. No one cares about me or anybody else."

"God cares."

The veteran snickered. "God? Which god?"

"There's only one."

"Hah! Just one. Maybe that explains why he's never around when you need him. I've got no time for such foolish nonsense."

I'd never encountered such stark cynicism before. "God's everywhere. He's always with us."

"I don't need some all-seeing eye following me around, though I can't imagine why he'd be interested. He must be pretty bored to have nothing better to do."

"Have you no hope?"

The veteran rolled his eyes and laughed. "Hope? What's to hope for? You mean like the Romans marching back into Britannia?"

Many people still clung to that hope; a dream that held the fraying fabric of our society together. I lifted my hand to the clouds. "I meant a better life in the hereafter."

The veteran scrunched his nose like Astor had defecated on his foot. "With the mess your god's made of this world, why would I want to see how he's ruined the next? I'll be content that it's all over." He tugged at his mare's trace. "Come on, Astor, we've wasted enough time on childish myths."

What could make anyone so bitter? Life had certainly not been kind to me. I hadn't lost an arm or eye, but I'd lost my parents and been abused by my real brothers. Without the

53

charity of the monks, maybe I would have grown just as lonely and morose as the old soldier. An unexpected sense of gratitude warmed my heart. The monks had instilled me with hope. They would never abandon me. A smile creased my lips. I tucked my head and chased after Bremen.

The sun glided into a cloudless blue sky as the morning's chill turned warm. I sweated in earnest as I caught up to the wagon. My thoughts turned to the cool water of the lake west of the monastery. Adalbert's ghastly dead face flashed through my head. I shuddered as I climbed up the sideboard to take my seat next to Bremen.

"Did you get the old fellow straightened out?"

"His wagon, yes. His sour disposition, no."

"Give you a rough time, did he?"

"Not really, but he never said thank you."

"Some men carry heavy burdens. It poisons the air around them. The past is not easy to forget. It can be cruel."

"Did you know Brother Adalbert well?"

Bremen cast a sideways glance at me then shrugged. "As well as most, though that isn't saying much. Adalbert did love my ale though, almost as much as I do." He winked at me. "We had a drink or two together. Just sampling, mind you. Making sure the brew hadn't spoiled."

"Did he ever speak of his past? Where he was from? Anything about his family?"

"He didn't need to tell me. I knew from his accent. He came from Gaul, near Troyes would be my guess."

"From Gaul? Why would he leave Gaul for here? Most people want to go the opposite way."

"Not if you've escaped debtor's prison."

"Prison?"

"We may be overrun with Scots and Picts, but if it's Roman law you're fleeing, Britannia is as good a spot as any. Don't act so shocked. Adalbert lost everything in some failed business venture. Believe me, there's those among our brethren who are fleeing worse crimes than not paying their debts. There are all sorts of mistakes and hardships that can drive a man to a vow of poverty and to hide away in obscurity. It's a hard choice, but sometimes not choosing it is an even a harder decision to make."

"And what about you?"

"Me?"

"What compelled you to take the vows?"

Bremen glared at me through the corner of his eyes. "Never mind about me, boy. Keep your nose in your own business."

Chastised, I kept my mouth closed.

We approached the city's southern gate, a wide arch with parapets on the far side of a wooden bridge spanning the hundred-foot-wide River Tyne. A ditch and low wall encircled the town. Eight armed guards, town watchmen, monitored the flow of traffic. A scruffy looking brute, twice my size, wearing an iron, pot-shaped helmet, blocked the roadway where merchants' wagons queued.

"That's interesting," Bremen said. "The usual tax collector is missing. Looks like big ol' Sunno is in charge." He leaned into my ear and whispered, "Hold your tongue, lad. I'll do the talking."

I nodded, happy to oblige, wondering what Bremen thought I could possibly have to say.

The tax-collecting process clogged the gate as some merchants argued over the amount extorted by the guards. Every argument ended the same. Those who had the coins paid the tax in silver. Those without money paid with a share of their merchandise. A considerable amount of booty collected on wagons inside the gate. When a tax wagon could hold no more, mules hauled it away, the loaded axles groaning with the strain.

Our turn arrived. Brother Bremen smiled, showing a mouth full of yellowed teeth. "Fine morning to you, Sunno. What a glorious day God has given."

The brute grunted. "Morning, Bremen. Beer as usual?"

Brother Bremen beamed. "The finest ale in the district."

Sunno raised his right hand, pointed his forefinger at the

barrels, and began a slow, deliberate count out loud. He reached eight. A white goat nibbling at his leather boot distracted him. He kicked his foot. The goat fled with a protesting bleat. Sunno looked back to the wagon's contents, shook his head, and began again. "One … two … three …" When he finally reached thirty-two, he lowered his chin and scratched his scalp. "The toll on beer is one-twelfth its value." He peered into the sky, frowning and scratching his head while silently mouthing numbers.

"Excuse me, Sunno," Bremen interrupted. "I hesitate to point out an error, especially when it works to my benefit, but my Christian conscience cannot abide that I should profit by your honest mistake. You have forgotten that the tax on beer is not one-twelfth, but a larger one-sixteenth. It hurts me to admit it, but I could not sleep well knowing I'd abused your confusion."

The guard's eyes opened wide with a look of avarice. A cunning grin creased his lips. "One-sixteenth you say. I thought one-twelfth, but if you insist." His eyes tilted skyward, and he resumed his silent arithmetic. He completed his math, tweaking his nose with his thumb and forefinger. "That's two barrels," he said proudly. "You'll pay in kind?"

"We're but poor monks," Bremen said, lifting his broad empty palms. He twisted in his seat. "Fritigern, be lively. Give the man two barrels and be quick about it."

Fritigern complied in a flurry. The town watchmen lifted the barrels, hoisting one to the wagon of booty. The second they rolled away to a shadowed corner near the wall where it disappeared behind stacked stones and knee-high bushy weeds.

Sunno smacked his lips and chuckled. "Off with you, monk. You're holding up traffic."

"Good day," Bremen said with a cheerful smile.

I'd been biting my tongue during the entire exchange but could no longer hold my words. "Brother Bremen, a twelfth is larger than a sixteenth."

"Shhh!" He glanced over his shoulder at the guards.

"Let's hurry before the half-wit realizes two-and-two-thirds barrels are more than two." He sputtered then roared with uncontrollable laughter. "Half-wit. Get it? The man's a half-wit. Oh Lord, have mercy I'll bust a gut."

I didn't know whether to be shocked or elated. I glanced back to Fritigern, who stared blankly at the cobblestones passing beneath his dangling legs. He had either missed the ruse or had no better understanding of fractions than the ill-educated guard. My gaze returned to Bremen. "Isn't that stealing?"

"Stealing? Who took barrels of beer from whom?"

"Yes, but it's a tax."

"Tax, my eye. When Bishop Ivus founded our monastery, the city fathers agreed that the church and all within its charge would be exempt from taxes. After Ivus died, the citizens elected Bonifatius as bishop, and the exemption lapsed. We labor night and day. All we earn we give to the poor and needy. It riles me to think what the city prefect and the bishop are doing with their loot. Not God's work I assure you."

While I pondered this explanation, the shadows of the two- and three-story buildings lining Via Praetoria gave way to bright sunlight reflected from the central plaza's wide concourse. It bustled with activity. My heart raced. Scanning faces, trying not to appear overly excited, I longed to behold lustrous auburn curls.

Bremen guided the wagon through the crowd to a two-story, gray-stone building on the northeast corner of the square. A rectangular wooden sign with a painted red dragon hung horizontally from two black iron rings. Lester, the obese tavern owner, stood at the entrance, his beefy hands perched on his wide hips. He waved and exchanged greetings with Bremen. They retreated inside, leaving Fritigern and me to unload the wagon. Keeping one eye on the barrels and the other the faces in the crowd, I set about the task. My distraction must have been obvious because Fritigern dropped a heavy barrel on my shoulders, laughing as I juggled it. Luckily, I regained my balance before the load burst upon the pavement. Cursing my foolishness, I vowed to keep focused on my duties. Then a feathery red swirl caught the corner of my eye.

My heart stopped.

She wore a white linen dress belted beneath her breasts with a second band tied at her narrow waist. Sheer sleeves draped to her elbows, revealing her milky white forearms, slender hands, and fingers. Her hair hung just beneath her shoulders, every bit as alluring as my memory had conjured. She inspected a pink bar of soap at the top of a stacked display, her delicate fingers caressing the glossy cake, making me instantly jealous for her touch. She laughed politely, more a birdsong's cheerful chirp than laughter. She looked up. Not at me, alas, but at a handsome blond youth standing before her. He lifted his right hand and brushed her soft cheek with the back of his fingers. A jealous hostility flared in my heart. I yearned to trade places, becoming the owner of the boy's hand.

"Julia!" her father shouted, shattering my daydream. A scowl spread across his lips. Deep furrows creased his brow. The broad-shouldered, black-bearded man stood beside his pushcart filled with stacks of folded wool.

His daughter whisked her hand from the soap display. She spun and hurried away to her father without giving the fair-haired boy another glance.

Julia. Perfect. Julia. One more delectable morsel to add to my fantasies. Julia. I savored the way my mouth filled with her name. My lips puckered. The luscious "Joo" curled my tongue and teased my throat. My cheeks strained with a bittersweet "lee." My jaw dropped with a poignant "yah." Tantalizing. Full of promise. Joo-lee-yah. I yearned to rush after her. Joo-lee-yah. I ducked my head behind the barrel on my shoulder and hefted my load into the tavern.

One day, Julia, but not today.

Chapter X

The market-day crowd filled every bench, stool, and table in the dingy interior of the Red Dragon Tavern. The doughy air smelled of stale, spilled ale and too closely packed humanity. Our arrival did nothing to diminish the patrons' thirst or the indecency of their conversations. A shrill voice to my left blurted, "And then she farted." The entire table exploded with boisterous laughter. On my right, a middle-aged woman with dark circles around her eyes haggled over the price for a trip upstairs with a gray-haired man wearing a multicolored robe over his brown tunic. She pouted. He rolled his eyes and crossed his arms. The woman shrugged, clasped his hand, and dragged him toward the flight of stairs.

I found Bremen talking with the obese tavern owner in front of an open doorway that led to the storage cellar. I stopped before them, the heavy barrel on my shoulder, intending to squeeze past their large bodies to reach the stairway.

Lester said, "Adalbert's dead you say. Such a pity. Seemed like a bright and friendly fellow."

Bremen's bushy eyebrows rose. "You knew him?"

"Not well. He came here a few times, talking to the locals, sharing their ale and their stories."

"I had no idea." Bremen scratched his chin. "Guess that explains some of his absences. What are you standing there looking at, Clodius?"

"Excuse me. Can I get by you?"

Bremen stepped out of the doorway and pulled at the tavern owner's elbow. They continued conversing about the price of beer and wine as I carried my load down the stairs. I stacked the barrel against a plastered wall, then made my way back up. Bremen had left the room. The tavern owner stood in the dust-filled light of a window, a stylus in one hand, a small plank in his other, scribbling figures.

If God had not chosen me for a divine investigation, then providence kept drawing me further into the inquiry. The fact that Adalbert had frequented the tavern inflamed my curiosity. Bremen had looked confused but not interested enough to dig deeper. I couldn't bear to leave without my questions being answered.

"Pardon me, sir."

Lester looked up from his wooden tablet. His eyebrows rose, wrinkling his broad forehead. "Clodius, is it?"

"Yes, sir. I overheard you speaking with Brother Bremen about poor Adalbert. I'm the one who found his body floating in a lake."

"How dreadful. Bremen said he died of a knife wound. He didn't mention drowning."

"You said he came here often to meet with your patrons."

"I don't know that I said often, but he came from time to time. I never knew when to expect him."

"Do you remember who he met with?"

The owner's eyes rolled to his right. "Who he met? No one in particular. Never even the same person twice, best I recall. Gave me the impression he came more for the stories than any person."

"What stories?"

"Oh, the usual folklore that men spin when they're drinking. Seemed mostly interested in the ones about when the Romans left, during the last big invasion by the Scots. You know, mountains of gold hidden by rich landowners before they fled south, that sort of legend."

"I'm sorry, but I don't know. The Romans left when I was a baby."

He shrugged. "It's just talk. No one takes it seriously."

"Did he?"

A table in a corner erupted with hoots and derisive laughter. Lester's gaze jumped to the racket. "Did who?"

"Did Adalbert? Did he take the stories about hidden treasure seriously?"

"How should I know? Excuse me, but it looks like there's a fight brewing." He hustled over to the men at the table.

I exited the tavern to Bremen's scolding eyes. "Stop your

dawdling, Clodius. We've another delivery to make."

Fritigern stood at the rear of the wagon, his burly arms crossed over his chest. He studied me, peering down his broad nose. I ignored his stare and climbed beside Bremen.

Bremen flipped the reins. "Move it, Castratus, or I'll stop at the butcher's shop to check on the price for stubborn beef."

The ox lumbered forward.

"Should we tell the abbot that Adalbert went to the tavern?"

Bremen looked at me as if I had suggested we pour the rest of his beer into the sewer. "Why in God's name would we do that? Let the poor man be. Whatever sins he carried; he bore to his grave. No need to sully his good name with gossip and rumors."

"But what if he met the killer at the tavern? Shouldn't someone ask questions?"

Bremen huffed. "Some demon-crazed barbarian killed Adalbert. There's nothing more to know about it. So what if he wandered off to Coria every once in a while? If he went to bars, met with men, or even met with the women who frequent such establishments, it's none of your business. Sticking your nose into it will only bring disgrace upon him, and then upon you for smearing his good reputation. Let it go, Clodius."

The finality in Bremen's voice made clear he intended an order, not advice. It did nothing to diminish my inquisitiveness. Obviously, Bremen believed Adalbert had been engaged in sins of the flesh. A scandal couldn't hurt Adalbert. He lay beneath six feet of dirt, clay, and rocks. On the other hand, a scandal might rock the monastery. Bremen did not want to needlessly stir controversy.

Our wagon rolled toward the White Hart Tavern. We passed back through the forum, then turned right on Via Principalis and bumped along the road in front of the Basilica of Martyred Alban, heading toward the western district of the city. The basilica, a brick, hexagonal, domed building, with an adjoining stone bell tower, rose higher than any other edifice in the city.

Bremen grunted and spat on the cobblestones. "You want to ask questions, you'd do better asking about the residents here."

I knew from the two years of my novitiate that Bishop Bonifatius and the abbot were not on the best of terms. Whatever the causes or consequences of the rift, they attracted little attention as the two patriarchs seldom came into contact.

Bremen straightened his back, raising his chin. "Hello. What's he doing skulking about here?"

My gaze followed Bremen's to a vendor's pushcart arrayed with leather goods, small wooden boxes, and ceramic jars. Brother Lazarus stood in front of the stall, fingering a boot while nibbling on a honey-glazed roll covered with crushed nuts.

"Brother Lazarus!" Bremen shouted.

The monk dropped the boot and shot down the adjoining alleyway faster than a rabbit that had seen a hawk's shadow. He never turned to see who had called him.

Bremen frowned. He tilted his head, creased his brow, and peered at me from the corner of his right eye. "That was odd."

Lazarus often behaved erratically. I'd seen him ride a mule backward, flap his arms like he expected to soar as he leaped from a stone wall, and rub his head with Castratus's manure in a presumed display of humility. The fact that he had bolted did not strike me as abnormal, but the sweet bun in his hand piqued my curiosity. Such pastries were not cheap, and we weren't supposed to have money. It could have been given in charity, but that seemed unlikely. In my experience, charity consisted of stale bread, not a nobleman's dessert.

"Did you know he's the bishop's nephew?"

My eyes popped wide. "No."

"Bad enough that Bonifatius has grown fat and lazy after two decades in office, but then he had to push the family lunatic on us. That's the only reason Lazarus is a monk."

"Is that why the abbot dislikes the bishop?"

"Who said the abbot doesn't like him?"

Bremen himself had insinuated it more than once in our many journeys to deliver beer. I lowered my head and stared back at him through the tops of my eyes.

Bremen pretended to ignore me. He focused his stare on Castratus's rolling haunches.

"Maybe he came here to visit his uncle," I said.

"Bonifatius didn't send him away to our monastery because he enjoyed his company. More likely he's on one of his crazy whims. Lazarus knows he's not supposed to be here. That's why he scatted."

A litter carried on the shoulders of four priests burst upon us from an intersecting alleyway. Bremen gave the reins a sharp tug. "Whoa, Castratus!" The wagon jerked to an abrupt stop. Bremen leaned into my ear and spoke softly. "Here's the bleeding prince of darkness himself, riding his bleeding throne."

The bishop rode high upon the litter in a fleece-lined straight-backed chair. He had a flowing gray beard, his sideboards mashed into the rim of a peaked, black cap, pulled down tightly on his broad forehead. Long drooping creases, etched by years of querulous frowns, lined his cheeks from his nose to his chin. A heavy gold chain hung from his collar, a jeweled cross larger than my hand bounced in rhythm with the carriers' steps upon the well-fed belly beneath the bishop's black robe.

Bremen opened his mouth with a toothy grin. "Good day, Bishop."

Bonifatius tapped the litter's rail twice with his staff, and the priests stopped, blocking our route.

"God bless you, Brother Bremen. Making your rounds, I gather."

Fritigern jumped from the rear of the wagon and prostrated his big body on the road.

Bremen rolled his brown eyes and returned his gaze to

63

the bishop. "It's a thirsty town. We do what we can."

The bishop gave Fritigern an approving nod. He closed one eye and glared with his open green eye at me. He snorted, then focused his gaze on the wagon's contents. "And what's the cost of a barrel of ale nowadays?"

"Ten denarii, Eminence, and a bargain at that price."

The bishop's fat lips silently moved, as he scanned the stacked barrels. His eyebrows twitched, like a man coveting his neighbor's new horse. "You're doing well then."

"Yes, thank you, Eminence. We'll just be on our way."

The bishop gave no indication of being ready to move. "My condolences for your tragic loss."

"Sir?"

"Brother Adalbert's death. Still a young man as I remember."

"News travels fast. We only found him yesterday."

The bishop smiled. "God's eyes are always upon you."

"And more than just his by the sound of it."

Bonifatius's smile flipped to a frown. He squirmed in his chair, readjusting his great bulk. "I worry about your little community, Brother. Times have changed. There's no law and order outside the city's walls. I do wish the abbot would agree to move within Coria's protection. There's plenty of room for you at the basilica."

"Thank you for your concern. I'll be sure to relay your offer to Abbot Mutter."

"Do that. Your men would be much safer."

"And so much easier to keep an eye on, not to mention the eternal benefits of placing everything we grow, make, and sell under the blessing of your watchful gaze and protection."

The bishop's lids narrowed. "You'd do well to consider your jeopardy."

Bremen looked skyward and made the sign of the cross. "And God's blessed angels who guard us against it. I thank you for your persistent prayers and blessings, Eminence."

"There are rumblings in the north, Bremen. It's only a

matter of time until raiders return. Your compound's walls and monk's prayers will not save you. Adalbert's death is a sign."

"Sign? A sign of what, Eminence?"

The bishop's face blossomed red. "That you're not safe. That danger is at your door. That you should move to the town."

"Ah, I see your point. I'll be sure to tell the abbot of your concerns, Eminence."

The big man frowned. He leaned back in his chair. "Good day." He tapped his staff twice to his chair's wooden side. The litter bearers hustled onward, clearing our path.

Bremen grunted. He glanced at Fritigern still prostrate. "Get back to the wagon, you dolt. The man's a bishop, not the bleeding Son of God."

Fritigern lifted from the dirty road and shuffled back to the wagon's rear.

Bremen shook his head, gazing at the bishop's retinue. "Lord, forgive me, but the man's an arrogant ass." He snapped the reins and guided the wagon toward the White Hart.

"He's probably right about more raids," I said. "Without the Roman army to guard the wall, sooner or later the Scots and the Picts will come south again."

"True, but I assure you it's not our well-being that's on the bloody bishop's mind. Technically, he may be the abbot's superior, but he has no real control over us. He'd love to get his grubby hands on our library, my beer, and our harvest. If we move into the city, we'll become his slaves. No, thank you. I like our nice little retreat just fine, thank you very much."

Just after the ninth hour, we arrived at the White Hart Tavern. A dappled sunlight played upon the north face of the buildings. A crowd filled the tavern and blocked the front door. The owner directed us to the rear of the building for our delivery. I stepped over two snoring drunks sprawled in the street to reach the rear door. Fritigern tripped over the second body. The man kicked at him with an inebriated thrust of his leather boot.

I set my barrel next to the back door then retraced my steps, trying not to disturb those sleeping. At the rear of the wagon, my heart fluttered when I spotted a familiar-looking pushcart loaded with folds of wool, its handles braced against the wall of the insula across the street. My gaze darted up and down the street.

Men tussled in the tavern's doorway. Julia's hulking father shoved his way through the bodies jamming the front door. Someone in the crowd extended his leg, catching the fuller at his ankles. He fell face forward, breaking his fall with his outstretched right hand, but not avoiding planting his jaw into the paving stones. He lay motionless, groaning. Mocking laughter echoed from the tavern doorway.

"Watch your step there, Rufus."

"Better to watch how much he swills," another man said.

I rushed to the big man, thinking far more of Julia than with any concern for her father's injury. I reached under his shoulder and gently rolled him to his side. The smell of beer on his breath almost made me gag. His smashed nose bled profusely. Dirt and loose pebbles pimpled his forehead.

"Sir, are you all right?"

He blinked. His dilated pupils skittered then focused on me. "Who the devil are you?"

"I'm Clodius."

Fritigern emerged from the alleyway and knelt to my right. "Can I help?"

"Who the devil is he?"

"He's Fritigern. We're from St. Antony's."

"I don't need a goddam priest. I need a drink."

My emotions jumped between embarrassment and offense. Sinister aspirations prickled my skin. "Can we help you up?" I lifted his elbow.

He flung his arm and snarled. "Bugger off, I said!"

Fritigern backed away immediately.

Auburn curls still lingered in my head, fogging my better

judgment. "I'm not a priest. I'm only a novice. Is your home nearby? I can run for a family member to help you. A son, or maybe, *a daughter*?"

He slapped my hands away, then staggered to his feet. He glanced at his cart. His hands balled into fists. "Where's that silly girl run off to? I told her to stay with the cart. She'd better not be with that boy again. I'm going to beat the tar out of her when I find her."

My dreams had always envisioned an idyllic home life, a chaste daughter, loving parents, a fiery brazier warming a happy home. Stunned, I stood like a statue, unable to speak or move.

Julia's father stumbled to the cart, grabbed the handles, then shoved it away from the wall and down the street, all the while grumbling. He stubbed his foot against an uneven cobblestone. He cursed loudly, hopping on one foot. After several heartbeats, he resumed his drunken stagger.

"Thank you for your kindness."

I turned around. Translucent green eyes melted my heart.

"My father can be … difficult."

Words that normally came easily evaded my lips like scattering crows. My heart sprinted, my face burned hot, my mind could only focus on Julia's creamy white skin, dazzling eyes, and auburn curls blowing about her face. "I-I-I—"

She spread her lips, revealing perfectly aligned teeth. "I think I've seen you here before. Isn't there usually a different boy with you?"

"Eu-Eu-Eutychus." I couldn't believe myself. My lips sputtered my friend's name as my first coherent word to my goddess.

"I do hope he is well."

I dug my fingernails into the heels of my hands, hoping pain would unfetter my traitorous tongue. "A snake bit him."

Julia's smile died. She pursed her lips. "Oh my!"

Inspiration hit me. "But I saved him—saved his life, I mean. Me. All by myself."

Her smile blossomed again. "Then he's fortunate to have

such a brave friend as you."

"Yes. He's lucky. Lucky to have a brave friend. A friend like me. Lucky." My tongue rambled out of control, answering to some blathering idiot who had kidnapped my mouth.

Julia lifted her hand to cover her smile and tittered. She took two steps away, then hesitating, turned her head. "Goodbye. Thank you again." And then Julia left, chasing after her father.

Words that had escaped me came flooding into my head. Wait. My name is Clodius. You're beautiful. I love you. But now my feet had turned to stone. I stood mesmerized, locked by some invisible chains shackling my wrists and ankles.

"Wake up, fool." Fritigern shoved my shoulder. "Don't expect me to unload the wagon by myself."

Not even my hairy companion's growl could shake me from my euphoric trance. My old fantasies obsolete, a newer version of reality formed in my head. Julia's father became a beast, she a captive beauty. She needed a hero, someone brave and fearless.

She needed me.

Chapter XI

Julia and her father dominated my mind as we returned to the monastery. The passing landscape blurred as a backdrop to my visions of rescuing my princess from the vicious ogre. I, the holy champion, burst into Julia's home, surely a dungeon cellar. Brandishing a sword, or sometimes an ax, I cleaved the chains binding her hands and feet and swept her into my arms while holding the monster at bay. The fantasy changed with endless variations. Sometimes I stabbed the beast in the heart. Other times my sword lopped off his head. At first, my daydreams concluded with us running into the street but then evolved to a fuzzy notion of some fortified sanctuary that existed nowhere but my head. In later versions, Julia and I escaped into the open country or into a bright but ambiguous future. No matter. Her eternal gratitude cemented our love. I'd encircle her narrow waist with my arms, and she'd press her soft, rosebud lips against mine.

Our wagon rolled through the main gate into the monastery's compound. Sweaty tonsured heads, homely faces, and eroded brick peeking through fractured plaster jolted me back to reality. Nero lay on his side near the kitchen's back door, flies buzzing around his head, his sad brown eyes hoping for scraps that the kitchener might throw his way. Two chickens pecked at the dirt. A red-capped rooster perched on the corner ledge of the main house, keeping a lookout. This was not the home of a valiant champion. It was a hideaway for destitute, broken-hearted men, fleeing whatever injustice or hardship life had tossed at them. They had traded their liberty for a secluded, austere existence. It was my home. My mind sank into a bog of hopelessness. I was one of them or would soon become one of them at the end of my novitiate.

My fantasies about Julia were foolish and impossible. If I burst into her home, I'd be brandishing a shovel at best. Though I was fit and healthy, her father was a bull to my yearling. He'd pick me up and toss me from his home like last month's soiled straw. Even if I somehow evaded the brute, Julia would look up at me with a mystified expression and ask, "Do I know you?"

I passed through the dormitory's doorway, darkness engulfing me, the air redolent of mildew and human habitation. My cell lay at the far end, nearest to the back door leading to the latrine. A faint, acrid odor of unburied urine seeped through my tiny window, reminding me of my punishment and the need to clean the nasty holes and pour lye. Beneath the aperture, my half-used tallow candle stood solitary upon a brick outcropping that served as a narrow shelf. The charred stub of the wick protruded through the melted globs of yellowed wax at the center and puddled at its base. Other than my straw pallet and clothes, that candle was my sole possession. Not much to offer a beautiful princess.

"Welcome home." Eutychus stood in the dark hallway, his oval face shadowed except for his nose and forehead that reflected the dim light passing through the window. He hobbled to my doorway, a yew limb serving as a crudely fashioned crutch wedged into his left armpit.

I smiled, the gloom in my head brightening. "How's your leg?"

"Better, thanks to you. I'm sorry for not saying it earlier. I don't remember much. Finnian says you carried me on your back all the way from the woods. You saved my life. Thanks."

My sagging shoulders straightened. My friend's gratefulness warmed me with a small measure of restored self-esteem. Had he also forgotten how I soiled my robes? Perhaps I could play the hero after all. My heartbeat quickened. I had more news to share. "Did you know that Adalbert had escaped debtor's prison?"

Eutychus's eyes lit up. "What? No. How did you find that out?"

"Bremen told me."

"What else did he tell you?"

"Nothing else useful."

Eutychus frowned. "Well, I guess it's something." He leaned his left shoulder into my door frame.

I inclined toward him. "But Lester at the Red Dragon told me Adalbert had been coming to his tavern, asking questions about buried treasure. He says the stories are just wishful legends, but I can see why a man hounded for his debts might be interested."

"Do you think it has something to do with his murder?"

I screwed my lips tight and rubbed the back of my neck. "Maybe. The abbot seems to think that someone from his past killed him. Someone might have been collecting an old debt. Haman told me just before Adalbert disappeared, he had asked if he knew how to cook a hog."

Eutychus scratched his elbow. "A pointless question unless he'd come across one, or the means to buy one."

I nodded. "Exactly."

My friend hopped to my pallet and slid his back down the wall to rest on my bedding. He sighed with relief, the weight off his leg. "I never told you, but I saw Adalbert several times in the woods, south of the lake."

"When?"

Eutychus bit his thin lower lip. "I have a confession to make. I've been sneaking out a lot … to go swimming … mostly at night."

I'd been horribly wicked to sneak away with my friend a few times during daylight. No wonder he'd been punished by the serpent. "Have you learned your lesson?"

"Lesson?" He tapped his leg. "You mean this? Yeah, I've learned a lesson. The next time I go, I'll be better armed."

I frowned. Not the lesson I had in my mind, but just like Eutychus to be impenitent. "What was Adalbert doing in the woods?"

"I kept my distance. That area is riddled with pits and caves. He appeared to be looking for something."

"Like buried treasure?"

"Based on what you've learned, I'd say that's a good bet. Maybe he found something … maybe someone found him …

someone with a dagger." He frowned and dropped his gaze to the dirt floor. "When we found his corpse, I immediately felt guilty. I didn't know what he'd been doing out there, but I knew it wasn't safe. I should have told someone. But I couldn't get past the notion of having to explain how I knew. I never said a word to anyone, until now."

"Let's just keep that to ourselves, shall we? Fritigern has already placed the knife in our hands. We don't need to bolster his slander with evidence."

"Is that why you hit him?"

"I didn't hit him. Who told you that? It was more of a stranglehold."

"Finnian said you apologized on your knees. That had to hurt. Doeskin's a loud-mouthed, self-righteous, tattletale. Whatever you did, he deserved it."

"Thanks. Abbot Mutter disagrees with you."

Eutychus lifted his left leg and rotated his foot, his ankle bone popping. "It'll be a day or so before I can get around well enough to help. What's the next step?"

My eyebrows rose. "The next step?"

"To catch the killer."

His question should not have surprised me, but it did, nevertheless. Finding the killer followed me like my shadow. My mischievous friend hardly seemed a likely vessel to carry God's prompting, but I could not deny that Eutychus's interest enthused me.

"I'm not sure. To search for caves maybe?"

"Count me in."

"If we get caught, Abbot Mutter will lock us up—maybe even expel us."

"Yeah, I know. Mutter gave me the same lecture." Eutychus cocked his curly head and remained silent for a heartbeat. He shrugged. "I don't know. Would that be so bad?"

"We'd have no food, no shelter, no home. Yeah, that would be bad!"

"Okay—okay! Don't get angry. I like to eat just as much

as anyone. It's just that … well … you know … as long as we're together … you know … ah … what I mean is … we could manage."

Blood surged to my head and warmed my face. I appreciated the shadows of my room hiding my rush of emotion. My friend and I shared this moment of awkward candor, his words coming as close as either of us dared to express about our feelings of loyalty and devotion. I knew exactly what he meant, but my sense of manly propriety embarrassed me.

I glanced at his bandaged leg. "The slopes in the hills are rocky. There are thorn bushes, wild animals, and … snakes. Are you sure you'll be up to it?"

His lips parted in a beaming smile. "Are you kidding? A dead body, buried treasure, murder, secret caves. It's the best thing that's ever happened here."

Chapter XII

The next day Prior Tomas assigned the novices to work in the fields. The barley's bright green and golden-haired stalks stood chin high, rippling and swirling like a vast amber sea under the sunny morning sky. The grain would be ready to harvest in the next week or so, whenever the monks decided, but more eyes than the monks' watched the grain. The crows, sparrows, field mice, rats, and squirrels, just to name a few, had already commenced their own harvest. The prior tasked us to hunt and shoo them away.

Walking among the stalks, I carried a pitchfork and jabbed the sharp prongs at whatever moved near my feet. Occasionally, I'd frighten away a brown or gray ball of fur hiding in the underbrush. Our most potent weapon, though, was noise, not iron. I stomped, whooped, and hollered at the top of my lungs, and otherwise joined with my fellow field hands in making the loudest racket possible. Flocks of blackbirds squawked in protest and beat their wings, rising into the air, while tiny, scurrying rodents dashed among the dense foliage.

What kept me on my toes, of course, was not the rodents, but rather my fear of what might be feeding on them. Monks had once hauled a six-foot-long serpent out of the tall grass. Most snakes were not venomous. Brother Michael even welcomed them, saying they ate the pests. But that gave little comfort. Wading among the thick growth presented little opportunity to inspect a snake for poisonous fangs. Good or bad, I poised ready to stab with my pitchfork at the first hint of slithering scales. There's no such thing as a friendly snake.

Someone shouted my name from the edge of the field. Brother Gunther's big blond head stood tall above the golden kernel silks, his hands cupped to his mouth. He motioned with his husky arms for me to join him.

"Clodius, you have visitors."

What? I'd never had a visitor. "Who?"

Gunther shrugged. "Prior Tomas didn't say. They're

waiting in the reception hall."

They? My mind raced through faces trying to imagine who 'they' could be. The only faces I could remember from Coria were Lester, the bishop, Julia, and her father. The bishop wouldn't visit me. If he had some reason to speak with me, I'd be summoned. Perhaps Lester had some news about Adalbert that he wanted to share. That seemed even less likely than a visit from the bishop. I remembered babbling something about my name and home to Julia's father. Had I offended him? I hadn't told Julia my name. My heart had been racing so fast and my thoughts been so fuzzy that I might have said anything—but not my name. If her father had seen us talking, maybe he'd deduced I threatened his daughter's virtue. Maybe he'd awoken from his drunken stupor and held me responsible for his bloody face. I squeezed the handle my pitchfork, wondering whether to carry it for defense.

"I'll take that," Gunther said. "I'll cover for you until you return." He tromped off into the tall grain with my weapon.

I dragged my feet to the compound, my nerves jittery, entering by way of the main gate, then hesitated before plodding into the main house and through the atrium. Crossing the peristyle, I drew a deep breath, braced myself, then stepped into the reception hall.

Rubicus and Pilatus, my real brothers, waited on a bench.

My blood turned to ice. I seized the doorframe to steady my wobbling legs.

Dust covered my brothers' cloaks. Dirt smudged their faces. They stood as I entered, their mouths agape. Almost three years had passed since they had abandoned me. My height had increased by at least a foot, and my adolescent frame had filled out with muscles thanks to years of hard work. I was not the intimidated whelp they had abandoned, either physically or mentally.

Rubicus bared his teeth in what I supposed he intended to be a warm smile. I saw only yellowed fangs. Thick black hair covered his head, falling to his neck and blending with his unkempt bushy beard. "Little Clodius! What a man you've become! Praise God, you look well!" He lifted his arms and stepped toward me as if he expected that I would rush to his embrace.

I stood my ground.

Pilatus slouched at Rubicus's side, in his shadow, where he'd always been most comfortable. He hunched forward at his shoulders with an unbalanced posture that made him look as if he might totter to his left. He grinned at me, not showing any teeth, assuming he still had any. He possessed my father's large earlobes and my mother's mousy brown hair and blue eyes. His semblance to Mater stirred my anxiety as to which of my mother's traits I might have inherited.

Prior Tomas folded his slender hands at his chest and padded toward me. He tapped my arm as he passed. "I'll leave you now."

My gaze locked on Rubicus. "This is a surprise."

Rubicus dropped his arms. "Such a frosty reception. Is this how you show your gratitude to your kin?"

"What exactly am I supposed to be grateful about?"

Rubicus glanced at Pilatus and shook his head. "Can you believe it? We've worked our hands to the bone. Provided shelter and food. Raised him to maturity. Gave him the opportunity for godly learning, never once asking for thanks, not caring about ourselves, doing it only because we wanted the best for him and to fulfill our pledge to our blessed father and poor demented mother. What do we get in return? A haughty frown. Can you believe our own flesh and blood could be so callous?"

Pilatus's eyelids narrowed to mean slits. "I wouldn't have believed it. Not even if the bishop of Rome himself had said so."

Rubicus again raised his arms and spread them wide. "Come now, Clodius. Forget whatever misgivings your addled brain has conjured. Give your brothers the warm embrace they merit."

My memory of our family's history did not jibe with my

brother's. My father had died unexpectedly before his fortieth birthday. He lifted a heavy wheel to an axle and dropped dead on the spot. There'd been no time for deathbed pledges to care for the baby in the family. As for my mother, she'd become more feral than human. She didn't know my name when she died. Yes, for sixteen years I'd lived under the same roof as my older brothers, but it had hardly been a saintly upbringing. They neglected to teach me my father's craft, instead training me to pilfer items from wagons their victims called them to repair. While they hemmed and hawed, occupying the owner's attention about price, they'd set me to climbing beneath tarps, unlatching baskets, and stealing whatever my nimble body and skinny arms could carry. And whenever the victims caught me in my brothers' schemes, who got the blame? Not them. They'd bluster and slap me about, begging for their irate customer's forgiveness, claiming my mother's evil spirit dwelled in me, promising to punish me for my sins. Aside from their cursing, their first mention of God that I could recall occurred on my sixteenth birthday when Rubicus announced they had decided to give me to the holy fathers forty miles away. Perhaps my unruly reputation had at last damaged their business prospects, or my growth spurt and awkwardness had diminished my abilities as a thief. For whatever reason, they saw no further use for me.

Our reception hall was the house's tablinum, a large room where Romans greeted their guests and conducted business. Four plain wooden benches and a small table supporting a bronze cross furnished the austere room. I moved behind the table, the only barrier in the room to shield me from the last remnants of my family. "Why are you here?"

Rubicus's beefy arms slapped to his side. "Because you're our flesh and blood, dear brother, and whether you know it not, you need us. We're here to protect you."

"That would be a first! Protect me from what?"

"Perhaps news travels slowly, Clodius. We've run nearly the whole way, carrying nothing but the clothes that we wear, living off our wits and the land."

"Living off the backs of innocent victims more likely. Why the urgency?"

"The Picts, dear brother. The Picts. There's a massive herd of blue-bodied savages marching east. They've crossed the old Roman wall, burning down every farm and hamlet in their path. They're heading this way."

"That's not possible. We'd know about it."

Rubicus sneered. "Don't believe me, your loving brother, if you want. But don't delude yourself. You'll hear about it soon enough. Those lucky enough to escape, like us, will soon be washing up on your threshold with the Picts on their heels."

My brother lied more often and better than most, but I could think of no reason for him to lie about an invasion. I decided to believe him. "And what does this have to do with me?"

"Pilatus and I are headed south to Eboracum and then to Londinium. We'll find a boat to carry us to Armorica. There's still Romans there and the Franks. It's safe. We can start over."

"I still fail to see how this involves me."

My brothers exchanged flustered glances. "You think we'd leave you behind? To suffer at the bloodthirsty hands of the Picts and their cannibalistic appetites? What kind of brothers would we be? You must come with us, Clodius. You'll die if you stay here."

I feared the Picts and the Scots and the Danes for that matter, but except for their random raids, they'd not yet shown a desire for permanent conquest. Deep down, I knew that someday it might happen, but what could I do? Besides, chasing blackbirds, saying prayers, and chanting hymns left little time to worry about the future. Why fret about things beyond my control—what no one could control—except for God?

I studied my brothers. Filial love didn't motivate them. My gullibility didn't stretch that far. They needed me for some reason. They could not expect that I'd resume my career as a thief after nearly three years of training to become a monk. I didn't have any money. I tried to picture myself traveling alongside them, fleeing south. The Genesis story of Joseph joining his brothers in Dothan sprang into my head.

"Let's say I believe you, Londinium is at least a three-week journey. How will we survive? And assuming we reach the port safely, how could we ever pay for transportation to Armorica?"

Rubicus smiled. "There. You see, Pilatus. Didn't I say Clodius was a smart one?"

Pilatus's weak chin bounced up and down. "That's what you told me. He said it, Clodius. Every day. Clodius is a smart one, he said. He'd know what to do."

Rubicus stepped to the table. He traced his grimy fingers over the edges of the bronze cross. "Food should not be a problem. Your good brethren can spare charity enough for three travelers, especially one of their own. But money is more difficult. After all, the monks take a vow of poverty."

"You're probably right," I said. "The monks would give us food. But it's a long trip for nothing if we can't buy passage to the continent."

Rubicus lifted the cross to his sweat-streaked face. He closely inspected the metal. "Such a pity, don't you think? Everything here will be destroyed or carried away by the heathens. So much beauty, so many precious gifts honoring the Lord, all to be lost to flames or melted for pagan devil worship. What a waste. More than a waste, I'd call it a crime, a crime against God."

He may have been right about the fate of the monastery. Time would tell. But a crime of a different nature occupied Rubicus's mind.

I stretched my lips in a feigned smile, then wrested the cross from his grip. I slammed it back to the table. "It's time for you to leave."

He bared his teeth, his face burning red. "What? You'd throw us out? Without even a crust of bread? What kind of

Christian are you?"

I walked to the doorway, extended my arm, and pointed at the atrium exit across the garden. "The honest kind. Please leave now," I said, my voice calm, but my insides trembling.

"Don't be a fool, Clodius! No one's going to miss a few trinkets! No one will ever care because they'll all be dead!"

"I'll know. God will care. That's more than enough."

Rubicus stomped his foot. He swung his arm and slapped the cross, sending it spinning across the table. I leaped after it, catching it just before it crashed to the floor.

"You can go to hell! All of you! Come on, Pilatus, we have no brother here."

My last two blood relatives stormed out of the room and headed toward the atrium. The tension in my muscles relaxed. I exhaled with a long, slow breath and prayed to never see them again. I returned the cross to the table and walked to the doorway.

The prior stood nearby, leaning his shoulder against a red column, watching me. Had he been there the whole time?

A tidal wave of shame slammed my heart. The same rotted roots that had produced my brothers had sprouted me. The less the monks knew about my sordid family history, the better. I'd come to presume that at the end of my training my enrollment into the monastery as a monk would be automatic, but I could be wrong. What might become of me if at the end of my novitiate the monks rejected me?

Tomas straightened. He folded his hands within the sleeves of his habit and stepped toward me. His brown eyes glistened, soft and sympathetic. "I heard shouting. Is everything all right?"

I glanced back toward the atrium. My brothers were gone. "I don't think they'll be coming back. They wanted me to go with them to Londinium."

Tomas sighed deeply. "Life's choices can be difficult. You refused; I gather."

I nodded.

Tomas placed a hand on my shoulder. His fingers pressed

into my skin. A reassuring warmth radiated through my arm. "You've done well to remain with us, Clodius. God is pleased. He will bless you for your faithfulness."

My reasoning had not been as noble as the prior believed, but nevertheless, pride swelled my heart.

Tomas lifted his hand and returned it to the folds of his sleeves. "We have all faced difficult decisions, Clodius. It's no small matter to turn your back on the world and embrace austerity. Some people accuse us of madness. Others say we are cowards." He grinned. "Maybe there's a glimmer of truth in both, but it's not the full truth." He looked skyward. "Those on the outside can't understand what it means to devote your life to a broader purpose than just filling your belly with rich food or wearing fine clothes. Nor do they see our unity. It's God's interest we serve. Bigger than any one of us." His gaze lowered to the atrium doorway through which Rubicus and Pilatus had exited. "It's what it means to be brothers, more truly than the loins that birthed us." He focused his gaze on me. "It binds us."

My chest warmed. Despite meeting my deplorable family, the prior accepted me.

An urgent memory grabbed me. "There's important news. My brothers said an army of Picts has crossed Emperor Hadrian's Wall. They're heading toward Coria."

Tomas's bushy eyebrows shot upward. For one instant, terror lit in his brown eyes, then vanished so swiftly that perhaps I had projected my own fears onto him. "That can't be correct. We would have heard something."

"Maybe we just did," I said.

Tomas stroked his square cheek. "I'll speak to the abbot. We can send a runner to the city. The prefect will know if there's been an invasion. Until we confirm it, don't tell anyone else. We mustn't cause a panic."

I bowed my head. "I should return to the fields, Father."

Tomas nodded and grinned. "Go, my son."

Chapter XIII

Dinner that evening consisted of boiled leeks and wheat bread. A chicken may have wandered near the broth as it boiled, but meat came no closer. Eutychus sat next to me, pushing his spoon at an opaque tuber floating on the surface of his soup. He frowned, sighed, and placed his utensil beside the bowl. He lifted his slice of brown bread to his mouth and nibbled it, making it last.

Brother Silvanius, the most recent monk to have taken his vows, disturbed supper's mandated silence as he rushed into the refectory through the center door. His skinny chest heaved. He hesitated, scanning the room. He hurried to the abbot seated at the head of our long table and whispered into Mutter's ear. Whatever the news, Mutter's dour face retained a stoic indifference. The abbot nodded, then motioned for Silvanius to be seated and eat. He grimaced, his eyes glazed as he scanned the table's meager offerings, but he bowed his narrow head and found an empty seat at the table behind me.

Eutychus nudged me with his elbow. He lifted his left eyebrow.

I had a notion of the news Silvanius carried but based on the abbot's reaction I could not be certain. I patted the table's boards with my fingertips, signaling Eutychus to be patient.

After we'd cleared the dishes, the novices assembled with the monks and proceeded in single file to the church. Abbot Mutter led us in prayers. Brother Lucius led us in song. Nero howled in chorus outside. It seemed ordinary.

The abbot raised his hands to give a final blessing but then paused. He lowered his arms, stepped from the altar dais, and walked to the center of our two rows. "Brothers, Silvanius has brought me grave news from Prefect Linus. One thousand Picts are marching east toward Coria."

The church echoed with gasps. Across the nave, directly opposite me, Eutychus's gaze bore into mine. I nodded furtively.

"We mustn't panic," Mutter said. "They're making slow

progress. The spring harvest is ready. The Picts are scouring the land, reaping every grain in their path in addition to their looting and killing. We have at least three days to prepare."

"Prepare?" Nebridius, the short almoner, squeaked. "How can we prepare except to flee?"

Bremen stepped forward. "I've got one hundred barrels of beer ready to sell. We can't leave them behind for the pagans to guzzle. We don't have the wagons to carry them."

Michael lifted his arm and pointed in the direction of the fields. "The barley is ready to harvest. That will take at least three days even with every man working. It's not enough time."

The room erupted with excited discussions between neighbors and shouts hurled across the room. Discussions became arguments. The noise escalated and reverberated from the stone walls, eclipsing Nero's droning howl. Eutychus just stared at me, grinning from ear to ear.

"Brothers!" Abbot Mutter's shout brought swift silence. The abbot continued. "Darkness is upon us, brothers. There is nothing we can do tonight. Retire to your beds. Get a good night's rest. You will need your strength in the morning. Prior Tomas and I will formulate a plan and issue assignments at breakfast. Now go."

Anxious, plaintive murmurs echoed.

Mutter silenced the dissension with a stern gaze.

Tight-lipped, we shuffled out of the church.

Eutychus pushed through the monks to reach my side. He tugged at my robe, slowing my pace, allowing the others to leave us behind. "Did you know?" he whispered.

"My older brothers showed up today and told me. They're running away."

"What will we do?"

I shrugged. "It's up to the abbot."

Eutychus shook his head. "No. I mean about finding Adalbert's killer."

The matter had completely slipped my mind. The approaching Picts worried me far more, but God would not let me forget. I was Jonah, my friend the whale. I resented God's adamancy. In three days, our world would be in flames. There'd likely be more bodies than poor Adalbert's to bury. What did it matter now? And yet with breathless excitement, Eutychus stared at me, his eyes brimming confidence in my leadership.

A lump rose in my throat. I could not disappoint him. "How's your leg?"

"I'm healed. What's your plan?"

"We need to search the caves. We can sneak out tonight. Wait until everyone's in bed. I'll meet you behind the balneary."

"Perfect. I'll be there."

A waning moon, nestled among billowy clouds, shined a faint light through the tiny window of my cell. The initial silence of bedtime had given way to a cacophony of snores, some rumbling so loud the earth trembled beneath my straw pallet. I rose from my bed and peeked through my doorway to make sure that the corridor was clear. Seeing no one, I stepped out, carrying my sandals to prevent their flopping. At the exit, I exhaled, laced my sandals on my feet, and searched the dimly lit landscape for any signs of activity.

The monastery compound had a different appearance from in the light of day. The heavily trod and pitted dirt looked less even and more hazardous. Rock outcroppings that littered the yard became shadowed boulders, somehow more cumbersome to walk upon. The buildings' weathered walls lost their imperfections, turned to silver, and became solid bastions. The church, more than three times the height of any other structure, loomed in the east. It cast a moon shadow over the roof of the balneary, rendering it almost invisible in the darkness. Nothing moved in the compound. I crouched low nonetheless, hustling toward the bathhouse to meet Eutychus.

A muffled shout paralyzed me. My gaze darted left and right, searching the landscape. A second shout rumbled but like distant thunder.

The Romans had enjoyed their privacy. All the villa's rooms looked inward to the peristyle garden. The back of the house nearest to the dormitory, where the abbot and prior had their offices, had no aperture connected to the sleeping quarters. The voices sounded like they were arguing. Stone, mud brick, and plaster muffled the words, but the heated tone and cadence of the exchange boomed clearly. The abbot had said that he and the prior would be meeting to discuss the best course of action. I had an odd sensation of eavesdropping on my parents fighting—somehow my fault. A disturbing schism had arisen between the abbot and the prior. Whatever the cause, my world felt less secure. Our peace was unraveling. I slinked through the darkness to the back of the main house, hoping to hear something more encouraging.

"… fighting … inevitable … be slaughtered …"

"God's will … faithful … Eboracum … hide …"

I couldn't tell who spoke or what they said, but the angry tone continued. My ears strained until the muffled shouts ended. I stepped away. A flickering candlelight at the villa's east corner arrested me. I dived behind a stack of oak logs used to make barrel staves. The steady tromping of sandals approached, but then veered away. I peeked over the woodpile. Prior Tomas's face glowed in the light of his candle, his tonsured head lowered, his eyes shadowy pits, his jaw tense.

I bit my lower lip, the uncertainty making me weak. The prior had spoken of unity. What if a rift divided us? The abbot against the prior? What would happen to us? To me? Who would I follow? My gaze followed Tomas as he strode to the dormitory. He disappeared through the doorway.

I inhaled slowly, bolstering my frayed nerves. I ducked my head and resumed my careful path to my rendezvous, almost bumping into Eutychus, who stood with his back pressed against the balneary's north wall. He raised a forefinger to his lips, then pointed toward the compound's outer wall. He followed me in silence around the church to the northwest corner of the complex.

The monastery's outer walls had been constructed when the Roman army had been garrisoned in Coria. They were built for seclusion, not defense. Though they stood seven-feet-tall, tree limbs overhung many locations. Cracks pitted the bricks, providing footholds. A small child would have no trouble scaling them. Should the Picts ever arrive, the walls would provide just a hiccup of security before the slaughter would begin.

Eutychus and I climbed the wall and jumped to the ground, landing in the cemetery, Adalbert's fresh grave on our right. We quickened our pace, less cautious of our footsteps, skirted the graveyard, then turned to find the dirt track leading to the Roman highway. I stumbled in the darkness.

Eutychus chuckled. "Follow me. I've done this a few times."

We reached the rutted path, and the footing became less treacherous.

I tapped my friend's arm. "When we get to the caves, what exactly are we looking for? Buried treasure doesn't just lie about. It's … well, you know … buried."

Eutychus glanced over his shoulder. "I've been thinking about that. We'll have to look for footprints and signs of activity. Rocks chipped or rolled away. Tree limbs broken. Dirt turned with a shovel. If we're lucky, there might be a recent fire pit. I don't know. Just keep your eyes open. I'm more concerned that if Adalbert found anything, the killer has already removed it."

His words did not encourage me. "We may at least find an empty hole. It would lend credence to our theory. But I'm optimistic that whatever Adalbert found, it's still there. If someone had shown up in Coria with a lot of old Roman coins or jewelry, I think we would have heard something. It's more likely the killer would leave it safe until he could figure out how to remove it without causing a stir."

"You may be right, especially now with the Picts descending upon us," Eutychus said.

"The killer wouldn't have known about the Picts."

"True."

"But maybe the news of the invasion will help us," I said.

"Help us?"

"The abbot said 1,000. The killer has got to be considering running, just like my brothers. If he does, he won't leave the treasure behind."

"You think he'll come to retrieve it?"

"Wouldn't you?"

Eutychus tromped on in silence. The vague outline of the pasture wall and the Roman road appeared ahead of us.

"It would be nice to catch him in the act," Eutychus said.

"That's what I've been thinking, too. It would require us to keep watch near the caves. The turmoil of the next few days can help us to steal away from time to time, but it will be hard for just two of us to maintain a vigil. We may miss the killer entirely."

We reached the stone wall. I climbed over it first, scratching my ankle and knee. Eutychus showed off by vaulting it.

"Your leg seems to be fully healed."

"Never better," he said.

I marched on, taking the lead. "I think we need to recruit a helper."

Eutychus groaned. "The abbot will find out. He'll lock us up."

"Olaf wouldn't betray us."

"What makes you so sure?"

"The way he looks at us. Especially you. I think he idolizes you."

Eutychus feigned a cough. "I hope it's not more than a role model he desires."

"What are you talking about?"

"Well, look at him. He looks more woman than man."

My breathing grew heavy as we ascended the hill into the

woods. "Trust me. I've seen him in the bath. There's not a female hiding under his habit."

"That's not what I meant."

"What are you talking about?"

Eutychus laughed. "You really don't know?"

"Sometimes you're a complete mystery. Pict gibberish is easier to understand."

My friend's laughter grew louder. He huffed and puffed between hoots. "Stop for a minute … my sides are hurting."

"I fail to see the humor." I stopped and turned; my face heated with anger. "I know something of human anatomy. What you say is physically impossible."

Eutychus's eyes became as bright as silver denarii. He howled and fell to the ground, clutching at his ribs. I crossed my arms, utterly vexed while he gasped and gulped choppy breaths.

He brought his laughing under control and struggled to his feet. "I'm sorry, Clodius … but you kill me … you really do." He caught his breath. "You are correct. God fashioned men and women to couple in a certain way, but, my friend, you may have overlooked an orifice or two."

My initial disbelief changed to shock. "That's disgusting. No one could engage in such filth."

Eutychus grabbed at his side. "Please. Enough. I can't take any more. You'll slay me with your innocence. Don't believe me. Ask the abbot or the prior. It's even in the Bible."

His seriousness convinced me of his sincerity. But could men really lust after men in the same wicked way that I relished my daydreams about Julia? It couldn't be true. But it must be.

Eutychus shrugged and pointed onward. "Anyway, I'm sure Olaf will be fine. When should we ask him?"

I spun and resumed my ascent into the woods. "Tomorrow morning. Don't bother yourself. I'll handle it."

We plodded into the forest, heading south to the foot of the limestone hills. I climbed atop a boulder. Behind me, the edge of the lake glowed like a silver crescent, peeking over the forest canopy. Ahead, the terrain became broken and undulating, with white cliff faces and shadowed crevices. It looked enormous and our task impossible.

"Let's start at the bottom," I said. "No need to make this harder than necessary."

"This way," Eutychus said. He strolled off to his left.

I scrambled off the rock and followed him.

We searched every dark corner and countless hole that we encountered among the rocks. I kept a careful watch on the moon's course across the heavens, as we must return to St. Antony's before the monks awoke for nocturns. The longer we looked, the more certain I became of the hopelessness of finding a secret hideaway. When the time came to return, Eutychus did not protest.

Our progress had taken us about one-fourth the way around the base of the hills. We made a straight line for the Roman road rather than retracing our steps through the woods.

Before we reached the road, Eutychus crouched in the waist-high grass. He grabbed my arm and pulled me down with him. He covered his mouth with his palm, then pointed to our left.

A tiny yellow starlight twinkled at ground level to our north. A hooded figure carried a shielded candle or oil lamp, walking into the hills we had just left.

My gaze shot back to the moon. If we delayed, our absence would be discovered. We didn't even know who this person might be. It could be a shepherd, a farmer, an insomniac, or a killer returning for his loot.

"We have to get back," Eutychus whispered. "If the abbot catches us …"

Locked in our cells, we'd never catch the killer. I hated it, but we couldn't risk returning late.

We crawled through the grass toward home until the twinkling light had disappeared. We then hurried back to the compound wall, agreeing to proceed separately back to bed to minimize our noise. Eutychus scaled the wall first. I counted to fifty, then followed.

In the yard, the moon's angle had changed, the church's east side now in the shadows with the dormitory and balneary fully exposed by dim light. The still air carried the drone of snoring across the compound from the dormitory. My nerves relaxed. I had not miscalculated the time of our return. Walking behind the church, clinging to its shadowed wall, I hustled across the gap between the church and the balneary, crouching just in case anyone might be about the yard.

"Ouch!"

I ran smack into a big strong body.

"Who the--?" Fritigern stood frozen before me, his palm pressed against his skull where our heads had collided. His wet hair dripped water on his robe. His eyes drew into dark trenches. "Clodius, what are you doing out here?"

I resisted the urge to run. "Me? What are you doing here?"

"None of your business! I'm asking the questions!"

Sandals shuffled behind Fritigern. Brother Lucius emerged through the doorway. He rubbed his scalp with a small towel. He froze the instant he saw me. His mouth and eyes shot wide; guilt written across his face.

A picture flashed into my head that would have been impossible a few hours earlier. My memory of male groans meshed with the implausible picture of men coupling. A blinding epiphany shot thunderbolts from my head to my soles. My jaw dropped to my belt. An image formed of Fritigern's thick, hairy limbs wrapping around Lucius's flabby body.

Fritigern's gaze oscillated between Lucius and me. His face glowed ashenly. "I-I took a bath—Lucius took a bath—we took a bath."

"I can see that," I said.

"Say nothing of it!" Fritigern said. "Or you'll have to explain your whereabouts this night!"

"Agreed." I dashed for the dormitory, noisily sprinting,

desperate to reach my cell before the laughter erupting from my chest could escape my lungs and shatter the tranquility of the night.

Chapter XIV

Sleep came easily, my fatigue overpowering the whirling questions taxing my mind. Slumber's oblivion transported me to the world beyond reality, that dreamy realm where years became seconds, seconds decades, and the supernatural reigns supreme.

A tiled platform overlooked calm lake waters, the crescent moon shining, white limestone columns glowing, growing, four playing upon lustrous glass, rippling, pulsating. My Julia, my jewel, danced upon the heads of fleece-lined serpents who gushed from the waters like crenelated geysers, catching her every step, twirling, vanishing, then again thrusting upward in an endless pirouette of serpent steppingstones scaling into the cosmos. I reached for her, chased her, the air droning with the groans of ancient seraphs, their throaty chants gliding upon the winds, their cry never ending, their eyes ever watching. Slipping beyond my grasp, my green-eyed temptress turned and beckoned, yet did not wait. The void between us expanded, separating me farther from her touch. The smell of musk and lavender trailed in sparkling stardust from her billowing skirt.

"Wait for me. I love you," I said.

Tittering laughter echoed, a clinking chime against the melancholy tunes of the six-winged angels. I shuddered, my entire organism rapt in delight, crazy with excitement, yet chained by the humble mumble filling my ears, fetters wrapped over my legs and ankles, weight dragging me deep into the waters, my lungs heaving, a rushing torrent bursting from me. And then she fell into my arms, her diaphanous, gossamer gown flapping in the wind, wrapping my thighs, my back, her eyes close to mine, her pupils, deep, bottomless caverns. Warmth and solitude enveloped me.

Her lips parted. The faintest whisper floated to my ears.

"Find the murderer."

Infinite ranks of tiny blue men, a phalanx of spears thrusting forward, their feet stomping, flattening the plain, tromping upon my skin, endless spiny creatures swimming then swirling over me, their pikes stabbing, their feet kicking me, kicking me, kicking me …

"Wake up, Clodius. It's time for morning prayers." Olaf's cherubic face filled my vision. He shook my shoulder. "Hurry up. You'll be late."

A burning sensation heated my groin. My inner thighs stuck together, moist and clammy. A delicious tingle lingered on my skin. I didn't know what had happened, but I felt ashamed. I curled my knees to my chest, rolling away from Olaf to hide my lap.

"Don't go back to sleep."

I twisted my face toward him. "I'll be right there. I have to go to the latrine."

"Okay. I'll see you at the church."

The idea of attending early prayers seemed especially unappetizing. I never liked this time of day, waking before dawn and dragging my weary body to mumble memorized prayers and chant cheerless hymns in the company of my bleary-eyed, unharmonious brethren. But my excitement and the rapid thumping of my heart made me feel especially unworthy, guilty even. I had strong, lustful, sinful desires, but no desire to repent.

I arose from my pallet and rubbed my thighs clean with scratchy straw from the floor. My irritated skin flared painfully. Spreading my feet wide apart, I scuttled away, out of the dormitory, toward the church.

Chapter XV

The entire complement of monks stood in the church, present for nocturns, apart from Lazarus, who probably wandered about on one of his mad larks. That seemed especially risky given the latest news, but the poor man had never demonstrated much of a grasp on reality and the dangers it posed.

Abbot Mutter led us in prayers. Brother Lucius led us in a hymn. Everything seemed the same, but also different. Every word spoken or sung had a nervous jitteriness, a subtle, anxious squeak, hinting that their minds focused not on the chants but on the uncertain future.

After concluding our prayers and hymns, we continued in silence to the refectory where Abbot Mutter blessed our wheat porridge then surprisingly, he remained standing as we took our seats on the benches. "Brothers, I hope you slept well. We have a long day ahead of us. There's no time to waste. Prior Tomas has your work assignments. Does anyone know where Brother Lazarus has gone?"

Heads shook. The brethren exchanged baffled looks. No one spoke. Eutychus raised eyebrows at me. Had we seen Lazarus last night?

"We can't spare anyone for a search party," Mutter said. "Perhaps he has gone to Coria. Bremen, when you're there today, you can make inquiries."

Bremen nodded. "Why am I going to town?"

The abbot looked to Prior Tomas.

The prior stepped forward. Rather than his usual, gracious demeanor, he had tired, bloodshot eyes and puffy lower lids. "We need to remove all the beer to Coria. We don't want to have anything in the monastery to tempt the Picts when they arrive. We've only the one wagon, so you'll have to make several trips."

My heartbeat quickened. Julia.

Bremen stood. "It will only take two trips. Castratus can handle fifty barrels." He grinned. "Should we save a few barrels for ourselves? We may get thirsty on the road when we leave."

Tomas did not smile. He glanced at the abbot, then back to Bremen. "We are not leaving."

Bremen's jaw dropped. He fell back to his seat.

Lucius's bald crown popped just above those surrounding him, then halted, lowered, and pushed higher again as he stood. "D-do you mean we will only go to Coria?"

Tomas shook his head. "We'll remain here at the monastery."

Lucius's flabby jowls shivered. "B-but we have no defense, no way to protect ourselves."

The abbot raised his arms above his head. "We have God's protection."

The cantor's trembling shifted from his cheeks to his hands. He glanced at the other faces in the room. No one stood to join him. "Yes, Abbot, b-but the Picts are heathens. They b-burn churches and slaughter the faithful."

"Courage, brothers," Mutter said. "When St. Alban faced execution for his beliefs, he did not flee. Even upon encountering a blocked bridge, he dried the river so that he could ascend with the axman to the executioner's hill. When the wicked governor of Egypt persecuted Christians, St. Antony did not hide. He marched proudly into Alexandria to accept his fate. God did not abandon them, and he will not abandon us."

These were well-known sacred stories. Alban had been sentenced to death for harboring a Christian in disobedience of the pagan emperor's persecution. He first endured scourging with joyful hymn singing, then his captors led him in chains to his place of execution. People crammed the road out of the city to the hilltop chopping block, rendering the bridge crossing the deep, swift-running river impassable. Not to be denied his martyrdom, St. Alban miraculously dried up the river so that the execution party could cross the bone-dry banks. When the group reached the hill, Alban complained of a thirst, and a pure spring gushed from the ground from which he drank. Stunned by the miracles, the executioner refused to carry out the death sentence. The judge ordered a Roman soldier to complete the task, but he fell to his knees, declared Christ as his king, and refused to obey. A third man showed no such reluctance. He lopped off Alban's and the Roman soldier's heads, but then the new executioner's eyeballs bulged and popped out. He dropped dead next to the beheaded corpses.

St. Antony's tale had a different ending. When he learned that Alexandria's governor persecuted Christians, Antony marched into the city declaring his Christian faith and demanding to be executed. Perhaps intimidated by the saint's dauntless spirit, or maybe thinking the man insane, the governor relented and ended the persecutions. It was never quite clear whether this was a happy ending, but my timidity prevented me from asking the monks to clarify the point. Both Alban and Antony had overtly courted martyrdom. Alban had been successful, aided by miracles. It seemed that therefore martyrdom must be greatly prized and desired. So too Antony must have thought. Yet, a weak-kneed, ambivalent governor frustrated his goal. Maybe if the emperor had been present, he could have replaced the governor with someone more courageous. Instead, poor, dejected Antony had returned to his life of solitude in the desert and died of inglorious old age.

"We must trust in God," the abbot said. "He is our fortress, a strong tower in times of trouble. Even if in his wisdom he sees fit that we should die for our faith, we will be welcomed into his loving arms to reign with Christ for eternity. Hallelujah!"

"Hallelujah," we echoed in response, though like the others surrounding me, my voice did not equal Mutter's enthusiasm. I held no eagerness to follow Alban's or Antony's examples.

The abbot sat, and the monks began to eat. I ate less than half of the bowl. My appetite had vanished.

The novices cleared the tables, and we joined the men in

the garden to receive our daily work assignments. Prior Tomas assigned Eutychus and me to Brother Bremen's beer delivery. I lingered long enough to hear Tomas assign Olaf to the fields where the monks would harvest and store as much of the grain as possible.

I grabbed Olaf's arm and pulled him aside. "Eutychus and I need your help on something."

Olaf's eyes shot wide, and he smiled. "You and Eutychus?"

"Yes, but first you must swear by all that is holy that you will tell no one. It's a secret."

He drew a sharp breath. "A secret? I won't tell anyone."

"Make the sign of the cross and swear it."

He crossed his chest with alacrity. "I swear."

"We're going to catch Adalbert's killer."

He gasped. "You're going to fight the Picts?"

"The Picts didn't kill him. Someone local murdered him. Someone who knew a secret that Adalbert had found."

Olaf's head sagged. "Huh?"

His mouth gaped as I explained our discoveries. When I finished, he swallowed and nervously scratched his forearm. "What do you want me to do?"

"Team with us to keep an eye on the hills."

"How? I'm working the fields."

"There will be lots of confusion. You'll have no trouble slipping away. With everyone in the fields, no one will miss you. Just keep a watch on the Roman road and let us know if you see anyone going into the hills."

"I don't know. It seems kind of—"

"Can Eutychus and I count on you or not?"

Olaf bit his lower lip. He nodded. "Okay. I'll try."

"Good. Just do what you can."

Olaf headed toward the barley. I marched to the brewery to help Eutychus and Bremen load the beer. Silvanius harnessed the ox to the wagon, and Michael helped in stacking the barrels in the rear.

"How's Olaf?" Eutychus asked.

"Shaken, but good. He'll do what's needed."

Bremen slapped me on my back. "I'm proud of you, boy. Taking the younger novices under your wing is showing real leadership."

I did not deserve his praise but smiled at him.

"What did you say?" Michael asked. His cheek twitched.

"Huh? Who?"

"Olaf. What did you say to him?"

I cast Eutychus an annoyed frown for having opened the inquiry. He smirked at me as he handed Michael another barrel. I hesitated, wondering at what point straying from the truth became sin. "That we're a team. He can count on us. We need to know we can count on him."

Silvanius grunted, tugging on the leather bellyband under Castratus's gut. "Do you think the stories about Picts eating humans are true?"

"Now there's a happy turn of subject," Michael said.

"You don't need to worry about it," Eutychus said. "I spent four months with them and never saw a human sacrificed or eaten. It's just a story the Romans told to frighten their children. Even if true, no one would want to chew on your skinny bones. Now Brother Bremen here, he's a different story. Look at those hams, would you?"

Bremen stopped in mid-stride and frowned at Eutychus. "Keep focused on your work, boy. We've enough troubles without worrying about the bleeding Picts' diet."

Silvanius glanced at the brewer. "One thousand. Did I hear that right?"

Bremen said, "Aye, a legion of the bloodthirsty savages. Hurry now. If they catch us on the road, there'll be no escape."

"But so many. I didn't think it possible. I've never heard of more than forty or fifty banding together."

Michael nudged Silvanius's skinny arm. "Since when did you become an expert on Pict warriors?"

"No, he's right," Eutychus said. "The village that enslaved me had less than one hundred, men, women, and children combined. They never showed much respect for or interest in their neighbors. A father might travel to a nearby village to seek a bride for his son, but never more than a few miles. The Picts are so isolated and have so many dialects they can barely even talk to each other. It would take something or someone special to amass so many warriors."

Bremen grunted. "Some bedeviled druid has united the clans no doubt. It happened once before, years before the Roman army left. Surprised it has taken this long now that I think about it. Emperor Hadrian's Wall is unguarded. There's not much to keep them away. Last winter lasted unusually long. Maybe hunger has brought the Picts together."

I carried a barrel past the big brewer. "Did you tell the abbot that we saw Lazarus in town?"

"What? When?" Michael asked.

"On market day," I said. "Near St. Alban's."

Bremen hefted a barrel to his broad shoulder. "Yes, I told him. He didn't seem interested but said he would investigate. What's the count?"

"Thirty-eight," Michael said.

"Twelve more and lash them tightly," Bremen said.

Michael cocked the wiry eyebrow over his good eye. "What was Lazarus doing in Coria?"

I said, "I don't know. He stood at a vendor's stall when we saw him. Bremen called him, and he ran away."

Silvanius said, "Sounds like he was up to no good then."

Bremen groaned. "Enough of the chatter. We'll not be spreading idle gossip about poor Lazarus."

We finished loading the wagon and strapped down the stacked barrels.

Bremen gestured toward the rear of the wagon. "You boys will need to walk behind this trip. The load is heavy enough as is." He mounted the driver's seat, flipped the reins, and the ox bellowed in protest. The wagon pulled forward, the axles squeaking at the hubs from the excessive weight. Eutychus and I fell into step behind it.

"Do you think it was Lazarus we saw last night?"

Eutychus asked.

"It would explain a few things."

"Like what?"

"When I saw him in the city, he nibbled on a fancy pastry. If he robbed Adalbert, it would explain where he got the money."

Eutychus scoffed. "Lazarus is crazy, but he's harmless."

Lazarus was often disturbing, but he'd never been frightening. Still, it was difficult to know exactly what thoughts brewed behind his mismatched eyes. "I hope you're right because if you're wrong, he's probably already collected the treasure and is long gone."

Approaching Coria, we encountered an unusual and increasingly dense stream of traffic traveling in the opposite direction, men, women, and children, carrying bundles under their arms or on their backs, despair written across their faces. A lanky man wearing little more than patched rags skirted the edge of the wagon with his wife and four children, the kids without shoes.

Bremen halted the wagon. "What's the news, friend?"

The man stopped and squinted. "Don't know which is worse, the Picts or the prefect. We fled our farm to escape the blue heathens, hoping for the safety of Coria. When we arrived at the gate, the town watch blocked our path. Prefect Linus has declared a new head tax. He's demanding one denarius for each person entering. Do I look like a man with six denarii?"

Bremen's big hands tightened on the reins. His face flushed. "I'm truly sorry, friend. The prefect can be a cold-hearted bastard. What will you do?"

"We'll keep going south. The people of Eboracum may be more charitable."

The man and his family carried no food. I pointed to our rear. "St. Antony's Monastery is a few miles to the south. You'll find it at the end of a dirt track leading east from this road. You and your family will be welcome there. The monks have food to spare."

The man glanced at his children and squeezed his wife's hand. "Thank you for your kindness."

"God go with you," Bremen said and slapped Castratus's back with the reins.

When we neared Coria's south gate, pandemonium reigned on the crowded road. Sunno and his guards stopped everyone from entering unless they could pay the newly imposed tax. They turned more people away than they admitted. Castratus slowly plowed his way through the chaos, people giving way to his blunted horns. Half an hour passed before we finally crossed the bridge and reached the gate. I clung to the ropes strapped over the barrels to avoid being swept away by the ever-shifting, unruly mass.

Sunno pushed a man to the ground who disappeared beneath the mob. Other people shoved their way forward. The guards cordoned off the entrance, pressing back against the rabble with interlocked shields.

Sunno screamed at Bremen, "The tax is one-fifth on all goods!"

Bremen sprang from the driver's bench like someone had shoved a pike up his rear. "What! That's an outrage!"

"It's the toll! Pay it or turn around!"

"Have you no shame? You'd hold us up for five barrels when yesterday the toll was only two!"

"I don't make the taxes. I just collect them."

"Shame on the prefect then! He's not robbing us! He's robbing every poor widow and orphan who we give the money to!"

"I don't have time to argue. If you don't like it take your beer elsewhere."

"Five barrels! Five barrels! I've got another wagon load to bring. How do I know you won't increase the taxes again when I arrive with the next load?"

"You don't."

"But ten barrels for two bleeding wagons! It's blasphemy!"

"Away with you, Bremen. There's plenty behind you

who will pay."

"Wait! Have mercy. Look, I'll make a deal with you. I'll give you all ten barrels right now if you promise me free passage for the next wagon."

Sunno's eyelids narrowed. He raised his hand to his chin. "Why should I do that?"

"I'll throw in one more barrel for you and your men. That's eleven barrels. Call it insurance against another tax increase."

Sunno scratched his chin. "Eleven barrels?"

"Right now. They're yours if you'll give me your word."

The giant guard nodded. He turned to his men. "Let the wagon through and unload eleven barrels."

The shields parted, and Castratus lumbered forward through the gate.

Eutychus and I untied the ropes and began handing barrels to guards.

Eutychus whispered, "One-fifth of fifty is ten. For two wagons, it's twenty."

"Shhh! I know. Ask me later."

We finished unloading the toll and re-secured the remaining thirty-nine barrels. Bremen, sporting a smug grin, nonchalantly steered toward the Red Dragon.

The crowd in the streets beyond the gate remained almost as dense as the one at the gate. The merchants' stalls that lined the road stood mostly empty. One vegetable vendor had a few bruised heads of cabbage, some moldy carrots, and radishes that looked like they'd been trampled by a bull. A shuttered bakery we passed hung a painted sign reading: NO BREAD. Every face we passed along our route looked on the edge of despair—and these were the lucky folk who could pay the prefect's new tax.

We made our way to the forum and across its concourse to the Red Dragon. Here the crowd became more boisterous and in a better humor with laughter and an occasional cheer.

Lester, the obese tavern owner, had a broad, toothy smile. "You're an answered prayer, Bremen. People are drinking like it's the end of the world. I've doubled the price, and they keep coming. I've nearly sold every drop you delivered. I need every barrel you've got."

Bremen scratched the back of his neck. "But I've only got thirty-nine. I need to make a delivery to Janus at the White Hart."

The owner wrapped his fat arm around Bremen's shoulder. "Be a friend, Bremen. I'll pay you double the price for all the barrels. It will be our secret."

"But I can't—"

"Triple the price! Think of all the good you can do with the extra money."

"Three times the price? Very well, but swear you'll never tell another soul. Janus would tar and feather me if he knew I'd sold you my last barrels."

"You're a good man, Bremen."

Bremen turned to us. He winked. "Unload them all, boys."

We rushed to obey. When we had finished, Eutychus and I climbed into the back of the wagon and Bremen steered Castratus toward the south gate. We again threaded our way through the crowded streets. Near the outer walls, stamping feet filled the air ahead of us. Twisting and craning my neck to peer above the wagon's sideboards, I saw Prefect Linus, wearing chest armor and a Roman helmet squeezed over his chubby cheeks, accompanied by ten men-at-arms marching toward the gate from the street left of the wagon.

"Whoa, Castratus."

The wagon jerked to a stop. The well-armed troop halted directly ahead of us.

Prefect Linus said, "Brother Bremen, I see your wagon is empty."

"Just making our deliveries, Excellency. But we'll be returning with another load."

"Then two of my men will accompany you."

"That's generous of you, sir, but it's not necessary. I've two men of my own."

The pudgy prefect chuckled. "Unarmed boys won't be of much use in a fight. I insist you take my men. They can make sure your cargo and your brethren reach town safely. You've little time to evacuate. Everything you bring will be secured in the town's warehouses."

"Ah, well then, one more reason your men aren't needed. I've only one more load to carry, and it's been promised to the White Hart."

Linus's face flushed red. "Nonsense! This isn't about profit. It's about survival. We must have ample stocks of food and drink in the event of a siege. And how many of your brothers are there now? Twenty? Twenty-five? More mouths for us to feed. But I'll waive the head-tax in exchange for your ale."

Bremen shrugged. "There again, Excellency, you've counted mouths that will not be eating at your table. We aren't moving to Coria."

The prefect's flabby jaws tightened. "Don't be foolish! Eboracum is a three-day journey south through open country. The Picts will catch you before you can reach the city."

"God's our bastion, Prefect. We don't need your soldiers. We won't be going to Eboracum either."

Linus sneered. "What? A handful of monks armed with pitchforks? You'll be slaughtered! I have one hundred trained men. Join us. I'll give you swords and spears. You'll survive if you stand with us."

Bremen scanned the men-at-arms behind the prefect. "Begging your pardon, Excellency, but if they have a mind to see Coria's forum, 1,000 Picts won't be stopped by one hundred soldiers, any more than by me carrying my pitchfork."

Linus's face turned a purple hue. "Then you're a fool!"

Bremen's nose twitched. His lips stretched flat. "It's like St. Paul said, Excellency. Sometimes God's wisdom is foolishness to men."

The prefect spun about, his clenched fists shaking with rage, and ordered his men onward. They marched down the street and disappeared behind buildings to our right.

Bremen's faith and courage impressed me. He did not strike me as a man eager to be martyred. He appeared to really have faith in the Lord's protection.

Bremen slapped the reins. "Don't let any of that talk worry you, boys. Linus just wanted to scare us. He cares about nothing except lining his bleeding pockets. Those are his warehouses he spoke of. If there's a siege, the greedy ass will keep the contents to himself or parse it out to whoever will pay him the highest price."

Eutychus leaned and whispered in my ear, "Bremen's more worried about his beer than his life."

Perhaps my companion judged character better than me. The brewer's fortitude had more to do with pride of ownership than faith in divine intervention.

Refugees still crowded the bridge and gate, but Bremen coaxed Castratus onward like a man on a holy mission, which I suppose he was. Eutychus rode beside me on the tail of the empty wagon as we rumbled along the road. As the crowd thinned, Bremen whipped Castratus into a trot. It took two hours until we neared the cut-off to the monastery. We had made good time, but clearly, darkness would come before we could complete the next delivery to the White Hart.

I leaned into Eutychus's ear. "When we get to the White Hart, I'm going to get lost in the crowd. You'll need to tell Bremen not to worry. I'm smart enough to find my way home."

"I'm going to get lost with you."

"No. You need to go with Bremen to St. Alban's. Lazarus might be there. If not, find out what the bishop knows."

"And where will you be?"

"I'll go to the caves to keep watch. With all this commotion, there's a good chance the killer will try to retrieve the treasure and run south."

"You don't even know if the killer is still here."

I shrugged. God wouldn't send me on a pointless

mission, but I couldn't share my divine inspiration just yet. "In which case, I'll come trotting home empty-handed."

Eutychus frowned. He slowly shook his head. "I don't know … all the refugees have made me wonder … maybe we should re-think what we're doing. The Picts are really coming. Their scouts are probably already watching the city. It might not be safe. Maybe we should wait until the Picts leave."

My eyebrows arched. "Since when did you become an advocate for caution?"

"It's just that … well … there's more than us to think about. If we get ourselves killed in the woods, we won't be able to help anybody else."

"Don't worry. If I see a Pict, I'll come running home. But I haven't seen one yet. Until I do, I'm not giving up on Adalbert."

"Hey! Wait for me!" Olaf ran behind the wagon.

I grabbed his extended hand and pulled him into the rear between Eutychus and me. "How did you get here?" I asked.

"A mass of people showed up at the monastery gate. They said a monk had sent them there promising they'd receive food."

Eutychus eyed me. "I wonder who did that?"

"I sent one family."

Olaf shrugged. "Well, word spread. There must have been two hundred. But don't worry. The abbot welcomed them. We've been passing out the grain. I worked my way through the crowd handing out food until I came to the woods. I had no difficult stealing away to keep watch on the hills."

I asked, "Did you see anything?"

Olaf frowned. "I'm not sure. A shepherd boy ran across the grassland heading to Coria."

"Why was he running?" Eutychus asked.

Olaf's head sagged into his shoulders. "How should I know? Clodius asked me to keep watch not ask questions, right? Besides, he ran too fast and far away for me to catch him even if I had tried."

Eutychus huffed. "What good does that do us?"

"I don't know. I did what Clodius asked."

"You did great," I said. I cocked my eyebrow. "Right, Eutychus?"

My friend nodded and cracked a smile. "Sure. It's a big help. Thanks, Olaf."

Olaf's neck straightened. He grinned. "I need to get back to the barley fields. I'll see you at dinner." He hopped off the wagon and disappeared into the trees behind us.

Five minutes later we passed through the refugees receiving handouts at the front gate. The big brewer steered straight for the brewery, and we hurriedly stacked the last fifty barrels into the wagon. Bremen then whipped the ox, who protested with a fatigued bellow. The final load headed back to Coria with Eutychus and me walking behind.

The sun held low on the horizon when we reached the city's gate. The crowd had dwindled to a handful of irate people arguing and being turned away. The guards had long since tapped into the eleventh barrel. Drowsy faces and drooping lids paid little attention to us. Sunno waved us forward with an inebriated wink and leer. We arrived at the White Hart Tavern just as the sun dipped beneath the city's western wall. The alleyways grew dark. While unloading the wagon, I had to be careful not to trip over the drunken bodies littering the street.

Bremen went inside the tavern to negotiate with the owner. The moment presented a good opportunity for me to become lost. Eutychus had disappeared. Although I wanted to wave goodbye, my fear that Bremen might re-emerge from the tavern convinced me to steal away. I lifted my hood over my head and headed into a dark alleyway, trusting that Eutychus would cover for me as we had planned.

The narrow alley made sharp turns around a two-story red-brick insula. As I made the second turn, my heart skipped a beat. I leaped backward, plastering myself against the shadowed wall. Ahead of me in the darkness, a cloaked figure blocked my path. Had Bremen left the tavern and wandered down the alley for some unknown reason? Then his belly laugh echoed up the street behind me. Whoever stood in my way, it wasn't the big brewer. I slowly leaned forward to peek around the corner.

The shape awkwardly hunched forward. As my eyes grew more accustomed to the darkness, the image became clearer. The person wore an undyed habit, a novice's habit. I released my breath, ready to curse Eutychus for causing me such a fright. Then came a moan—a female moan.

I stood paralyzed.

Arms crossed Eutychus's back, but not his arms. White, smooth, graceful, female arms, squeezed his body. Slender fingers kneaded his muscles.

Eutychus's hips lurched forward once, a second time, then repeated with rhythmic thrusts. Feet and legs wrapped around his thighs beneath the folds of his robe, squirming, jerking. A female's urgent groan joined Eutychus's heavy pants.

"Julia," he gasped. "Julia. Julia. Joo-lee-yah!"

Chapter XVI

Why did I feel betrayed? Julia, my Julia, did not even know my name. Eutychus had no inkling of my fantasies. They were far too intimate and sinful to share even with my best friend. It made no difference. An irrational, depressing sense of loss flowed through me, settling in my stomach like rancid milk. I stood totally immobilized, frozen by the writhing bodies, shocked by the sight and sound of ecstatic urges far exceeding the imagined embraces of my childish dreams.

Somehow, in my traumatized state, I slunk around the coupled forms, down the alleyway, and into the shadows. The lovers wouldn't have heard a Roman legion marching past them. My legs then broke into a run. Why I ran, I couldn't be sure. My head became a morass of confused emotions—jealousy, anger, betrayal, love—all fueled by an insane energy raging beyond my control. I had to escape, but the lovers' specters chased after me, gaining ground no matter how fast my legs pumped.

My foot caught the raised edge of a paving stone. My sprawling body flew forward. My chin crashed to the street. Stinging pain shot through my tongue. I tasted blood. My head whirled dizzily. For an instant, I forgot my location, even my identity. Then her name drifted through the dank air. Heartache slammed down on me.

Julia! Julia! Julia!

A part of me had died, a part of my heart. I pushed up from the dirty street and stumbled onward, still dazed by the fall. My next steps must have been directed by divine grace because Sunno's deep voice soon bellowed to my front. I don't remember how I arrived there. The big guard yelled at some unfortunate merchant begging to enter the city. His cursing returned me to some sense of reality and purpose.

Adalbert's floating corpse called me.

I squeezed through the inebriated guards blocking the gate. They stopped people from entering the town. They did not care about any fool wanting to leave.

The slender crescent moon had risen just slightly above a line of clouds bordering the eastern horizon. Its light helped me to avoid tripping over the potholes of the vandalized Roman highway. I bolted many miles down the road, then crossed into the grasslands ascending to the limestone rocks, all the while replaying Julia's limbs wrapping around Eutychus's body, his groaning ecstasy. How foolish to be so distracted. A horde of Picts could have surrounded me, and I wouldn't have noticed or cared much for that matter. Maybe then she would notice me if I died, mauled by Pict warriors. Even better, if the Pict chieftain would challenge me to single combat, I'd slay him. His warriors would kneel. I'd save the city. Maybe that would make Julia run to me. She'd kiss me, wrap her arms around my back, her legs around my thighs. She'd forget about—I couldn't bear to think of his name— she'd know who was the better man.

God! I was such an idiot! Julia would never love me because she loved *my best friend*! He'd never even told me about her, but now his clandestine late-night escapes came into far better focus. I imagined them meeting at the lake, swimming together, caressing each other, touching, kissing, the cold waters an exciting elixir stoking the fires fueling their passion. Like in some pagan orgy of Rome's past, their bodies intertwined upon the ancient limestone platform, squirming, writhing, thrusting, squeezing one another with extreme urgency.

"Aaahh!" I screamed. Exhausted, I collapsed to my knees, jabbing my fists at the heavens, glaring at the moon's silvery smirk. The reality of my foolishness fell upon me like a collapsing stone tower. Julia, the precious jewel in my eye, was a fool's dream. I was the fool.

The dark solitude of the night folded over me, hiding me from the rest of the world. I knelt alone. Truly alone. There'd be no Julia in my life. Not her and no one ever like her. I'd grow old and die in some musty dormitory surrounded by ugly, unwanted misfits who had chosen to hide from life instead of embracing it. And so be it. I was one of them.

"Find the murderer."

A tiny voice echoed in my head.

"Find the murderer."

I could not help but feel that another foolish delusion spurred my quest. Adalbert lay dead and buried. No one seemed too worried about the loss. Yet, some ember glowed within that made me yearn for an answer. Who killed Adalbert and why? God had appointed me to this task. I could not disobey.

The moon did not smirk. It faded. In another day, it would vanish and then be born anew, growing until it reached its brightest glory. And so life progressed. Every day turned to darkness, to be reborn in the brilliance of the sun's golden glow. The sun would rise tomorrow and shine afresh on me. I could choose to hate my circumstances or to embrace them. Would the world be less beautiful with Adalbert's murder unsolved? Not likely. But God still wanted me to find the killer and to fulfill his justice. Like Moses, Gideon, and Jonah before me, my insecurity made me doubtful. But God was God. When he called, I must answer.

But really, Eutychus, how could you do this? To me? Your best friend?

"Find the murderer."

A gentle breeze blew through the vast plain, swirling the silvery stalks of seed-laden grass. A calmness descended upon me, a renewed rectitude in my purpose.

"Find the murderer."

I stood alone. The night expanded, awesome and deep. Somewhere out there, I would find Adalbert's murderer.

Chapter XVII

The night's breeze died, the air becoming deathly still as I reached the base of the limestone rocks jutting into the forest. A white stone crag, far above and beyond, glowed faintly in the moonlight, shadowed by rounded clefts and jagged crevices scarring its face. An owl hooted, hidden among the branches of the tall pines. The leaves of nearby scrub brush rustled; some nocturnal rodent foraging among the undergrowth.

The firm ground changed to sliding loose rocks on my path, making my footing more difficult. I picked up a walking stick the length of my arm from among fist-size stones, then used it to probe into dark recesses and pits, too fearful to stick my hand or foot into them. Time stood still as I progressed, steering along moonlit paths, jabbing and prodding with the stick, keeping a hopeful watch for a torch or candlelight, scrambling atop stacked rocks, leaping from boulder to boulder, searching every pit or shallow cave.

The night's darkness seemed endless. I finished probing an L-shaped hole, then climbed up a slanting dead tree trunk wedged between stacked boulders and found myself standing atop a ledge. The sky formed a black canopy sprinkled with millions of glittering stars. Far to the northeast, the dark silhouette of Coria's walls rose, barely visible above the faintly glowing landscape. Flickering pinpricks of torches burned from the town's watchtowers, sparkling like heaven's lights above.

Eutychus and Julia might still be there. I pushed the image from my head, looking skyward, focusing on Orion's twinkling belt. Julia's legs wrapped around it.

Life had not been fair. Better to have never seen the fruit than to have beheld its glory and be forever tormented by its tantalizing luster. Instead of sweetness, a lingering bitterness soured my tongue. It fouled my mouth and my mind. Rather than keeping careful watch for my quarry, the awful moment of seeing their coupled bodies replayed in my head. Worms writhed in my gut.

My feet rolled with my next step, the rocks shifting, throwing my weight backward. My left foot flew skyward, my right knee bending back. My arms flailed uselessly. My shoulders crashed, sharp rocks digging through my clothing. My helpless body slid down a steep declivity, rocks tumbling, dust rising, choking my breath. The back of my head bounced hard. Purple swirls and tiny lightning bolts joined jumbled, flashing stars.

My fall stopped. My senses, numbed by shock, slowly awakened to the pain of cuts and bruises down my legs and across my back. A trickle of liquid flowed from my scalp down my neck, coating the gritty limestone dust and dirt kicked up by the tumble.

Painful, but I would survive. I slowly raised up on my elbows, then sat up to look at my legs. Grime covered my skin except for the dark wet spots where I bled.

Staggering to my feet, I groped for my stick, finding it a few feet behind me, up the rocky incline. The view of the city had disappeared behind the trees' dark curtain. My fall had been ten or twenty paces. Maybe farther. Nearly killed myself and what had I accomplished? Nothing. I was no closer to finding Adalbert's killer than when I had found his body. I'd wasted my time on one more useless exercise.

The moon hid behind the rocky hill looming above. I had lost track of how much time had passed and my sense of direction. The landscape leveled to my left and led into the black woods. The lake must lay somewhere in that direction. If I found its shoreline, the lake would show me the way home. I could wash and cleanse my injuries, remove the evidence of my accident, and avoid unwanted questions. Lying had become a bad habit.

Near the tree line, I sensed another's presence. I froze, holding my breath.

A dark human shape, sitting, and leaning against a small white boulder, watched me, the whites of his eyes reflecting the faint starlight. His form did not move.

My confusion held me immobilized. The man had to have seen and heard my fall, yet he had not come to either help me or finish me off. So, neither friend nor a foe, what did that leave?

"Hello," I said, breaking the night's quiet.

The man's gaze remained frozen upon me, not even blinking.

I cautiously stepped toward him. "Hello?"

He remained motionless.

I stepped closer, prodding his leg with my stick. He did not move. I shuddered. The man was dead.

I knelt to examine him. He had a tonsured scalp. He wore a monk's habit. I gasped. Lazarus.

My instincts screamed run. Picts hid among the trees. Snakes slithered upon the ground. A murderer lurked among the shadows. Nowhere seemed safe. Instead, I froze upon the rocky flat, paralyzed by indecision, my gaze locked on Lazarus's dead face.

Noisy panting shattered the quiet. Mine. I covered my gaping mouth with my hand and forced my heaving chest to slow. My rapid breathing subsided. I squatted alone beside a corpse. No hidden threat watched me.

In the darkness, I couldn't see any sign of Lazarus's injury. He sat, and but for his frozen features could have been relaxing against the rock. I touched his chest with my stick, then marshaled enough courage to lay aside my probe and touched his arm with my hand. His stiff flesh resisted my prod. I traced my fingers across his chest, then toward his abdomen. The smooth fibers of his habit changed to a rough-textured brittleness, soaked with dried blood. Loose, torn, and stiff fibers marked a puncture in the cloth three fingers in width just beneath his sternum. I slowly pushed my trembling fingers into the tear. Cold, wet, dead meat enveloped my skin. I yanked my hand from his chest. The ooze first clung to my fingers, then released me with a slurp.

What should I do? Lost and by now long overdue, my return would raise questions. If I carried Lazarus's body back to St. Antony's, there'd only be more questions about what I had been doing out in the hills. The abbot would lock me up for sure. If I left him here, sooner or later someone else would come upon him, and if they didn't, I could pretend to stumble across his body after the Picts had left, assuming I still lived. If I did not survive, well, no one would care, except for the murderer. He'd emerge from behind the safety of Coria's walls, bundle up his hidden treasure, and carry his blood-stained bounty south to live out his years in wealth and luxury, escaping all justice except God's final judgment. It angered me, but the night grew old. I had no choice.

I stood, turned back to the trees, and pressed onward into the woods. By more luck than cleverness, my legs carried me to the lake's shoreline. The white columns and platform glimmered directly before me on the far shore. Home waited two miles away, its direction now clear. I tossed off my clothes, washed my cuts, bruises, and dirty limbs, then redressed. Refreshed, I trotted homeward.

Near St. Antony's, sporadic torchlight stretched along the Roman road to the south, following the course of the highway. Where the road met the dirt trail, fewer lights burned but marked the way to the monastery. As I neared the road, dark shapes became families, carrying their few possessions, frightened and despairing.

A gray-bearded man wearing a frayed leather cap glumly shook his head. He grabbed my arm as I passed him. "Have you seen my wife?"

His grasp frightened me. I tried to shake free. "Your wife, sir? I'm sorry I don't know her."

"Don't know her? She's my wife. Everyone knows my Maggie. Have you seen her?"

"Truly sir, I don't know her. I'm sorry."

The man released my arm, staggered several feet down the track, then grabbed at another stranger. "Have you seen my Maggie?"

"Don't let him worry you." A younger man carrying a sleeping infant in his arms addressed me.

"I wish I could help him."

The young man shook his head. "No one can. His wife died three days ago. The Picts split her head with an ax. Right before his eyes."

I gasped. "Dear God, no wonder he's in shock. How did he escape?"

"He strangled the Pict with his bare hands then ran away like a man demon possessed."

"How do you know all this?"

The man's lips stretched flat and grim. "I'm his son. My wife died too. I saved my daughter and went running after my father."

"I wish I could do something."

"Thank you, Father. The monks gave us soup and bread. It's the first meal we've had in days."

"I'm just a novice. My name is Clodius."

The man adjusted his grip on the child in his arms. "Well, please thank your brethren for their kindness. I have to catch up to my father and guide him toward Eboracum." He took a step.

I touched his forearm. "How far are Picts?"

He stopped. "Not far. One day, maybe two. Their scouts are already watching us. Be careful."

"God go with you," I said.

I weaved through the other refugees, joining those ascending the dirt track to St. Antony's. Outside the main gate, exhausted faces glowed around small campfires. Michael and Haman dispensed a hot liquid from an iron pot to a line of people carrying bowls and cups.

"Where have you been?" Michael asked.

"I got lost." Half-truths came easy.

Haman said, "Go find the abbot. He's been sick with worry about you."

I nodded then entered the compound, the grounds lit with fires and busy with monks rushing about.

Olaf strained, carrying a bucket of water. He stopped when he saw me, dropped the bucket and rushed over. "I'm glad to see you."

"I've been scouting the caves."

"You worried me. Remember that boy I saw running? Turns out he found a body among the rocks. Prefect Linus sent word to warn us. The Picts have arrived."

The dead body was Lazarus, but I wasn't ready to let on. Olaf was a good boy, but he'd tell Eutychus. My hurt feelings hadn't yet healed. My best friend had a secret he had failed to share with me. I wanted to get even.

"Have you seen Abbot Mutter?"

Olaf jerked his thumb over his shoulder. "Try the library. Cassius and Fabian have been locked in there all day. The abbot's got them working on something."

I thanked Olaf and went to the estate house. Torches lit the atrium and the peristyle walkway. Across the garden, the abbot's office and the library door glowed with candlelight. Cassius and Fabian crossed the doorway several times, their arms loaded with books.

I walked through the garden and rapped on the abbot's doorframe. The monks stopped their frantic work and peered at me through the adjoining side door. Fabian's dark eyes glared at me from beneath his bushy brow. Past their heads, the library's shelves were empty. Leather-wrapped and tied bundles lay on the floor.

"What do you *want*?" Fabian asked.

My head recoiled. I stepped back. "I'm looking for the abbot."

"He's not here. Try the main gate."

"I did already."

"Then look elsewhere. We're busy."

I scanned the bundles. "I see that. Can I help?"

"It's none of your business."

Cassius raised his hand and patted Fabian's shoulder with his slender fingers. "No need to be so harsh, Fabian. The boy is just looking for the abbot. I'm sorry, we don't know where he's gone. It's been a busy day for everyone. If he returns, can we give him a message from you?"

"Just that I've returned. There's no reason to be worried about me."

"I'll make sure he knows," Cassius said. "Now, if you'll excuse us, we're rather busy."

I retreated from the light, turned about-face, then headed toward the brewery where I hoped to find Bremen.

"There you are," the big man said as I walked into the glow of a fire outside the building. "Where have you been? And don't tell me you were lost. Not even a skilled liar like Eutychus could make me believe that fable."

"Have you seen him?" I asked, hoping to deflect the question.

"Answer me first."

I puffed my chest and feigned indignation. "I *did* get lost. Where else would I go?"

Bremen's eyelids narrowed. "This is no time for playing games, Clodius. Poor Adalbert dead. Crazy Lazarus missing. The Picts marching to our threshold. I don't want to find your corpse floating in the lake or half-eaten by bleeding savages."

"There's no chance of that. Where's Eutychus?"

"He's working in the fields. The abbot wants to save every grain possible."

I gazed at the glow of a bonfire burning near the crops. "I should join him. Did the bishop say anything?"

"The bishop?"

"Abbot Mutter asked you to inquire about Lazarus."

Bremen grunted. "He said he hadn't seen his nephew. But I don't know that I believe him. He might be hiding the coward for the sake of his sister."

"I thought he didn't like Lazarus."

The burly brewer snorted and spat. "What's that got to do with anything? The man's his kin, like it or not. Besides, I know his sister. She's a rosy-cheeked virago who'd never forgive him if he let her boy die."

I swallowed hard. "Is that what you think? We're going to die?"

"The Picts show no mercy to holy men."

"Then maybe we should go."

His gaze slammed me, his brow furrowed. "Against the abbot's orders? We swore an oath of loyalty to Christ and his church. We can't leave unless Abbot Mutter consents." His glare softened. "Besides, where would we go? No other monastery would accept us without the abbot's written authorization. No, to disobey the abbot is to disobey Jesus. We might save our skins from the Picts but at the cost of burning for eternity. Enough jabbering. Off to the fields with you. They'll be no rest tonight."

Small bonfires burned where the fields had already been cleared, providing illumination for the monks working with sickles, thrashing the stalks, while others rushed about with heavy bundles of the harvested grain on their shoulders, loading pushcarts manned by still others. Eutychus appeared from the dense greenery, laboring with an armload of grain he tossed to the back of a cart.

A tired smile dawned on his face as I stepped toward him. He wiped sweat from his forehead. "What a night. Did you find anything?"

"Nothing worth mentioning."

Eutychus leaned forward, examining me more closely. "You've got blood on your head. What happened?"

"I fell. Just a clumsy accident. What about you? You disappeared at the White Hart. Where'd you run off to?"

His gaze avoided mine. "Nowhere. You're mistaken. You just lost me in the dark."

Liar!

"Odd, because I looked for you. I don't know how I could have missed you."

"Hey! You two!" Brother Michael stood next to a bonfire, glaring at us with his good eye. "Stop your gabbing and get back to work!"

Eutychus slapped my arm. "Come on. Gunther's slashing through barley faster than I can keep up. We can use your help."

Eutychus hustled toward the standing grain with me at his

rear. He had lied. How many other times? My resentment festered with each passing heartbeat. If that was how he defined friendship, fine. I had a few secrets of my own.

We worked without rest deep into the night, halting only when Prior Tomas called the brothers to nocturns. Our prayers and hymns echoed more feeble than usual, everyone exhausted. Poor Olaf nearly collapsed when he fell asleep at my side. I caught him when his body sagged, helped him to straighten, then periodically jabbed him with my elbow to keep him awake.

We completed the last hymn, and Abbot Mutter gave us the option of eating breakfast or retiring directly to the dormitory. Slurping cold gruel felt unappealing. A few monks headed to the refectory, but the majority of us tromped in a herd to the dormitory. When I reached my cell, my knees folded. I fell face forward to my pallet. Sleep immediately took me.

Julia waited.

She floated at the end of a narrow alley, her eyes shut, darkness surrounding her, a brilliant, virginal white light glowing behind her. A breeze blew through her hair, the folds of her white tunic undulated over her body. Her lips parted, her tongue tracing their contours, the membranes moist, sticky, delicate. Her chest heaved, releasing a barely audible gasp, followed by another, then another, each building in intensity, becoming urgent groans. Her head rocked in rhythm with each explosion from her lungs, her auburn curls tossing from her cheeks to her throat, her soft skin blushing, turning hot. Her body convulsed violently, her hands clenched, her legs bending and kicking, her mouth opening, screaming in ecstasy, "Eutychus! Eutychus! Eutychus!"

"Clodius, wake up," Eutychus said. "The sun's up. Prior Tomas wants everyone to assemble at the refectory."

My confusing dream left me resentful and ashamed, yet with a yearning to return. I closed my eyes, hoping to see her face again.

Eutychus kicked my leg. "Don't go back to sleep. We

need to plan."

I rolled my face to the wall, curling my legs, seeking sleep's numbing embrace.

Pain shot through my rump.

"Stop kicking me!"

"Get up! We don't have time to waste. We have to decide what to do."

I folded my back erect, rubbing my eyes with my fingers. "Do about what?"

"About Adalbert. About finding his killer. What else?"

"It's hopeless. We don't have enough time. We don't even know for sure what we're looking for."

"No, listen. I've been thinking. It has to be Lazarus."

I shook my head. "It's not him."

"How do you know?"

I squinted bleary eyes at my traitorous friend. "Call it a hunch. Anyway, if Lazarus killed Adalbert and stole the treasure, he'd be half-way to Londinium by now. There's nothing we could do about it."

"That's where you're wrong. His whole family is in Coria. He'd be hopelessly lost without them. But think about this. What if he conspired with the bishop? Bonifatius could easily hide him in the basilica."

"You think the bishop of Coria conspired with his half-mad nephew to kill Adalbert—that's your brilliant theory? I suppose you want to go back to Coria so you can search the church."

"You said yourself Bonifatius has grown fat and greedy."

Eutychus couldn't fool me. He had a completely different motive for wanting to return to the city. "That's what Bremen told me. He was just spewing sour grapes," I said. "Look, it wasn't Lazarus. Whoever killed Adalbert, if the treasure is still in the hills, our best hope is that the murderer will try to recover it."

"Then what should we do?"

I pointed out my door. "Get assigned to a work detail outside the compound. It will be easier to get away. Then

121

keep a lookout on the hills and pray for a miracle."

Chapter XVIII

During my few hours of sleep, a storm had blown in from the northeast, covering the sky with a thick blanket of angry black and gray clouds, the wind swirling loose dirt and straw about the garden outside the refectory where the monks had assembled. Abbot Mutter and Prior Tomas stood together in front of the door, the abbot gesticulating and lecturing the prior about something I could not hear. Tomas remained silent, his face sorrowful, his shoulders slumped. His dejection affected the men around me.

"Any news of the Picts?" Silvanius whispered to Michael.

Michael shrugged and shook his head.

Nebridius, the almoner, tasked with accounting for all gifts and money we received, tugged on Silvanius's sleeve. "Word circulated among the refugees that the Picts are no more than a day away. We should expect them tomorrow."

Silvanius asked, "Any chance the abbot will change his mind?"

Nebridius stood only slightly taller than a dwarf. He scowled. "I doubt it."

"Lord help us," Lucius said and whimpered.

"I'm fairly certain that's exactly what Mutter expects," Michael said.

Feet shuffled to my left. Olaf slid through the assembly to reach my side. The edges of his blue eyes drooped. He cracked a half-smile. "Can I work with you today?"

I cast Eutychus a sideways glance.

The traitor cocked his head and arched his eyebrows.

"Sure," I said, "if the prior allows it. Here he comes now."

Tomas stood on the edge of the peristyle walkway, his head higher than the assembled monks. "Brothers, praise God for your labors. Yesterday, by his grace, we emptied the brewery and almost completely harvested the barley. Every man here did the work of three. You've shown great faith and fortitude." A mizzling rainfall began. Many in the group covered their heads with their hoods. The prior peered skyward. "We'll have to hurry to complete the harvest before the storm comes. Gunther, Michael, take as many men as you think are needed. Where's Nebridius?"

The almoner raised his hand above the taller heads and shoulders surrounding him. "Here, Prior."

"What's left that we can give to those fleeing?"

Nebridius supervised the disbursement of alms to the needy, who had significantly increased since the Romans' departure. While Nebridius kept watch over the treasury, Prior Tomas kept a careful eye on Nebridius. Temptation could be an awful burden. Lord help me, I knew it only too well.

The almoner lifted his empty palms. "The alms box is empty, but we've still plenty of grain. The people were especially grateful for our soup. They can't prepare a hot meal while on the run."

Tomas said, "Then we should prepare more and continue to distribute whatever grain they can carry. How many men would you like to help you?"

Nebridius lowered his hands. "The flow of people has dwindled. Four should do."

"Very well. Pick your team. Anyone not going with Michael or the almoner, come to the church to pray."

"What about the walls?" Gunther asked. "They're in need of repair if we're to repel the Picts."

"Aye," Malthius said. "And there's blades to sharpen."

Several others echoed the sentiment.

Tomas glanced at the abbot, who remained silent, his face an unyielding bastion. The prior looked back to us. "Prayers, brothers, they are our arrows. Our hymns are our walls. The Lord will not desert us."

A grim silence reigned over the assembly.

"Very well," Tomas said, "Gunther, Michael, Nebridius, select your men. The rest of you will follow Abbot Mutter to the church."

I jumped toward Nebridius. "Can I help you?"

"And me," Olaf said.

Fritigern shoved ahead of Eutychus. "Me too."

"Hey don't push. I'm with Clodius," Eutychus said.

Nebridius's wispy black eyebrows raised high. "What's this sudden interest in charity by the novices?"

"I'm not much good at praying," I said. "And you know my fear of snakes. I'm better used serving the people."

The almoner scratched his narrow chin. "Well, I need the kitchener's help for the soup, but three of you can help distribute food. Clodius, Olaf, Fritigern, come with me."

"What about me?" Eutychus pleaded.

Nebridius's eyes slanted with an incredulous gaze. "You've never shown any interest in helping me before. Why now?"

Eutychus's mouth opened wide. He drew a sharp breath. "Well, I—I—"

"No. You're the strongest. Gunther and Michael can put you to better use. You three come with me."

Nebridius marched toward the kitchen. Fritigern, Olaf, and I fell into step behind him. I glanced back to Eutychus, who watched us leave with a forlorn frown. I should have regretted our separation, but my bruised ego had yet to heal. Spending my last day on earth in the company of Fritigern did not appeal to me, but at least he would not be a constant memory of my frustrated lusts.

Nebridius first went to the kitchen and asked Haman to prepare a vegetable broth. Fritigern and I manhandled a heavy iron basin to the front gate while Nebridius dispatched Olaf to retrieve dry wood we could use to build a warming fire. We had to drench the wood with tallow, but we soon had a substantial blaze despite the constant drizzle.

The numbers outside the gate had greatly decreased, and only a trickle of refugees journeyed up the track from the Roman highway. We set about shuttling grain from the granary to the front gate in wooden buckets, piling the kernels beneath an oil-slicked leather tarpaulin to keep them dry. We quickly accumulated far more than the dwindling demand required. Olaf and Nebridius ladled hot soup into bowls, but soon Fritigern and I stood idly above the stacked grain.

My opportunity had arrived.

I pointed to the piled barley. "Brother Nebridius, the grain will spoil if we don't give it away. There are more people on the road. I can carry it down there to them."

Nebridius scanned the empty path. He nodded. "Good idea."

"I'll go with him," Fritigern said.

I said, "Someone should stay here in case more people arrive. I can do well enough alone."

"No, Olaf and I can take care of anyone who comes to the gate. You two stay together. Not everyone on the road is seeking charity. Some want to help themselves without concern for the harm to others."

I filled two buckets, secured their lids, and trudged down the now muddy track. Fritigern followed close behind me with two more.

"I've got my eyes on you," he said as soon as we left the compound.

"Make sure that's all you put on me."

"What's that supposed to mean?"

"I think you know."

For the next few paces, we kept silent.

"I don't know what you're up to, but you won't get away with it," Fritigern said.

"I'm not up to anything."

"Then explain why you've been disappearing and prowling about at night."

I halted and fixed my stare on my hairy companion. "Really? Do you really want to discuss nighttime prowling?"

Fritigern glared at me. "It's about Adalbert's death, isn't it? And Lazarus too. You know something you're not telling."

I ignored his accusation and resumed my steps down the

sloping path. "Your imagination is getting the best of you. I had nothing to do with Adalbert's death. Don't forget, I'm the one who found his body."

"Or you're the one who knew its location."

I stopped again, pivoting to face him. "What's *wrong* with you? What's this fascination you have for Adalbert anyway? What was he to you?"

Fritigern's face paled for a heartbeat, then his eyelids narrowed. He bared his teeth. "Someone murdered him. Isn't that reason enough?"

I grunted. "Fine. Do what you want. You're wasting your time." I stomped away.

We came to the Roman road, but like the path to St. Antony's, the flow of refugees had dwindled. I offered food to the first people I encountered, an elderly couple who scooped the grain with their wrinkled hands into folds of cloth slung over their shoulders. Next followed a melancholy bearded man with a bloody rag tied around his forehead.

"Thank you, Father," he said scooping a handful of grain.

I'd grown tired of explaining my lowly rank. "How far have you come?"

"I own a pasture west of Luguvalium. The barbarians descended on my home while I tended my sheep. They killed my wife and two sons. I fought with one savage. He gave me this," he said, pointing at his bandaged head. "No way to save my family, though."

Fritigern moved ahead, allowing refugees to spoon out whatever they could carry.

I said, "I'm so sorry for your loss. God be with you."

"God's abandoned us, Father. Just like the Romans. Thank you for the grain." He left me. I couldn't think of anything to say.

"Bless you, Father," said another man with a scraggly beard and a short-brimmed leather cap pulled down over his stringy black hair.

"Take as much as you can carry," I said, feeling helpless.

"Thank you, but it's my wife and children that need your

help, Father."

I glanced about. He seemed alone.

"No sir, I've sheltered them over there, among those trees." He pointed up the hill toward the forest. "My son and daughter have a terrible fever. My dear wife's keeping them out of the cold rain."

"I'm sorry, I'm not a healer. All I have is this grain."

"It's not food they need, Father. It's your prayers and blessing. They're near death. Could you please lay your hands on them and bless their poor little souls? It'd mean so much to my wife."

Under the circumstances, even a novice's blessing would be better than dying unsanctified. Fritigern had wandered far ahead of me. He engaged with a haggard woman traveling with a young girl.

"Here, let me carry those for you," the man said, reaching for the buckets. "My family's just there among those trees."

"Okay," I said. "Just carry one. I've got the other."

"Bless you, Father."

I followed him off the road, climbing over the crumbling stone wall, across the brook, and up toward the trees.

"Just there, Father. It's only a short way."

We scaled the hill to the edge of the woods where a huddled figure squatted beneath the shroud of a makeshift tent of dirty, patched rags, secured by ropes tied to pine trees. The worried husband slowed a stepped as he labored up the hill, lagging to my rear. The bucket plopped to the ground as he rested and gasped for breath. A long-haired, skinny figure emerged from the tent's shelter. The person's scruffy beard momentarily confused me, until my gaze locked on the dagger in his hand.

"Don't give us any trouble and we won't hurt you," the liar behind me said.

I dropped my bucket, its contents spilled at my feet. Though frightened, I did not panic. Two cutthroats couldn't compare to a six-foot viper.

"I don't have anything, just this grain."

"We'll decide that. What's under your clothes?"

I turned to face the liar, his hand also filled with a knife. "Just me. I'm just a novice. I don't own a thing."

"Off with it."

"What?"

"Your clothes, boy. Take them off."

I raised my empty hands to my waist. "But I told you I have nothing."

"Then prove it, or I'll gut you."

Reluctantly, I withdrew my arms into my sleeves, reached to my neck, and pulled my habit and tunic over my head. The wind and drizzle sent shivers through my nakedness. "See. I have nothing."

The long-haired bandit sneered. "Nice job, dimwit. You really know how to pick them."

The liar raised his hand to the top of his leather cap and screwed it tighter down on his scalp. "How was I supposed to know he's penniless? Maybe the priests will pay a ransom."

"We have no money," I said. "We're not priests. We're monks. We give everything to the poor."

"Nice arse though," the man behind me said. "It's been a long time since I've had some fun."

My sphincter squeezed shut. "I-I'm a novice, pledged to serve God. You wouldn't dare."

"Yaahhh!"

Fritigern leaped from behind a tree, crashing his head into the ribs of the liar.

The man's terrified eyes shot open, his hands jerked upward, the knife flying from his grip. Fritigern's bulk slammed the man into the mud.

I launched at his knife, catching it before it hit the ground. I wheeled around to face the second assailant. He flipped his dagger upward, caught the blade, then reared back and threw it at me. I ducked my head and shoulders. The knife missed me and landed with a thud to my rear.

Fritigern cried out.

I turned. The knife had landed in his left shoulder. The

man he had tackled shoved Fritigern aside, scrambled to his feet, and sprinted deep into the woods. His partner ran the opposite direction.

"Go after them!" Fritigern yelled.

"Are you crazy? You're hurt!"

The blade had pierced his back at a shallow angle. He reached with his right hand and yanked the dagger out. "I'll survive. Let's get them!" He pushed to his feet and dashed after the man he had tackled.

The hairy oaf was an obnoxious busybody, but no coward. Shamed, I gulped down a breath, grabbed my clothing, and charged into the thick ground cover after the man who had thrown the knife. What exactly I might do with the fiend should I catch him had not yet registered. The man fled like a rabbit. I chased like a fox. The consequences must await the catch. Regrettably, the rabbit ran much faster, especially after I tripped and tumbled while pulling my tunic and habit over my head. After several minutes of hard running, the scoundrel had disappeared deep into the woods.

I slowed to listen for his footsteps. The silence of the dense woodland closed around me. My foe had escaped. Discouraged and gasping for air, I gave up the hunt. I looked about me then froze, a chill coursing down my back. I did not recognize anything. I whirled, searching for a familiar landmark. My spirits sank. Lost—this time for real!

"Fritigern!"

My voice carried into the woods and died without echo or reply. The steady rain and clouds dimmed the forest to nighttime darkness. Help would not be coming. Once night fell, the forest would grow pitch-black. The wet wood wouldn't burn for warmth or light. My best choice seemed to keep walking, but which direction? The lake, the stream that curved east from its source, the old Roman road, and the limestone hills to the south, hemmed the woods. Whichever direction I headed, eventually I must encounter one of these features if I maintained a straight path.

Little distinguished the trees or undergrowth in any

direction. The liar's knife had a cheaply forged steel blade showing rust spots with a slotted wooden handle bound tightly with leather straps. I stepped to the nearest pine tree, then scored the bark with an arrow pointing to my front. Walking ten paces and only so far as I could still see the marked tree, I scratched an arrow into another tree pointing in the same direction. Aligning myself on these two markers, I locked onto another tree straight ahead of me, then walked to it. I marked its bark, then fixed on another tree in the distance.

The process consumed time and energy but proved sound. A few paces past the eighteenth marked tree, stacked limestone boulders appeared ahead. Triumph replaced my fear of snakes, bandits, and being lost as my plan led me to the base of the hills. I climbed the rocks, ascending high enough to see above the canopy, and congratulated myself on my ingenuity when the serpentine line of the lake appeared. East lay to my right and my way home.

My pace quickened with my certainty, and soon my muddy feet had carried me entirely out of the forest to a grassy vista overlooking the road to Coria. The sky had darkened, the rain grown fiercer, angry thunder grumbled overhead. My stride lengthened, my legs breaking into a run, thoughts of hot soup and buttered bread compelling me onward, my stomach griping about not being fed.

Lightning flashed. The bolt struck an oak tree to my left. Sparks flew. Wood groaned as a heavy limb collapsed to the turf. The blast stunned me, throwing me off balance, my feet becoming tangled, my body flying headfirst into the rain-soaked sod. Grass and mud choked my mouth and blurred my vision. The sharp sting of a laceration pulsated across my forehead. I groaned, spat out grime, then slowly rolled onto my back and folded upright. Dull pain throbbed from my knees and hips. Was God aiming at me? Mercifully, I'd been spared serious injury.

I lifted my face skyward and showered under the heavy droplets, wiping my mouth and eyes clear. My rapid breathing eased. The landscape lit up, another zigzagging white bolt shattering the darkness. Successive flashes unveiled frozen images, glistening stones of a dilapidated pasture wall in the distance. Beyond it, the Roman road and the spur to the monastery would be nearby. By now, the dirt path home would have turned into a river. My journey would not be getting easier.

I drew a deep breath, pressed my hands into the muddy ground, and pushed myself up. Another string of flashes lit the sky. Two cloaked figures straddled the stone wall to my front. Darkness returned.

Had my eyes lied? I froze, waiting for the landscape to be re-illuminated, hoping my imagination had conjured the image, in no mood to deal with more strangers.

The sky exploded again. Fright seized me. The hooded figures had grown larger, heading my direction.

Hide! Shrinking into a tight ball, I lay among the tall grass, trusting the darkness to conceal me.

Heavy, sloshing footsteps drew near.

"Slow down a bit. The pack is killing my shoulders," Fabian said.

Cassius answered, "Stop complaining. We've got a lot more to hide. If we don't hurry, we'll never finish in time."

"Aw, give me a break. Just to adjust the load. There's a sharp edge digging into my backbone."

The sloshing footsteps halted near my head. Fear seized me, jumbling my thoughts. These were monks, my brethren, surely no threat, yet my instincts screamed caution, paralyzing me.

Cassius said, "Make it quick. We must be done by morning. Don't want the whole world to see us."

A huffing breath accompanied the splash of a heavy load dropped to the mud. A hand slapped against leather. Shifting and sliding noises punctuated heaving breaths. Someone released a straining grunt. A pack clapped against a wet back.

"That's better," Fabian said.

Their sloshing resumed, growing louder, coming at me!

My lungs froze. I squeezed my knees and prayed to shrink and become invisible.

Someone stomped so near my legs I felt certain he must have seen me. My heart thudded against my chest, but their footsteps continued, gradually diminishing with increasing distance.

I wanted to return to a hot meal and a dry bed, but a spirit inside commanded, "Follow them." Picts, refugees, Fritigern, bandits, rain, calamity, and devastation, they had brought me to this moment. Find the murderer. All this must be connected to Adalbert in some way.

The darkness made it difficult for me to follow the scribes. Too close and I might be discovered. Too remote and I might lose them. Fortunately, they made no effort to quiet their steps, sloshing and stamping across the drenched terrain. Both men hunched low, laboring under the weight of their burdens. Lightning provided bright glimpses of them. Their packs were oiled sheepskin caged by wooden frames wider than their bodies, rising above their heads, harnessed by ropes passing over their shoulders. They had been bundling volumes during our prior encounter in the library. They were probably carrying the books to a place of safety.

Just as the Romans had hidden their gold, Abbot Mutter hid his treasure. He accepted the personal hazards posed by the invasion, but he would not risk his precious books. He cherished them dearer than—well—his life. How this could be connected to Adalbert's death escaped me. Adalbert had died before anyone had known the Picts had invaded. The deeper into the woods I followed Mutter's pets, I feared I chased another phantom.

As Cassius and Fabian entered the forest, tracking them became more difficult. The trees shielded them from the flashes of lightning and blocked my field of vision. I risked closing my distance to them. Fortunately, their bulky loads made them clumsy and noisy, bumping into trunks, breaking dead limbs, crashing and scratching through needle-filled branches. Worried I'd become lost again, I paused to make notches in the trees with my knife.

The scribes reached the south edge of the forest where trees blended with limestone boulders before the steep ascent of the hills. The men's breathing became heavy and pronounced as they started to climb through the rocks. Fabian slipped on loose stones, sending a small avalanche toward me. I cringed, cradling my head beneath my arms. A rock bounced hard against my scalp, making me dizzy. I gritted my teeth and held my breath to keep my lungs from betraying my position. The pain faded. My head cleared. The men had disappeared.

Energy shot to my arms and legs. I scrambled upward, following in the scribes' path, my feet sliding upon an incline of loose stones where Fabian must have also slipped. A few feet beyond, the rocky climb came to a shallow ledge providing a narrow footpath leading to my right. I hugged the rock face and sidestepped my way about twelve paces to where the ledge wrapped around the bluff's corner, then led toward two huge boulders leaning against each other, a dark, narrow passageway visible at their base. The ledge left me exposed should the monks unexpectedly emerge from the hole.

Ignoring my fear of discovery, I scurried to the boulders and ducked my head inside the opening. The air within the pitch-black cave smelled stale and musty, but the floor felt dry. I cautiously entered, my eyes useless, I probed forward with my hands.

A voice echoed ahead of me. I stopped and held my breath. Hollow, indiscernible words bounced from the invisible walls. I crept onward. A dim glow appeared against a rock wall twice my height. A few steps further, the glow grew brighter, revealing a wide vault filled with jagged boulders. The ceiling reached as high as our church. Ghostly, torchlit shadows danced upon the rocks at the edge of the cave's complete darkness. As I continued, hollow echoes focused into discernible language.

"...favorite of mine," Fabian said.

"Don't start reminiscing. We've at least two more trips."

Leather slapped against leather followed by the creak of a book's binding. Pages rustled.

"The glorious city of God is my theme in this work, which you, my dearest son, Marcellinus, suggested. Funny, I copied every word of this one but hardly remember what it says."

"We don't have time to read, Fabian."

"I remember the illuminations, though." Pages turned. "Especially this one. I had fun drawing the tumbling columns, the flames licking the broken arches. See here. You can feel the terror on this lady's face. More fun than endlessly painting enshrined apostles and crowned heads."

"Please, Fabian, really."

The book slammed shut. "Guess this is what burying your child must feel like if I had any."

Cassius released a heavy sigh. "Don't give up hope, Brother. We may yet be reunited."

"You don't really think so, do you? I mean, I've got my hopes, too, but I can't stop seeing blue heathens bursting into our church, painting the floor red with our blood. I can't help myself, Cassius. I don't want to die."

"Courage. Glory awaits us. Draw comfort knowing that our dear children will survive."

"Who do you think will find them?"

"God will guide a righteous man here if it comes to that. Our works will be resurrected, and future generations will marvel at your artistry."

Fabian snorted a laugh. "Wish I could be there to see it."

Cassius grunted, the empty pack squeaking as he hoisted the basket on his back. "Let's go. We still got more unpleasant business to finish."

Fabian shouldered his pack, and the monks stepped toward the cave's entrance.

"I don't know," Fabian said. "You ever thought about hiding here. I mean, we could delay our return. Get lost, you know, for a day or two."

Cassius stopped abruptly and faced his partner. "To what end? To save our skins? And should we survive and crawl out of our warren like terrified hares, what kind of world would we emerge into? A scorched earth, the city in ruins, the monastery burned to the ground, our brethren dismembered, their corpses stacked and charred. Could you live with such a sight? Or even worse, what if we should emerge into a world redeemed, God's holy armies having descended from the sky and routed the Picts. Could you hide your shame? Do you think God's eyes can't pierce cavern walls to see our cowardice? Could you look into Abbot Mutter's eyes without pain, guilt, and depression? No, Fabian. It's Satan's temptation putting those thoughts in your head."

"It's not like we don't have other sins hanging over us. Think of what we've done. These books are a millstone around our necks."

"It's not a sin to preserve knowledge for God's glory. The abbot's right. We have to trust him."

Cassius turned back to the entrance and resumed his path toward me, Fabian following him. Boulders and huge slabs of stone littered the cavern floor. I crawled behind a pile of rocks away from the monk's path, lying flat to hide from their approaching torchlight.

"I know he's right. I didn't mean we should do it. Just wondered if you were as worried as me is all."

"Of course, I'm worried, Fabian, but I'm not willing to trade eternity in paradise for a few more years in this grubby body, eating gruel, wearing coarse wool, going blind copying ancient texts all day."

The men walked past my position. The sound of their breathing faded, and the torchlight dimmed as they walked on. The cavern turned black and quiet.

My senses became disoriented. The direction to the exit had been fixed in my memory, but as I crawled about on all fours, mounting doubts grew into a rising panic. My hands grappled with grainy walls and sharp edges. My feet searched for firm purchase. Images of steep cliffs and bottomless pits worried me. A rock rolled beneath the flexed balls of my feet, my ankle scraping against rough sandstone. I lifted my leg, testing the footing, fearing some chasm had opened beneath me and that the dark earth might swallow me. One more step. Then another. I inched onward. Dripping water broke the silence. The sound came from above. I crawled toward it. Faint gray light filtered to my eyes, curing my blindness. A rush of energy propelled me to the cave's rain-battered entrance.

Extinguished torches lay inside the entrance next to a bird's nest of tinder, flint, and steel. I struck the fire starters, sparks flying. The kindling caught fire quickly. I re-ignited a torch. Its brightness soothed me, restoring my courage. Dark chasms and bottomless pits vanished, the cavern returning to a tall chamber cluttered with fallen rocks. I breathed deeply, then trod back into the lair.

Deep in the cave, the enormity of the cache startled me. Hundreds of books formed irregular ranks, stacked in neat piles, eight or ten volumes in height. Far more than the 108 from the abbot's library. On the front row, familiar bindings and titles had been the most recently added. Crawling to the rear of the stacks, I retrieved the farthest volume I could reach, assuming it would be the cave's longest tenant. The book weighed heavy, its leather binding cracked, one corner of the binding scorched black. Inside the cover, large block letters on the first page read: *Sayings of the Desert Fathers*. The title rang familiar, but I couldn't remember why. I grabbed another book. The first page showed: *On Nature*. It meant nothing. I scanned the first few words, an introduction devoted to God, but it gave no hint at the author or purpose of the text. A third book displayed Greek letters. I could not read Greek well but knew enough to translate its title. *Thalia*. Grace.

The discovery perplexed me. Fabian and Cassius obviously hid the abbot's library from the Picts. But for some reason, the cave concealed other older and more numerous books. Certainly, Mutter knew about it. His pets never acted on their own initiative. How did this pertain to Adalbert? He could have stumbled upon this stash in his search for Roman treasure. The books had immeasurable value, but Adalbert could not easily carry or sell the volumes. Nor was this some Roman aristocrat's long-lost abandoned riches. The books belonged to the monastery. He'd be stealing from us. Even if he had decided to commit that grievous sin and been discovered, Mutter and his scribes wouldn't murder Adalbert to silence him. Would they? And what about Lazarus? He couldn't even read as best I knew.

Returning the books to their original places, I checked to make sure there'd be no other evidence of my intrusion, then headed toward the exit. The heavy rain continued to fall outside. I extinguished the torch with the wet fabric of my habit, lifted my hood over my head, then stepped outside.

Fabian and Cassius were long gone, making my descent easier and less cautious than the climb, a good thing because my head churned with questions distracting my attention. Why had Mutter been so quick to drop the investigation of Adalbert's death? He adamantly wanted to keep us out of the woods and the caves beyond. Lazarus was his antagonist's nephew. These pieces connected somehow, but how? The books must be the key.

Damn my ignorance. I needed help.

Chapter XIX

The heavy rain had changed to a persistent drizzle by the time I finally reached the open pasture that descended to the long-neglected Roman road. Along my route, I'd become increasingly careless, my head knotted with questions.

Tired and distracted. I almost ran straight into the wayward scribes' path a second time.

"Heavy bugger for being so small," Fabian said.

I dived headlong into the tall grass.

"Stop your complaining," Cassius said.

"Don't see why we couldn't just plant him where he lay. No one's going to miss him."

I peeked out from the weeds, relieved that they had not spotted me. The monks carried a long pole over their shoulders. A human-sized form slung on the pole swayed between them in rhythm to their steps. They trudged along the side of the crumbling pasture wall only a dozen paces from my hiding spot.

"Have a heart, Fabian. He's got a mother, you know. The bishop's sister. She'd care, for one."

"Don't think she'd care much, Brother. Have you even once seen her visit the monastery?"

"No, but can't say I've ever seen your mother either, assuming you ever had one."

"Everyone's got a mother, you lout. At least I had one. She and my pater died of consumption before I'd grown ten if you must know. That's how I landed here."

"Sorry. I didn't mean anything by it. If she were still alive, I'm sure she'd want to know where your miserable bones lay. It's the least we can do for poor Lazarus, after all he's been through. We owe him that much even if—what was that?"

"What was what?" Fabian said.

"I heard something. A gurgling sound. Like a hungry stomach."

"It's your own starving innards, you dope. Been twelve hours since we had a proper meal."

"I haven't had a proper meal in thirty-five years, but it wasn't my stomach grumbling."

"Then it was mine," Cassius said. "Move on. My shoulders are aching."

The men walked past me, only a few feet away. My head pleaded for my stomach to stop growling. I waited for their shadowy forms to disappear into the dark, then rose from the mud. I headed toward the dirt track leading home more cautiously. I slowed several times, the monks' soggy footsteps splashing ahead of me. They went straight to the front gate. I left the trail, skirted the graveyard, and scaled the wall at the corner of the compound, not wanting Fabian and Cassius to have any inkling that I had tailed them.

Eutychus waited in my dormitory cell when I entered. "My God, where have you been?"

"Is Fritigern back?"

"In the infirmary with a bandaged shoulder. He says you were butt naked and went chasing after a robber. He thinks maybe they killed Adalbert."

I shook my head. "No chance. They were just two bandits."

"You look terrible. What happened?" Eutychus's eyes slanted with worry. He leaned forward, his hands ready as if to catch me should I faint.

I hated that I could not trust him. Julia's squirming body and ecstatic moans still haunted me. Bitter juices soured my gut. "I got lost."

He eyed me through squinting lids. "What again? You've been gone half the night."

I turned my shoulder on him and gazed at my straw pallet. "Leave me alone. I need to sleep."

"First tell me the truth."

My face heated. "I got lost! Now go!"

"Okay, okay. Calm down. Does Mutter know you're back?"

The mention of the abbot's name jolted me. "I-I … no. I climbed the wall."

"Lay down. I'll let him know you've returned and that you're exhausted."

I sank to my bed. "Thanks."

Eutychus stepped toward the door, then stopped and turned back. "I'll tell him you need to sleep, but when you wake up, I hope you'll have a better story. Getting lost is wearing thin."

My eyes weighed so heavily tent poles wouldn't have held them open, but as soon as my head hit my pallet, Eutychus's warning did what tent poles could not. My head buzzed with excuses and fabricated scenarios to explain my absence. I pictured Abbot Mutter staring me down, probing me with clever questions, blistering me with a biting cross-examination, exposing my lies, then tossing me to his pets to be gagged and permanently silenced.

Cassius and Fabian had known where to find Lazarus's body. They never seemed the least bit distraught by his murder. I could not escape the feeling that they knew how to find him because they had left him there to die. I could not figure out why they had decided to retrieve him unless they thought the monks' fear of the Picts would provide them with an alibi. At this point, it would be easy to believe Lazarus had run afoul of Pict warriors or bandits and been killed.

I rolled over and squeezed my eyes shut, praying for God to grant me sleep and greater wisdom.

Sleep did not come.

Every blade of straw on my mat became a pricking needle, every shallow curvature of the floor a prodding lump. I drew my knees to my chest, then stretched my legs straight. I lay on my right side, then tossed to my left. I folded my arms for a pillow. I rolled onto my back. No matter my posture, Morpheus's bliss evaded me. My mind churned with Adalbert's ghastly face, Lazarus's bloody robe, the books piled high in the cave, Julia's ecstatic moans, Eutychus's pumping hips, the cutthroat lusting after my flesh, the earthy groans from the balneary.

Who could I trust? Anyone? Had I gone crazy? Hearing God's voice. Really? Who did I think I was? Moses?

It was madness. A madness driving me to suspect the abbot of murder and conspiracy. I admired the abbot, wanted to be like him, to have even a thimbleful of the knowledge and wisdom he commanded. What foolishness possessed me?

Find the murderer. I recalled the whisper, the words echoed in the darkness of my shabby cell. Chance had not sent me into the hills. God had used the cutthroats to guide me to Lazarus's body. Julia and Eutychus had broken my heart, but my torment steered me into the forest and God's thunderbolt to Mutter's nefarious pets. The books must be the key, but to what? Why would Adalbert want them? Why would the abbot hide them?

I beat my forehead with my palm. Think, Clodius. Think.

Was this insanity? Had my mother's demented seed sprouted anew in me? My God! Was that what happened? Could I never escape the family curse? Would I never know happiness? All I wanted was to belong, to be cherished, to know the warmth and security of a parent's love. But not for me. No, no! My friends, I detested. My mentors I demonized with conjured depravity. Did this dementia infest Mater? Never trusting or loving anyone? Did it now thrive in me?

Sandaled feet shuffled outside my doorway. A flame's glow bounced on the walls of the corridor. A wrinkled hand carrying a candle poked into my cell. I squinted, the light blinding me. My sight adjusted.

Abbot Mutter stood in my doorway, his eyes dark pits, his forehead and cheeks lined with shadowed creases. "Clodius, thank God you're unharmed."

I propped on my elbows, then readied to stand.

"No, Clodius. You needn't rise. The prior and I just wanted to make sure you were all right ... and to have a few words."

Mutter stepped into my cell. Prior Tomas emerged from the corridor's shadow and filled my doorway.

I folded at my waist and sat straight. "Forgive me. I should have reported to you. Eutychus said he would tell you."

"He found us," Mutter said, "but I wanted to see for myself. You've caused me an awful fright, Clodius."

"I'm sorry, Father. I'm fine."

"Whatever were you thinking? Don't you realize how dangerous it is? Dear Lord, chasing after bandits. You're lucky you've not been killed like Adalbert and poor, simple Lazarus."

I jerked my head and gaped, feigning surprise. "Lazarus?"

Tomas inched forward. "They found his body in the limestone foothills. Someone stabbed him, like Adalbert. Probably the same men who tried to rob you."

I glanced at the abbot. "Then even a greater shame that Fritigern and I did not catch them."

The abbot's hand trembled, jostling the candle, bouncing its light across the monks' faces. His mouth arched in a frown. "Enough of your foolishness, Clodius. Brother Bremen says you've been asking questions about Adalbert, prying, sticking your nose where it has no business. Then there's the matter of your getting lost not just once— repeatedly. I warned you. If you refuse to heed the danger, refuse to obey my warnings, you leave me no choice."

"But I got lost! I—"

"Enough I said! Hold your tongue before you stray beyond redemption!"

My lips clamped shut.

Mutter drew a deep breath. "You're confined to the compound's walls."

"But Father—"

"Another word and I'll confine you to your cell!"

I drew my legs to my chest and pressed my mouth into my knees. My head burned.

"It's for your own good, Clodius. There'll be no more forays into the forest. You need to spend more time on your

143

knees at the altar, with your nose in the gospels."

I dared not open my mouth. Anger swirled in my head. One syllable and an avalanche of words I would regret would follow.

"Goodnight," the abbot said and strode toward the door.

Tomas moved out of his way by stepping into my cell. "I have a few things to add."

Mutter paused, glanced at the prior, then nodded. He pushed the candle toward him. "Do you want this?"

"No, thank you. What I have to say passes just as well in the dark."

The abbot's eyelids narrowed. "Humph." He nodded and passed through my doorway. Darkness swallowed us as the candlelight retreated down the corridor.

Prior Tomas squatted, his head drawing even with my eyes, peering over my squeezed knees. A faint light glowed through my small window but barely illuminated his shadowy silhouette. "The abbot is doing what he thinks best, Clodius. He only means to protect you."

I pressed my forehead against my knees.

Tomas paused as if waiting for me to reply. After several heartbeats, he said, "This is your home, Clodius. I ... the abbot and I worry about you. You're smart and brave, but you can be reckless. I don't want to see you get hurt, son. Do you understand that?"

I lifted my head. The blood rushing to my face had cooled, the bitterness in my throat dissolved. I wanted to tell the prior what I had learned but held my breath. I'd just as well spill my guts to Fritigern. The story would fly straight to the abbot. I couldn't trust anyone.

The prior's dark form rose. He shuffled to the doorway and stopped. "I'll speak to the abbot. In a day or two maybe he'll relent. Try to sleep, son. You'll see. Things will be better in the morning. Goodnight."

Chapter XX

"The Picts are here!"

The panicked scream awoke me. Early morning sunlight filtered through my tiny window. Jumping up from my pallet, I ran from my cell to the empty hallway, expecting to see monks' faces. The dormitory was deserted. I ran to the entrance. Eutychus raced across the muddy compound from the direction of the church.

"What's happening?" I asked.

Eutychus bent double, gasping to catch his breath. "Picts are at the front gate. Come on. We can stop them." He straightened and sped off toward the main gate.

Before my head fully registered the import of his words, my feet sprinted after him.

Five men stood in the open gateway, blocking the entrance. Hulking Gunther held a sharpened sickle. Michael and Bremen carried pitchforks. Malthius wielded a large knife. Prior Tomas stood behind them, unarmed, his face pale, his hands trembling. His voice quavered as he spoke. "Boys, what are you doing here? Go back to the church."

Eutychus said, "Sorry, Prior, but I'm better at fighting than praying."

Tomas's face flushed red. He bared his teeth. "Don't be absurd! You could be killed!"

"Leave them be, Tomas," Bremen said. "We may need them."

The prior's body trembled. "Need them for what? Tools are no match for swords and spears. You'll be slaughtered. All of you."

Bremen grabbed Tomas's arm. He gave it a forceful jerk. "Steady, Tomas. Maybe you should return to the church. We can manage here for now. I'll see no harm comes to the boys."

Tomas's gaze darted about at the men staring back at him and landed on me. A rush of color returned to his face. "Clodius, you shouldn't be here. The abbot—"

"I won't leave the compound, Prior, but I can guard the gate."

Tomas's jaw tightened. "Don't be silly. You're just a boy."

Bremen stabbed his pitchfork's handle into the muddy ground. "Pardon, Prior, Gunther and I may be bigger and stronger, but there's not a one of us who can run as far or fast as Clodius and Eutychus. Look at them. They're not boys anymore. They're men."

I straightened and rolled my shoulders back. "My place is here, Prior, at the gate with my brothers."

Tomas's mouth hung open for a heartbeat. His gaze shot back to the gate. The color left his cheeks. He shivered. "Do nothing rash. I must speak to the abbot." He turned and stumbled in the direction of the main house. "Stay inside the walls." He broke into a trot.

"Good riddance," Gunther said. "His fear started to infect me."

"He's a good man. Just not a fighter," Bremen said.

The prior hesitated before entering the villa's front door. He cast a shuddering glance over his shoulder, then disappeared through the archway.

Scales fell from my eyes. I couldn't judge the man. How could I? I knew the symptoms all too well. Beneath his mask of discipline, shattered nerves trembled, terror knotted his guts and drained his courage.

I turned to the gate and pushed forward between Michael and Bremen to peer outside. Three muscular men with spiked hair stood like statues in the middle of the muddy trail more than a stone's throw from the gate. One had a sharp chin, a ferret-like nose, beady black eyes, and hawk feathers knotted in the back of his hair, his skin adorned with painted blue sunbursts and clawing talons. Beside him, a shorter, thick-waisted man had fox-skin armbands and anklets, a foxtail dangling from his hair, and snarling animal faces painted on his legs and torso. The third and largest warrior had a scarred face. The side of his torso and bulging legs were decorated with images of huge, blue snakes. Other than their paint and amulets, the men stood completely naked. My shocked gaze locked on their dangling genitals.

"What are they doing?" I asked.

"Watching us," Bremen said. "Just like we're watching them."

Gunther squeezed the handle of his sickle. "I say we rush them. Show them we're not afraid."

"Calm down," Michael said. "I think they're just scouts, but we can't be sure. There could be a whole army of them in the trees."

I said, "I didn't see any of them last night."

"Last night? Where were you?" Michael said.

Eutychus glanced at me, his eyebrows arched. "Yeah, where were you?"

"I got lost. I wandered all over the place. If the Pict army had been nearby, I would've tripped over them. Michael's right. These have to be scouts."

"Then let's charge them," Gunther said. "We can make sure they don't report back to their chiefs."

Bremen scoffed. "No offense, Gunther, but look at them. They're built like stags. You're strong as an ox, but as slow as one, too. And I'm no better, I run out of breath chasing after a butterfly."

"I can catch them," Eutychus said.

"Don't even think it," Bremen said. "They'd have your bleeding head at the end of a spear before you laid a hand on them."

The Picts pivoted about-face.

"They're leaving," I said.

The six of us watched in silence as the Picts loped down the trail and disappeared.

Michael said, "Whatever they were looking for, they seem to have found it.".

Malthius said, "You suppose they'll be back?"

Eutychus laughed sarcastically. "I'm sure we scared them away, especially you with your great blade, Barber. One look at your shaved scalps and they be terrified you'd cut off their pretty pointy spikes."

"I fail to see the humor in it," Malthius said.

"They'll be back," Bremen said, "and with more of their bleeding blue brethren."

Gunther jabbed his sickle in the direction of the trail. "There must be something more we can do than just wait for them to return."

"Pray," Michael said. "Like the abbot says."

Gunther frowned. "Prayer is not much use in a sword fight."

Michael lifted his pitchfork skyward. "It chased those three away."

"Maybe." Gunther shrugged. "Maybe they just didn't like the look of your ugly mug."

"Enough, Gunther," Bremen said. "Unless you're prepared to disobey Abbot Mutter, prayer is our only option. I suggest you return to the church to join our brothers and lift your voices to heaven. Except for you two." He pointed at Eutychus and me. "I want a word with you. The rest of you go. I'll stand guard and sound the alarm if the Picts reappear."

Gunther grunted, then lowered the sickle he brandished and joined Michael, Silvanius, and Malthius in sloshing toward the church.

Bremen stepped to the gate, checking the trail. He turned back. "I want you to gather the other novices and go to Coria."

His words hit me like a hammer.

A big smile sprouted across Eutychus's face.

My head shuddered; my thoughts jumbled. "W-we can't. I-I've been confined to the compound. The abbot has ordered everyone to remain here."

Bremen shook his head. "No. None of you have taken your vows."

I said, "What difference does that make?"

"We swore eternal obedience when we took our oaths.

Monks can't disobey their abbot. But none of you have made a pledge. You can leave without consequence. And as for your confinement, well, the Picts' arrival has changed everything."

It took me several breaths to process his words. The notion of fleeing to the city appealed to me. Our recent visitors had brought home the seriousness of our plight. But it did not feel right. I felt ashamed of my eagerness to run.

I glanced at Eutychus. He nodded. He needed no more convincing, but my conscience nagged at me. Fleeing the monastery amounted to abandoning the men who had been my family. "Why hasn't Mutter allowed the novices to leave if they're not bound to his orders?"

Bremen grimaced. "I'm sure he wants to but consider his position. Right now, he's leading prayers in the church, asking for God's protection. What kind of faith would he show if he whisked all the novices away to the safety of Coria's walls?"

I said, "And you, what about your faith?"

The big monk lowered his head and drew a deep breath. "I'm not expecting any miracles."

"Then come with us," Eutychus said.

"I can't, lad. I've taken the vows. I must obey the abbot."

"And what if he wasn't the abbot?" I asked.

Bremen's husky frame stiffened. "I don't know what you're thinking, boy, but put it out of your head. He's the abbot until he dies. The abbot he stays."

"But what if—"

His face glowed red. He balled his hands. "I'll not listen to blasphemy! Whatever you're thinking, forget it! Do you hear me?"

I cowered. "But—"

"Not a word, Clodius! Not one word!"

My head shrunk into my shoulders. Bremen thought I meant to kill the abbot, but why would he jump so readily to such a conclusion, and so vehemently silence me, unless the thought hadn't crossed his mind? If Mutter died, the prior would take charge. Tomas would order an evacuation.

Bremen turned back to the trail. "You asked me once how I ended up here." He stepped away from the gate, grabbed his stool, and sat. "I was a runaway, born to a slave and would have died a slave if not for the abbot." He looked over his shoulder at me. "I escaped the iron mines at Burrium. I killed a black-hearted fiend who enjoyed beating slaves. He deserved to die, but that makes no difference." Bremen paused. He returned his gaze to the dirt track and drew a shuddering breath. "You know what they do to murdering runaways when they catch them."

"Crucify them," Eutychus said.

"They do the same to anyone harboring fugitive slaves." He paused and inhaled slowly. "No older than you two, I ran half-way across Britannia. Nearly died of exposure. Mutter was just a monk back then. He found me and hid me in one of the caves in the hills. He brought me food for months until I healed. Then he vouched for me with Venicius, the former abbot, and I joined the brothers."

I bit my lower lip. The suspicion and anger simmering in my heart cooled. The abbot had risked his life to save a slave. What noble act had I done that gave me the right to judge him? Bremen's loyalty made perfect sense, but almost two decades had passed since then. People changed. Bremen himself had told me that Bishop Bonifatius had once been a good man but had grown fat and corrupt. The abbot didn't pine for food or money. He lusted for knowledge, his books. I wanted to tell Bremen what I had discovered about the cave, but it would be useless.

"That's how I became a monk," Bremen said and shot me a second glance. "Now, off with you, before I lose my temper and forget that you're just novices. Get the other boys together and leave. The Picts could return at any moment." The big brewer rose from the stool, turned his back to us, and assumed a sentinel's watch at the gate.

Eutychus grabbed my sleeve and pulled me away. I followed him toward the church, where'd we find the other novices.

I said, "He doesn't understand. I meant to remove the abbot, not kill him."

"Bremen's in no mood to listen to whatever you have in mind. Besides, how could you remove him? Only the bishop has that authority, and it requires a trial."

"The idea has only just occurred to me. I haven't worked out the details."

"Even if we had time for a trial, ordering the monks to stand on their faith is hardly a church crime."

"No, but murder is."

Eutychus stopped abruptly, still clinging to my sleeve. "Okay. Enough of the lies. Tell me. What did you find?"

I swallowed my regrets about Julia. I needed help. "A cave."

Eutychus's body turned rigid. "A cave? What? Adalbert's cave?"

"I don't know. Maybe. I think so."

He grabbed my arm and spun me to face him. "Where? When?"

"Last night in the storm. In the hills, as we had guessed. I followed Fabian and Cassius there."

His mouth gaped. "Fabian and Cassius? What are you talking about?"

"They've hidden the library there. They're protecting the books from the Picts I'm sure, but there are more books than just our library. A lot more. And they've been there a long time."

Eutychus's steady gaze burned into my eyes. He froze in silence. Wheels and gears turned inside his skull.

I pried his grip from my sleeve. "I think Adalbert may have stumbled upon the books during his treasure hunt. They're valuable, right? He may have tried to sell one. Somehow Mutter found out."

"And he murdered him? It's a good thing Bremen cut you off, Clodius. Otherwise, he would have killed you on the spot for slander."

"I know it doesn't make sense. I couldn't believe it either until I saw Lazarus's body."

"*You* found Lazarus? Why didn't you tell me?"

My lungs froze. Julia's arms and legs wrapped around Eutychus's body. "I-I couldn't."

"Why not?"

"This isn't about us, Eutychus. It's about Adalbert. It's about Mutter and saving the monks from his lunacy."

"Who said anything about you and me? Of course, it's about Adalbert. Why would you even say such a thing? Why have you been lying to me?"

"Because you lied to me!"

"You're off your head. You've turned paranoid. First, the abbot's a murderer, then I'm a liar. Who will you accuse next? Bremen? Tomas? Olaf?"

"I *saw* you." I seethed. "You and her … together … you and Julia."

Shock, guilt, outrage, Eutychus stood paralyzed by the emotions slamming inside. My old feelings of jealousy and betrayal flowed back into my heart. What had we been arguing about? I couldn't even remember. The image of Julia lingered, writhing in his arms, her stuttered gasps, his ecstatic moans.

Eutychus's eyes narrowed. "You've been spying on me."

"No." I shook my head. "That's a lie."

He stepped closer, his jaw rippling, his fists balled. "So how long did you stand and watch us? Did you get your fill?"

"I didn't … I wouldn't."

"How do you even know her name?"

"I-I—"

Eutychus's fist crashed into my jaw. I tumbled backward to the muddy ground, hitting my head hard.

My friend stormed off, flashing lights spinning before my eyes.

Chapter XXI

I didn't know how long I lay in the mud. The gray sky floated above me, misty, unfocused, unfriendly. A dizziness swam about my head, joined by a throbbing from my jaw and the back of my skull. The hard edge of a stone dug into my scalp. My full senses returned with a shiver, my skin chilled from the drizzle drenching my clothes. I rolled to my side, then propped upon my elbow. I inspected the puddle formed where my head had lain. The water had a pinkish hue.

What happened? Eutychus's angry face flashed. Oh, yeah.

Folding my legs beneath me, sitting hunched, my hands holding my head, the hopelessness of my quest pressed down upon me. Maybe I should just run off to the safety of Coria with the other novices and forget everything. Mutter wanted to be martyred. No one appointed me to save the fools who wanted to follow him to the grave. They'd never believe me. I didn't even believe me. None of it made sense. I had missed something—an important fact that would bring the conspiracy to light. What God? Show me.

Footsteps approached me from behind. A gentle hand squeezed my shoulder.

"You all right?" Olaf's sympathetic blue eyes looked down at me.

"Not really. I think I cracked my skull."

He knelt beside me and examined my scalp, probing with his fingers. "There's blood, but I don't think its broken. What happened?"

"I fell."

"Eutychus told me I'd find you here. Odd that he'd leave you if you'd fallen."

"It's complicated. Help me to my feet."

His hand gripped beneath my armpit and lifted. "We're to meet him at the main gate. He's getting Fritigern from the infirmary. We're going to Coria."

"What about the abbot?"

Olaf frowned. "I think he knows. He didn't say anything when Eutychus came to get me."

"And the monks?"

"Everyone's on their knees in the church begging for God's mercy."

"You can let go of my arm. I'm all right," I said.

"Come on. They'll be at the gate by now."

I shook my head. "I'm not going. At least, not yet."

"Then I'll stay with you."

His loyalty moved me, but I could not keep him with me. The plan brewing in my mind seemed desperate, more like one of my foolish fantasies. I had to try but couldn't risk Olaf's life to save my own. "No. Join the others. Eutychus and Fritigern will get you safely to the town. You can trust them."

"What should I tell them?"

"Not to wait for me. I'll come later."

Olaf chewed his lip. He took my hand. "Be careful."

He meant well but considering bloodthirsty Picts surrounded us, a murderer roamed freely, and my head bled, his warning felt somewhat condescending. What did he think I would do, act foolishly? Based on my prior behavior, perhaps his concern had merit. Be careful. Ha! The lines had become so blurred, I didn't know where prudence ended and folly began.

Olaf released his grip and left.

Prior Tomas had gone to the villa, not the church, where he would have found the abbot if he really wanted to talk to him. Maybe he had good reason to retreat to his office instead of joining the monks in prayer. He had been arguing with the abbot. The Picts terrified him. Perhaps he had no faith in the abbot's judgment or the prospect of divine intervention. Nor did he show Mutter's ready willingness to be martyred. The prior would flee if given a chance, but no doubt felt constrained by the same regulation restraining Bremen. If Tomas had the authority, he would order an immediate evacuation to safety. Unlike Bremen, maybe

Tomas would be willing to hear my story and help fill the gaps. Then we could close the net on the abbot. Prove he had murdered Adalbert. The other monks would abandon Mutter and Tomas could lead them to safety. Could I trust him?

I headed toward the main house. The atrium and peristyle garden were empty. I walked to the prior's office. Tomas leaned forward at his desk, his eyes closed, his head in his hands.

"Prior Tomas, may I interrupt you?"

His head jerked upward. "Clodius. You startled me."

"I'm sorry, Father, but I need to speak with you privately."

He pushed back into his chair, motioning with his hand for me to be seated. His eyes were bloodshot, his skin patched with reddish blotches. "Of course, Clodius. What have you done to your head? You're bleeding."

"It's nothing. I fell." I lowered myself onto a stool.

"What is troubling you?"

"I'm worried about the abbot. Some things that I've discovered. I don't know who else to go to."

Tomas's black eyebrows shot up. "The abbot? What on earth do you mean?"

"I found a cave in the hills. It's loaded with books from our library. Cassius and Fabian have been hiding them."

Tomas's cheeks flinched. "Yes, I know. They're there for safekeeping. If … when the Picts have left, they'll retrieve them. Only the abbot, Cassius, and Fabian know the exact location. The fewer who know, the less likely the location can be betrayed, either by negligence or … under torture. I'm afraid that your discovery may jeopardize you. It's best you do not mention it to anyone else."

"I believe Adalbert may have discovered them, too."

Tomas's head jerked back. "Adalbert? Why would Adalbert have found them?"

"He's been searching the hills for buried treasure left by the Romans before they fled. I think he stumbled upon the books instead."

Tomas's mouth pursed to his left as he shook his head. "You're confused. Adalbert died before the books were moved."

"I know, except there are more books than just the ones from our library. A lot more. Adalbert could have found them and then … well … maybe someone didn't want him to know."

Tomas's face flushed. "Be careful what you say, Clodius. I can excuse youthful ignorance, but I'll not countenance defamation."

I bit my lower lip. Had I'd misjudged Tomas? But I had no one else to tell. "I looked at some of the books. One seemed vaguely familiar, *Sayings of the Desert Fathers*. Others I didn't recognize, *On Nature*, *In Defense of Free Will*, and one written in Greek entitled *Grace*. I thought maybe you would know about them."

Tomas leaned back. He lifted his hand to his chin, fingers stroking his unshaved black stubble. He focused on the blank wall above my head. He held this contemplative pose for many heartbeats. Would he betray me? Tell the abbot? I glanced at the open doorway. Should I run?

Tomas's lips twisted into a scowl. "That's not possible. The books have been banned. We burned every copy. The abbot would never allow it."

"I'm not lying. I've never even heard of them. How could I make up such a story?"

Tomas shot up.

My heart fluttered. I leaned toward the open door.

Tomas spun away. He paced behind his desk, his lips mouthing silent words. He pressed his palms to his temples, seeming to forget my presence. He halted once and turned to me but then resumed his pacing without a word. I had lit a fire in him. Would the flame be turned on me? How foolish to think that I could persuade the prior, or anyone else that the abbot had murdered Adalbert. Even I found it hard to believe, but my own eyes had seen the books, my own ears had heard Cassius and Fabian. I could find no other explanation.

After half-a-dozen about-faces, Tomas stopped. He lowered his hands to his desk. He leaned toward me. His stare paralyzed my legs. The shadowed wrinkles lining his face darkened. Pits opened where before he'd had eyes. He spoke slowly, his voice steady.

"Abbot Mutter had a teacher … a monk … whose name we no longer speak … Pelagius." Tomas drew a deep breath. "Mutter traveled with him to Rome almost fifty years ago, long before I or anyone else knew him." He straightened and lifted his hands from the desk. "Years after I came to the monastery, after the Romans abandoned Britannia, an edict arrived from the bishops in Gaul, endorsing the resolution of a synod held in Carthage. Pelagius had been declared a heretic."

Tomas paused. He rubbed his forehead. His gaze shifted to his desktop. "We were ordered to collect and destroy all Pelagius's texts, anything he had ever written or even copied. By then, Bishop Bonifatius had appointed Mutter as the abbot, and so it fell upon him to carry out the edict in this district. I participated in the purge. We seized every copy we could find. I watched the books burn in a bonfire, stacked beneath a huge pile of fagots."

He lifted his chin, his gaze briefly fixing on the candle. His lips wrinkled, and he swallowed like bile fouled his throat. "The Greek text, *Grace*, is different, even worse than Pelagius's books, penned by Arius, a heretic whose blasphemy persists among the Germanic barbarian tribes to this day. Anyone with a copy risks being branded a heretic and being condemned to eternal damnation."

My chest burned. I'd forgotten to breathe. I gulped air and swallowed. "If the books are banned, why are Cassius, Fabian, and the abbot hiding them?"

"Cassius and Fabian will do whatever Abbot Mutter tells them. As for him, perhaps his allegiance to his old mentor lives."

A flame sparked in my head. Mutter's culpability at last

made sense. "If Adalbert stumbled onto the books, he might have threatened the abbot. Even if he didn't challenge Mutter, his knowledge of the secret would be an awful risk. Maybe—" I caught my breath. "Maybe too great a risk to suffer." I stared back at Tomas. "Maybe he had to be silenced."

The prior's lips stretched flat, his eyelids narrowed. "Who else knows about this?"

"Fabian and Cassius. I followed them to the cave. I told Eutychus about the cave, but he wouldn't listen. There's no one else."

"Did Fabian and Cassius see you?"

"No. I hid behind rocks."

"Good. Tell no one else. I don't know who we can trust."

"But if we go to the church and expose him, the brothers will follow your orders."

Tomas sneered. "What? Believe the word of a naughty novice over Fabian, Cassius, and the abbot?"

"They will if you back me."

The prior's face paled. His back slouched. "I wish it were true, but to my shame, I fear I've lost the men's confidence. That's why I prayed as you entered, asking forgiveness for my fears. I've seen it in their faces. Don't deny it. I saw it in your face, too. They'd sooner believe I'd invented the story to usurp the abbot's authority. And then what? We'd be locked away in a cell to await the Picts' slaughter."

Tomas's eyelids flickered. He lowered his head. He looked away from me. I sympathized with his humiliation, acknowledging his weakness, confessing the irrational, paralyzing fears that gripped him. No one knew fear better than I did.

"What can we do?"

"We must go to Coria to see the bishop."

"But there's no time for a trial."

Tomas's neck stiffened. "We don't need a trial. The bishop can suspend the abbot's authority and place me in charge pending a trial. I can order the monastery's

158

abandonment, and we can flee to the safety of the city. It's our only hope."

God had led me to Tomas. I could trust him, of this I felt certain. Now I understood the abbot's guilt and the reason for God's call. Adalbert's murder was a tragic prelude to a monstrous injustice that must be prevented. God wanted me to save my brothers from a pointless slaughter. We had to renounce Mutter's authority and free his captives from his suicidal command. Just one problem remained.

One thousand Picts stood between me and my brothers' salvation.

Chapter XXII

Prior Tomas grabbed a leather satchel, slung it over his shoulder, and we hurried out of his office to the colonnaded peristyle walkway. When we exited the atrium, he turned in the direction of the main gate.

"Wait." I tugged on his arm toward the church. "Bremen's at the gate. He may try to stop you. I know a better way to leave without anyone seeing us."

Tomas smirked. "Why doesn't that surprise me?"

He followed me around the house, past the balneary, and to the corner of the compound's wall. He scaled the wall and jumped to the cemetery with surprising agility, considering he had nearly forty years on me.

I said, "We must stay clear of the trail and road. The Picts will see us. We'll have to travel cross-country."

Tomas glanced at the dense woods. His lips quivered as he spoke. "Are you sure? We can't afford to get lost. The road would be faster."

"Not if the Picts catch us. Trust me. I'll get us there."

The anxiety in his gaze showed he had not truly considered the hazards of our journey. He nodded, then pointed a shaking finger at the woods to our north. "I'll follow you."

The undergrowth changed from trampled weeds to tangled vines, tall ferns, and thorny bushes soon after we crossed into the forest. When the monastery's walls disappeared behind us, I made careful note of an oak tree with a fallen limb covered by wiry gray moss. Eighteen paces farther, before losing sight of the oak, I aligned it with an elm tree sprouting prickly ferns from a knotty scar.

"What are you doing?" the prior asked.

"Keeping us on a true heading."

"North is that way," he said, pointing toward a rotted stump in the distance. "Just walk straight."

I checked the trees' alignment. I pointed at a slight angle from Tomas's aim. "Actually, north is that direction."

"How can you be sure?"

"It's easy to lose track of your direction in the forest. That's why I memorize landmarks. The trees, the bushes, the rocks, and the groundcover are all different. I look for distinctive features, then keep three markers in alignment to follow their straight line. Coria and the River Tyne lie in that direction. If we keep a true heading, we can't miss them."

"Who taught you to do that?"

"No one. I used to mark the trees with notches, but it slows me down. The more I've wandered the forest, the more obvious distinctive traits have become. Like that pine tree up ahead. It's my next marker."

Tomas squinted into the distance. "There's a thousand pine trees ahead of us."

"Yes, but the one I'm fixed on has a patch of bark rubbed clean from the trunk about three feet from the floor. Maybe some stag used it to sharpen his antlers."

"I can't see what you're talking about."

"It's there."

The rain lifted, but the sky remained overcast. A bright shaft of sunlight pierced the canopy. Water droplets adhering to fern stalks and tree branches glinted like jewels. The light faded. A somber gray resumed. We came upon an enormous spider's web draped between two pine trees. Dew beaded on the threads. At its center, a long-legged, yellow and black spider awaited its next victim.

Tomas whispered, "How much farther?"

"I can't be sure."

Thunder rumbled overhead. The steady pit-pat of rain resumed.

"You said you knew the way."

"I said I could get us there."

His voice trembled. "What? It's too dark. You can't see where you're going."

"That's why I'm constantly aligning the trees."

"You'll get us lost!"

"Shh! Quiet. Don't worry. The trick is to fix on a target

161

ahead of us. I look for a good marker like that spider's web, or those three trunks growing together ahead of us. It keeps us from walking in circles."

"What three trunks? Where?"

I pointed straight ahead. "There, next to the fern shaped like a hawk's wings."

"I can't see a thing in this darkness."

"I've got good eyes. We'll get there."

Wood cracked to my right.

I crouched, waving my hand downward at Tomas.

"What?"

I held a forefinger to my puckered lips. Tomas's face turned white. He crouched beside me. We held motionless until my calves began to burn. Even with good eyes, the shadows made it difficult to see shapes among the trees. I had heard something, but the forest masked my vision.

Leaves rustled. A curling fern frond bounced. I held my breath as a long-haired Pict warrior stepped from the shadows fifty paces ahead of us. He took two soft steps then froze, only his gaze shifting, searching the woods. Swirling blue spirals ran the length of his muscular arms and legs. Talons, feathers, and stone amulets festooned his shoulder-length hair. He carried a long broadsword, its blade etched with fantastic mythical animals. A leather band strapped over his shoulder and across his chest held a fur-lined sheath over his back. Other than his baldric, he did not wear one stitch of clothing.

Tomas whimpered. I glared at him, imploring with my eyes to keep quiet. He squeezed his eyes shut, his lips compressed into straight lines, his cheeks as hard as stones.

The Pict stepped two paces toward us and stopped again. His head jerked left and right, then fixed directly at us. He looked right at me! I didn't dare move though my nerves urged me to jump and run. He had to see me. I held my breath and willed my hand to stop shaking, but my heart raced so fast I feared the warrior would hear it thumping against my chest.

He took two steps away from us, then paused, looking to his right. A trilling whistle sounded from a distance. The Pict burst into a sprint after it. He disappeared into the forest's depths.

I released my breath.

Tomas collapsed to the ground beside me. "What was I thinking? We'll never make it."

I shared his pessimism, but our options appeared limited. We could turn back and be slaughtered by the Picts in St. Antony's, or venture onward and be captured and killed somewhere deep in the forest. Either way, the prospect of death appeared certain. Our chances of reaching the town, and then returning to liberate our brethren remained desperately slim, but the only hope for our survival.

I straightened, keeping a careful watch on the trees into which the Pict had disappeared, and whispered, "We have to try."

Tomas lifted himself. His body shuddered. He gritted his teeth and waved me onward.

The farther into the forest we proceeded, the more confident I became in my sense of direction. Details in the plants that I would not have previously noticed jumped out at me. Many trees had a shadowy discoloration on the north side of their bark, where moisture hung, and a greater density of lichens and mosses clung to their trunks. Some trees grew slanted, tipping to the southwest, bent by weeks of prevailing winds blowing in from the northern seas. Boulders also provided hints, their mottled colors with varying shades of green and gray lichen pointing north.

"Slow down." The prior huffed behind me.

My gait had unconsciously quickened. Ahead, a glimmer of sunlight splashed across a clearing. A few steps farther, the light became a broad bright band stretching beyond my sight. I motioned for the prior to rest. "Let me scout ahead. I think we've reached the river."

Tomas nodded. He sank to the wet blanket of dead leaves and pine needles.

Using the concealment of ferns and fallen timber, I inched to the edge of the forest. The landscape opened to a broad clearing of tall grass and scattered brush at least fifty paces from the south bank of the Tyne. Near the water's edge, a dozen blue-painted warriors patrolled the river's north side. I dropped to my chest, praying they had not spotted me. The blue forms continued their route undisturbed. I crept backward until the undergrowth swallowed me, then slouched and ran with loping strides back to the prior.

"The river is just ahead, but there are patrols."

"How do we get across?"

"I don't know."

"Where's Coria? How far?"

"We're downstream from the city, maybe a mile or two."

Tomas screwed his lips and stared at the river. "We can swim across. There's another Roman road on the other side."

I shook my head. "It's a good fifty paces from the forest to the water on this side. They'll see us before we reach the water. Besides, the road isn't safe."

"Then we wait for nightfall."

The cover of darkness would help, but we'd be wasting precious time. After we crossed, we'd still have to risk the journey upstream near the road. Even in the darkness, we'd be at great risk of being spotted.

"I have an idea," I said.

Tomas rolled his eyes skyward. "God help us." His gaze fixed on me. "Okay, let's hear it."

"You won't like it."

Chapter XXIII

"You'll get us killed." Prior Tomas's wide eyes and gaping mouth protested my insanity.

"It's the only way to avoid being spotted."

The prior folded his hands and shook them at his breast. His lips moved with a silent prayer. He pulled his knees to his chest, then rocked in silence. A moment later, he raised his chin, pressed his palms to his thighs and exhaled. "Okay … I can't think of anything better."

"All right then. Follow me."

Scanning the woods, my gaze fixed on a shattered gray trunk to our rear. I walked to it then picked out a pine tree scarred by a fallen branch. We continued traveling deeper into the trees until the forest canopy completely shrouded us. We then turned west, my sight locked on a V-shaped fir tree to our right. We progressed through the forest following my sense of direction until at last we reached our first dangerous obstacle.

The old road running north to Coria lay before us. A cleared grassland stretched from the forest's ragged edge to the road forty paces away, and then another forty or fifty paces to the opposing forest's edge beyond the road. When we crossed, we would be exposed. Unlike the flat land adjacent to the river, the terrain here formed low hills and hollows, traversed by waist-high fieldstone pasture divides. The undulating landscape obstructed clear fields of vision and hopefully would conceal us from any Picts nearby. It also meant we would be blind to what might be waiting for us beyond a rise, but I preferred not to think about that. God had brought us this far. Surely, he did not intend for our journey to end here.

I turned back to Prior Tomas. "Ready?"

He signed the cross on his forehead. "God be with us."

A dilapidated stone wall no taller than my waist reached to the forest's edge to our left, then jutted westward across the adjacent pasture before intersecting more walls defining the fields. We held to the woods until we reached the wall, then crawled on all fours behind it as we followed its lie through the tall grass. A stiff wind picked up when we left the trees, whistling across the top of the stacked rocks, bending the green grass stalks to the north. The raindrops fell heavier, soaking into my clothes.

We reached the walls' first intersection. I peeked above the stones, thinking I could risk climbing over the wall into the next pasture. The field looked clear. I drew a deep breath, raised my hands to the wall's edge, and prepared to vault it as I'd seen Eutychus do. I nodded at Tomas, then sprang upward and over.

If I had landed in a nest of vipers, I could not have been more terrified.

My terror matched that of the blue-tattooed face that I landed upon.

Maybe he had lain down to take a nap, or just to escape the chilly stiff wind, but for whatever reason, a naked, blue-painted savage lay beneath me.

The shocked white terror in his eyes changed to a painful cringe, a squeaking whimper escaped his lips. My knee had landed in the squishy ball sack between his thighs.

Before I had recovered from my fright, Prior Tomas came bounding on top of both of us, driving my kneecap further into the man's scrotum, so far that his gonads might have popped out of his rectum. His whimpering transformed into a whining cry, his body convulsing with such force that he threw both of us off him, sending us rolling into the grass.

The prior's reaction mirrored mine. Blind terror. We jumped to our feet and ran like scared rabbits for the road and the sanctuary of the trees beyond.

Voices shouted from my left. My sandals landed on the road's stones. I bounded over the far curb and landed on the soft turf. I glanced to my side. One hundred paces away, four Picts carrying spears sprinted down the road toward me.

"Run Prior!"

"I'm right behind you!"

We crossed the pasture and plunged into the welcoming shadows of the forest. We leaped a fallen pine, avoided slamming into any trees, and ducked under low branches.

"They're gaining on us!" Tomas screamed with choking gasps. He could not outrun them for much longer.

To my right, the forested terrain gave way to a deep ravine cut by a purling stream. A huge oak leaned precariously away from the stream, its massive tangle of roots exposed by the waters and ripped from the earth by the tree's weight. Driven more by fear and instinct than cleverness, I jumped into the ravine, splashing into rounded stones. Tomas landed beside me. I wrapped my arms around his waist and dived with him into the side of the bank beneath the tangle of roots. He understood my intent. We burrowed as deeply beneath the leaning tree as possible, while at the same time smearing our faces with mud.

Shouts and heavy footsteps approached us.

I froze, fighting to control my gasps and shaking limbs.

The footsteps slowed. Then stopped. Near.

A voice whispered in the gurgling Pict language. Silence. A different voice answered.

A rotted root crackled under a man's weight directly over my head. I could not move, my arms and legs helpless. I'd be found. Blinding lightning shot through my brain. I wanted to scream.

"Yaah!"

Not me. Another's voice split the air.

The man above me jumped back from the tree's roots. He screamed in fright.

Tomas squeezed his eyes shut. His lips mouthed silent prayers.

I twisted my neck, straining to roll my eyes upward as if to see through the back of my head into the earth above.

A root over my head shifted.

It breathed.

A fanged, loathsome creature, with copper-toned eyes split by black lozenges, slipped through muddy shoots. Its diamond-shaped head, armored with scaly plates, descended. Black jagged lightning coursed from its crown down its spine. A skinny black tongue, Satan's fork, spat from its tope mouth, tasting the air, exploring the roots, searching for me.

My heart battered against my chest. The slithering form dangled in space. Its head shifted. It rose. Then dived. Its brown, scalloped skin uncoiled endlessly. It dropped across my forehead. Hesitated inches from my nose. Tiny, perfectly regimented plates filled my sight. Its snout bobbed twice, faced away from my lips, then inch by inch, foot by foot, the serpent unwound. Its tail released its grip. The heavy body flopped to the earth, smacking dirt and rocks covering my foot. The coarse texture of its scales grated over my muddy toes. The serpent's body slid over my sandal and into the water of the fast-running stream.

I gulped in air. The sound of my heaving lungs blasted the forest's mist.

Tomas's eyes shot open. His hand flew to cover my mouth and silence me. My lungs, starved to the limit, jumped in my chest. The prior's effort to restrain me failed. I folded at my waist and collapsed to my knees, gasping for life.

My breathing slowed. My head cleared. No war cries. No piercing spears. No sword severing my head.

"It's a miracle," Tomas said. "They've left."

Strength returned to my arms and legs. If this was how God worked miracles, then I didn't care to witness another. The Picts had left us, but not by divine intervention. They'd seen the snake and knew that not even a crazy man would hide anywhere near it.

Grabbing at an overhanging root, I pulled up to my feet. My knees wobbled. "We need to get to the river." I pointed across the stream. "That way but watch for the snake."

"Snake! What snake?" Tomas cringed back into the mass of roots. His eyes had been closed the entire time. He had no idea of the horror I'd experience, and perhaps a good thing, too.

"Just keep your eyes open," I said.

I staggered forward, splashing through the water, searching the woodlands to keep our heading true. We trudged onward in silence until we reached a solitary, egg-shaped boulder, covered with green and gray mosses and small ferns on its top like green hair. We'd surely put at least a mile of forest between us and the road. Hopefully, it would be sufficient to place us outside the Picts' patrols.

I pointed to my right. Tomas gave a fatigued nod. We headed north. I memorized the twisting trunk of an ash tree, my next marker. Just beyond it, we reached the forest's edge. Down a grassy slope, the River Tyne's banks had flooded. Murky brown water churned and swirled toward Coria.

The sun had not yet set. Despite the unrelenting rain, ample light revealed the east-west road beyond the river. Across it, hundreds of shadowy forms moved about the highway in the direction of the town's western gate.

"We wait for darkness, then go," I said.

Tomas's knees folded. He melted to the ground. "This is foolishness. I never imagined it would take so long. We should rethink our plan."

I rested on my knees and maintained a careful watch of the river. "How do you mean?"

He pointed south. "How do we know the Picts haven't destroyed St. Antony's? Everyone could be dead. We may be risking our lives for nothing. If we're lucky enough to reach Coria, we'd do best to stay. The return is too risky."

I tumbled to my rear. "But we've come this far … we can't give up."

Tomas's jaw muscles rippled. "Can you tell me they live? That the monastery has not been destroyed?"

"Of course not, but—"

"Can you assure me we can return safely? That we will not die or be captured?"

"No, but—"

"But what? I should trust your instincts?"

I clenched my fist and beat it over my heart. "It's more than instinct. What about God? He hasn't abandoned us."

The prior closed his eyes. He lowered his chin and pressed his interlocked fingers to his forehead. He rocked silently.

My heart sank, but I couldn't blame the prior for his doubts. We'd already faced more danger today than any monk expected to see in his lifetime. And compared to our next steps, slipping past 1,000 Picts and sneaking into a garrisoned city, what we had already survived had been a carefree frolic.

I needed Tomas to trust me but could hardly condemn him for what I could not do myself. Oh, I had great eyesight, quick wits, strength, and stamina. My body and senses were sound. But when it came to good judgment, I had little to offer. Why? What curse afflicted me?

Tomas's head sagged, his body limp and exhausted. His breathing slowed. His chest rumbled. He fell asleep.

No wonder he'd lost courage. I'd run the man ragged. No. Not me. The One who sent me. And nearly killed us. I gazed skyward. God, what are you thinking?

The forest canopy blocked all but patches of the darkening overcast sky. It would be night soon. When the prior awakened, I needed to say something to fortify his courage. What God? What?

I ran my fingers through my coarse red hair and pressed into my skull. I closed my eyes. The river's roaring sounded distant. A nightingale twittered and chattered. The air smelled fresh and clean.

And yet … I'd gotten us safely here. There'd been close calls for sure, but we had survived. The prior would have never made it here on his own. Was that why God picked me? He knew I could guide the prior safely to the town and back. He knew I would not fail. Not because he'd make my path easy. My heart sprinted, and my head tingled.

God knew because God trusted in me.

Tomas stirred. He rubbed his bleary eyes. "Where are we? What time is it?"

"It's almost time to go, Prior. We should get ready."

He gazed at the river. "The water's running fast."

I glanced at the splashing current. "Just means we'll get to town faster."

Tomas squeezed his eyes shut. He blinked open. "I'm sorry, Clodius."

"Sorry, Father? For what?"

"For what I said earlier."

I stood and extended my hand. "Nothing to be sorry about. We're tired. It's easy to feel discouraged. We can't fail. Our brothers are counting on us."

The prior grabbed my hand, and I pulled him to his feet. "What would I do without you, Clodius?"

"Probably not this." I lifted the bottom hem of my habit. "Our clothes are too big and heavy. They'll pull us down in the current. We'll have to strip."

Tomas's nostrils flared. "Am I supposed to go to the bishop stark naked?"

I chuckled. "No. Bundle your habit and tunic and strap them on your back."

Following my own instructions, I stripped, folded my clothes, then secured them to my back with my belt. I helped Tomas do the same, averting my gaze from his nakedness. He scrupulously avoided mine. We were learning much more about each other than either of us desired. I thanked God he'd not thrown me among Lucius and Fritigern.

"When we reach the water, slide in quietly. Don't make a sound. We can drift with the current. Grab whatever you can when you reach the bridge. Whatever you do, don't get washed past it."

The forest around Coria and on both sides of the river had been cleared long ago by the Romans to provide unimpeded lines of sight, but since their departure, the defenses had been badly neglected. The once open field now sprouted with bushes, pine saplings, and thick weeds. As dusk began, we crawled away from the trees using whatever cover we could to hide us until we reached the water. At the river's edge, the current flowed with alarming speed. I slipped into the freezing water. My grip on the slimy bank slipped, and the current towed me into the swirling center. Tomas vanished as the malevolent waves tossed me about and tried to drown me. The muddy water concealed boulders and sharp edges beneath its torrent. My knee slammed hard into a submerged object. The current tossed me, my body spinning in a vortex. Stinging pain ripped across my buttocks. My back slammed into something hard, the swift flow trapping me against it. It would have knocked the breath from me had my back not been cushioned by my clothes.

A shaved scalp with drenched black hair bobbed near me. I grabbed Tomas's flailing arm. I hauled him to me. His head popped up, his mouth coughing and choking.

"It's a piling!" I screamed above the water's roar. "Can you reach for the next one?"

His eyes flashed white with desperation. He nodded. He flung himself to the adjacent timbers and held on for his life.

The pressure from the current plastered me against the vertical beam. I inched upward as high as I could manage, pushing with my legs until I reached the broad crossbar spanning the pilings overhead. I latched my arms around the beam and pulled myself up, grimacing as splinters stabbed into my forearms. I locked my legs around the beam then shimmied until I perched above Tomas. I reached down and hauled him out of the water, hoisting him by the belt strapped under his arms.

"Wait here!" I yelled.

The crossbar had a stub where it joined the bridge's facing, providing a slender foothold on which I braced and reached to the planks above. My hand groped about, but I could not find an edge to grasp.

A strong grip seized my wrist. My body flew upward, swung over the side of the bridge, and flopped hard upon the decking.

Sunno's mystified face stared at me. "What the devil?"

"Help. Prior Tomas is on the crossbar below. Throw him a rope."

Sunno's head recoiled. "What's that you say?"

I pointed at the boards spanning the bridge. "Tomas, the prior of St. Antony's, he's clinging to the transom beneath us."

Sunno barked an order, and two guards came running with a thick cord. They dropped it over the side of the bridge, and moments later Prior Tomas lay wheezing next to me, both of us naked and shivering.

"What were you doing under the bridge?" Sunno asked.

I coughed, spitting out dirty river water. "We have urgent business with Bishop Bonifatius. We floated down the river to avoid the Picts. They're everywhere."

"How do I know you're not spies?"

"I'm Clodius. Don't you remember me? I help Brother Bremen deliver ale."

Sunno scratched the stubble on his wide, square chin and studied me through narrow slits. "You look kind of familiar."

Tomas stood. "Do you think Picts would be swimming about with habits tied to their backs?" He unbuckled his belt and unfurled the drenched cloth. "And how many Picts have you seen with a tonsure?" He pointed at his scalp.

"I guess you can't be Picts," the big man said.

"Have you seen any other novices?" I asked. "They'd be wearing a habit like mine." I held out my drenched robe.

He shook his head. "Sorry. You're the only two I've seen since the Picts surrounded us. No one else has left or entered."

Eutychus, Olaf, and Fritigern had left before us and should have arrived long ago. Had they tried the road? Surely not. Eutychus would know better. Please God, he should know better. A pang of guilt stabbed my gut for having abandoned them.

Tomas lowered his habit over his head. He adjusted the wet folds clinging to his body. "Come, Clodius. We've no time to waste."

Chapter XXIV

Coria looked like a different town from the bustling market center I had become accustomed to. The Tyne had spilled over its banks, flooding the ditches surrounding the outer walls, and flowing into its lowest-lying paved streets. Torches blazed from random perches on buildings, the flames' reflections bouncing eerily from the black water. From the city's south gate to the central forum, water flooded Via Praetoria, sometimes rising above my ankles and as high as my knees at dips in the cobblestone road. A patchwork of blankets, rugs, and clothing, dingy with dampness, smelling of mildew, draped from balconies and windows of the two- and three-story insulae that lined the streets.

Despite the darkness, people waded in and out of swamped doorways, some cradling jars and bottles, others carrying water-stained furniture on their shoulders. A middle-aged woman with red, blotchy skin rocked at the top of three stone steps, just inches above the grimy water. A tallow candle burned at her side. She cried softly, holding a blue bundle at her chest, a tiny, pale arm hanging limply from the cloth. Farther down the road, we passed three boys playing at the water's edge with rolled-up sleeves and trousers, splashing and kicking water at each other. A woman with long gray braids stuck her head out a window above, scolding the boys for their playing.

The prior seemed unfazed by the devastation, not even pausing to console the poor woman lamenting her child's death. He turned down an alleyway, and I followed him as we wended our way through the dark canyons of packed buildings. The street level rose consistently as we moved onward, away from the bridge and toward the heights on which the basilica had been constructed. Soon we walked on dry stones.

Tomas walked with long, determined strides, showing no sign of confusion. He turned to the right at the corner of a shuttered butcher's shop and the great brick walls of St.

Alban's loomed ahead. Torches lit the broad limestone steps at the front of the basilica where people crowded, some sitting, some lying on pallets and rugs. A few black-robed priests circulated among them offering prayers and passing out small squares of hard-crust bread.

"Where can we find the bishop?" Tomas said to a thin priest with a brown beard.

The man looked up from an elderly, blue-shawled woman he had been consoling. "Prior Tomas. What a surprise. You look dreadful."

"It's been a terrible journey. I need to see the bishop. Urgently."

The priest cocked his head at the church's bronze door. "He's inside in his office. Gout has swollen his legs. He's in awful pain. Not much in the mood for visitors."

"This can't wait," Tomas said. "Wait here, Clodius. I'll speak with the bishop privately."

"But he may have questions."

Tomas lowered his head to my ear. He whispered, "Don't take offense, but I'd prefer that the bishop not know the accusations come from a novice. If I need you, I'll find you. For now, let's keep all of this to ourselves. Tell absolutely no one. Let me do all the talking."

I did not like being excluded but could hardly argue with his reasoning. The words of a nineteen-year-old, often-in-trouble novice would probably not count for much against a venerable, seventy-year-old abbot. If the bishop could be moved to suspend Mutter's authority, the prior's words were more likely to succeed.

"Stay here and help the priests until I return," Tomas said. He turned toward the basilica's front doors and scaled the steps.

The thin priest smiled and handed me the basket of rolls. "Just one per person. We have to make them last."

I circulated among the refugees, passing out the rolls. Three small children held out their hands, their eyes begging for food. I handed each a small loaf. A young blond boy with a dirty face reached into my basket to help himself. I slapped away his hand. He gave me a hurt, pouting look. My heart softened.

"You cannot steal what God gives freely," I said and handed him a roll.

He crammed the bread into his mouth, swallowed, then thrust his cupped hands at me again. "Please, sir. Can I have one?"

"But I already gave you one."

"Not me, sir. That was another."

His sad eyes reminded me of the boy I had been, stealing and lying for my brothers. I handed the boy a second roll. "No more. Make it last."

Someone tapped my right shoulder. I turned to look, then felt the tugging weight of hands pressing into the basket at my left side. I whirled around.

The boy had an armful of rolls. He fled down the steps.

"Wait! Stop him!"

My first step sprang after him. My second sent me sprawling headfirst into the paving, his unseen accomplice's foot tripping my ankle.

The basket of bread flew into the air, the rolls scattering across the steps. A mad scramble commenced among the people where the bread landed.

A trickle of blood dripped from my eyebrow to the corner of my eye. My hands and knees were scuffed and throbbing. I rolled onto my back, feeling angry, disappointed, tired, and ashamed. Curse my gullibility! Outsmarted by a street urchin. An awful thought shot through my head. What if the prior had lied? What if he sneaked out the back door of the basilica while I lay here helpless? What if—

"How awful. Can I help you?"

Anxious green eyes and auburn tresses brought instant energy to my body.

I scrambled to my feet. "I'm all right. Thank you."

"Thieves are everywhere. They have no shame. Stealing bread from the church. I wouldn't have believed it had I not seen it."

Julia's concern warmed me, but I couldn't suppress my lingering feelings of betrayal.

"Desperation can turn any heart evil," I said. "I should have been more careful."

"Are you alone? Are the other novices with you?"

"You mean Eutychus, your *lover*?"

Her eyelids flared, and her lips parted with a look of surprise. She turned her head and glanced at the people arrayed around us, avoiding my eyes.

"Don't worry. I won't tell anyone."

She lifted indignant green eyes to mine, her fists on her hips. "I'm sure I don't know what you mean."

Lying did not become her. A mole that I'd never noticed before became prominent on her cheek. Her nostrils deviated with imperfection, right of center over her lips. Her nose had an ungainly hump at its bridge. The goddess of my imagination turned into a pillar of salt. Despite this epiphany, my snide remarks gave me no satisfaction. Instead, a depressing sensation of shame filled me. My naive longings had turned me against my friend and into a complete ass. I had vented my unwarranted frustrations on the innocent target of my sinful lust. My childish acrimony had ambushed her, forcing her into a corner that she had defended with a lie. I hated myself for it, wishing I could take back my words.

"Forgive me. I'm rattled by my fall. I didn't intend an accusation. Eutychus is my friend. I'm worried about him. He should be here. No one has seen him."

Her challenging look of effrontery faded, replaced by wrinkled, quivering lips.

I reached for her hand, no longer a precious vessel I feared to touch, squeezing it between my palms. We shared something precious. We loved the same man.

"I'm sure he's okay," I said. "He escaped the Picts once before. He's too clever to be caught again. I'll find him. I promise."

She gazed straight at me. She pulled her hand away to

wipe a tear escaping the corner of her eye. "Thank you." She pivoted and walked down the steps, joining the traffic of despairing souls wandering on the street beneath. She disappeared into the night.

Chapter XXV

"I have what we came for," Tomas said, patting the leather satchel slung over his shoulder. "Now all we have to do is get back to St. Antony's. Let's hope the return trip will be less eventful. What happened to your head? It's bleeding."

"I fell."

Tomas reached up and brushed aside my red locks from my forehead. He squinted to inspect the damage. "I haven't properly thanked you. I would have never made it here without you. Thank you. Your bravery will be rewarded. Your cut isn't bad."

Tomas's gratitude should have swelled my head but did not move me, too many lives were at risk. "We should go," I said. "I just hope we get back in time."

"The bishop says the main body of the Pict army remains to the west. What we've seen are the scouts and advanced elements. Prefect Linus is confident the Picts won't attack the town when they see its defenses. There are too many easier targets to pillage."

Having seen the damage from the flood, the confusion in the town, and the desperation on so many faces, I did not share the prefect's optimism. Coria looked ready to collapse even without the invaders. But what did I know? I had no military skill or training. "You mean easier targets like St. Antony's."

"I'm afraid so."

The prior's calmness amazed me. He feared the Picts as much as I feared snakes, yet he spoke of them without betraying his trepidation. He poised ready to journey back into the darkness, beyond the safety of Coria's walls, to face his nightmares anew. He had real courage.

"So, how do we get back?" he asked.

"The same way we came, though this time without a ride down the river."

"That's welcome news. My fate is in your hands."

"In God's hands, Prior."

He nodded. "Just so."

We walked back through town, following the same back alleyways, avoiding the flood and congestion near the center of town. The guards at the bridge watched us warily as we emerged from the city's gate.

"Any sign of my friends, Sunno?"

He shook his big head. "There's been no one. Haven't even seen a Pict in this darkness. Just where do you think you two are going?"

Tomas said, "Bishop Bonifatius has dispatched us to St. Antony's to rescue our brethren."

"There are only two kinds of fools outside these walls. The dead and those about to be dead."

"We cannot abandon them," Tomas said.

"Lady Fortuna go with you then. Can't hardly see past your nose in this cursed darkness. No moon. No stars. Be careful you don't run smack into those blue bastards."

"Keep an eye out for my friends," I said.

"I've only got two, and they're already busy. I'll not make any promises."

"Then make me only half a promise."

"Huh?"

"Should you see them, tell them to keep safe. We should return by midday … or else not return at all."

"You're damn fools, both of you," Sunno said.

The prior followed me across the bridge. We climbed beneath its trestles and waded into the fast-moving waters, but only ankle deep. Using the flooded shrubs and reeds along the bank as cover, we escaped the glow of the guards' torches. Soon the darkness surrounded us so completely that but for the wetness and strength of the current retarding my stride, the river became invisible.

When we had gone far enough that I could no longer see the bridge, we turned south, crossing the grassy clearing at a run to the forest's edge. I nearly bumped into a tree. If any Picts hid close at hand, we could have gone right past them in the blackness.

The lack of visibility challenged my abilities beyond what I had considered. Navigating the forest in the daylight had become second nature, but without light, my eyes became blind and useless. If we ventured deep into the woods, I'd get us lost.

"It's too dark," I whispered. "I can't see anything."

"What do we do?"

I paused to consider alternatives. Only one came to mind. "Try the road."

"The road? Are you crazy?"

"Not on the road. We can follow the edge of the forest. There's a good chance any Picts will build a fire. We can steer wide of any we see."

"And those we don't see?"

"Their eyes are no better than ours in this darkness."

Prior Tomas remained silent for a few heartbeats, then sighed. "What choice do we have?"

"We could go back to Coria," I said, and silently cursed my stupidity. The prior had bottled his fears so well, I'd forgotten his courage had worn threadbare.

Tomas sighed. "Die out here or in the city. Not much of a choice."

I clapped his arm. "We'll make it, Prior. Trust me."

"Lead on," he said.

We crouched and sneaked along the edge of the trees until a hazy glow hung in the darkness ahead of us. As we drew closer, the haze became leaping flames, a dense smoke rising from wet wood. Silhouetted figures moved through the fire's light. My jittery nerves warned me we should go no nearer. I cut back into the woods, leading us away, using the glow of the Picts' campfire as a guiding beacon to avoid bumping into trees.

Tomas hung close to my side. His hands trembled.

Our heading brought us to trees bordering a band of turf alongside the Roman road leading back to St. Antony's. A tiny light far to the south had to be another Pict fire. It confirmed the danger of traveling on the road, but thus far hanging close to the trees had provided ample cover. At some point, we had to cross the road to reach the monastery. But not now with the glow of the fires.

We proceeded south, my eyes searching for any movement, my ears alert for any sounds. I couldn't blot out my concern for Eutychus, Fritigern, and Olaf. I feared we might find their corpses littering the road. My last words to Eutychus had been ugly and harsh. Julia was right for him and had always been wrong for me. She truly loved him. Would he forgive me for my fickle loyalty? My anxiety distracted my focus.

Tomas grabbed my habit, pulling me to stop. He raised his forefinger to his lips. He pointed to the trees to our right. Within the darkness of the forest, a slightly darker shadow balled on the ground.

"Uhhh," the figure said. He had not seen us, though less than ten paces away. His grunt sounded personal in nature.

A flatulent blast shattered the stillness. The man grunted a second time with the sound of gastric satisfaction. He rocked to and fro, then stood and jogged from the woods back to his companions at the roadside fire.

Tomas whispered, "Be careful where you step."

Had Tomas not stopped me, I would have bumped right into the man engaged in his organic business. My anxieties about the other novices were not solely to blame for my carelessness. My eyes and ears were tired. I needed to sleep.

I tapped Tomas's shoulder. "You take the lead. I'm getting drowsy."

"I'll get us lost."

"Just follow the edge of the woods. I'll keep you on track."

Tomas nodded and stepped to the front. He inched forward when his footfall made a squelching noise.

"Shit," he murmured.

I did not know if he meant to curse or was simply being observant. I declined to follow in his footsteps.

We sneaked onward to the south, delving deeper into the

woods whenever we discovered Pict campsites, returning to the forest's edge when we believed it safe. After many hours, a band of brightening gray skies appeared to the east. Dawn awakened the forest with birdsong. I recognized walls, pastures, and trees along our path.

I whispered, "We're almost there."

Tomas shot me a miffed look over his shoulder. "Are you sure?"

I pointed toward an oak tree standing alone on a rise to our left. "I recognize it. We're a quarter-of-a-mile from the trail to St. Antony's."

Tomas's lips cracked with a smile. "Then we've made it."

"Almost."

Tomas rubbed his eyes. "You take the lead again. My eyes are tired."

I nodded and stepped past him. The familiarity of the landscape cheered me. My feet felt lighter, my neck and shoulders less stiff. We descended a declivity to a saddle that stretched east to west across the road to the forest's edge on the far side. With slopes shielding us on both sides, it would be the safest place to cross the road. I pointed the way to the prior, and he nodded. I took two steps into the tall grass.

Green stalks surrounding me shot upward.

Three Pict warriors, their heads and shoulders camouflaged with plants, blocked my path. The warriors looked familiar—the ferret-faced man with his feathered hair, the warrior with animal skin armbands and foxtail, and the scar-faced muscular man adorned with huge blue serpents—the same men who had scouted the monastery. Only one chance to escape.

"Run!"

I whirled around. Tomas's mouth hung open. His hand held a blade pointed at me. I didn't even know he had a knife. What was the fool thinking? His short blade could not match the Picts spears and swords.

"Run!" I screamed again.

His eyes shot wide with terror. He spun about-face and pelted into the trees. I sprinted after him.

A sharp pain flared in my hip. My legs became weak and clumsy. I tripped and fell forward. I reached back to my burning thigh. A Pict's spear hung from my backside.

"Keep running!" I yelled.

Tomas disappeared into the forest's depths.

Three pairs of hands grabbed me, hauling me to my feet. Someone jerked the spear from my buttocks, the pain buckling my knees. Darkness surrounded the edges of my vision, then crept inward. My face planted into the wet turf. Mud and wet grass filled my mouth. I lost consciousness.

Chapter XXVI

Human voices filtered through the darkness. The words sounded foreign, incomprehensible. Pain throbbed in my rump, radiating up my spine, joining hundreds of aches, cuts, and bruises signaled from the rest of my body. I opened my eyes with difficulty, my lids glued shut with a grimy crust of dirt and blood. My awkwardly stretched shoulders hurt, my hands bound behind my back and tied around a waist-thick pine tree. Thirst burned my throat. I lifted my head, searching for the voices' owners.

Twenty paces to my front, scorched wood smoldered in a fire pit. A spiked-hair, naked Pict poked embers with the butt of his spear, sending swirling clouds of sparks and gray ash skyward. A second savage, squatting near the pit, chewed off the last piece of animal fiber from a bone. He tossed the remnant into the embers.

The area around the fire was trampled and cleared of debris, once occupied by many more than just these two blue pagans. I saw no others. My three captors must have dumped me and departed.

The sky remained overcast, a lighter gray hue to the west hiding an afternoon sun. A dry, chilly breeze blew through the trees, its gusts stirring the fire's blaze, the smoke swiftly dissipating in the wind. Pine trees surrounded us in a part of the forest I did not recognize.

Thank God, Tomas had escaped. We had been near enough to the monastery that if he had survived, he could have found his way home. Our quest would not have been in vain even if my part had ended. Perhaps I'd served my purpose. God had finished with me. Tomas could denounce the abbot and save my brothers from pointless martyrdom. I'd be the one martyred. The thought gave me no comfort. I didn't want to die.

The Picts used slaves to mine iron and tin and sold them to neighboring barbarian tribes. They enslaved only the young and strong, those who could survive wretched forced labor, or who would fetch a high price among slave traders. Stories told of prisoners being eviscerated as human sacrifices by druids. I didn't know which I dreaded more, grueling slavery or painful butchery as druids offered my entrails to Satanic idols. God help me. Even a serpent's venomous bite seemed a better alternative.

The squatting Pict slapped the leg of his companion. He jerked his thumb at me. He babbled something in the Pict language. The second man gathered a bloated animal skin hanging from a branch and walked toward me. The warrior had blazing red hair, mottled and spiked with dried mud. His bright green eyes scrutinized me from beneath a bony, protruding brow. Curling blue lines decorated his face, blue hands his chest. The proximity of his nakedness sent a prickling chill through my skin.

He mumbled words I did not comprehend. They did not sound threatening. He lifted the animal skin, dribbled water to his lips, then offered me the skin. My fright eased. I nodded and opened my jaw wide. He squirted a line of water from the bag into my parched mouth. I swallowed huge gulps, not stopping to breathe until I choked and gagged. He lowered the animal skin. He grunted with a nod, re-secured the water bag to the tree, and rejoined his companion near the warmth of the fire pit.

Time passed with agonizing slowness. The water had cut my thirst, but soon my bladder protested. I pled with my captors to untie me to let me piss. They paid me no attention. I relieved myself into the skirt of my habit. The humiliation deepened the awful abyss of my depression. I felt alone, forgotten by God, abandoned to misery.

"Wa-oooh!"

A muscular, naked Pict warrior came running through the forest in the direction of the guards. Blue images of serpents covered his face. Lightning bolts covered his torso, legs, and arms. He carried two pottery bottles, their lower bulges protected with woven wicker. I recognized them instantly. They held our sacramental wine.

If Tomas had been successful, the monks would have never left the wine behind. Tomas must have failed. St. Antony's lay in ruins. My brethren had been slaughtered.

"Wa-oooh! Wa-oooh!" the warrior yelled, his running stride accented by leaps and skips.

The men at the fire stood and grabbed their spears. The worry on their faces changed to lascivious grins when the approaching warrior stopped, held the bottles high, and laughed. He tilted one, pouring wine into his mouth. He smacked his lips and thrust the bottles at his comrades.

The guards dropped their spears and seized the wine. They flooded their mouths with the precious burgundy liquid. Their guzzling sickened me, a grotesque celebration of the defeat of my friends. Anger welled in my chest. I gritted my teeth and struggled to free my arms, but my effort proved useless. I could do nothing but watch the savages drink in drunken revelry.

Movement disturbed the distant trees. Two more Picts appeared from the forest's shadows. They carried crude, wooden-tipped spears. They ran toward the clearing. One had spiked blond hair, the other a dense forest of black hair covering his body. The heathens were returning in driblets from their looting. I prayed that some of the monks might have survived, but guilt nibbled at the edges of my hope. I desired their companionship as much as I wanted their survival. My loneliness made me yearn for a friendly face, but my comfort would mean a dreadful life in captivity for my brothers. Better a quick death than the slow decay of slavery or the torture of human sacrifice. God forgive me, the monks were better off dead.

The newly arriving Picts slowed to a walk as they neared the campfire. The two guards swallowed mouthfuls of wine, the red fluid drooling down their chins. They extended the bottles to the new arrivals.

The guards' eyes shot open, their mouths spewing purple spray as their grinning comrades plunged spears into their bellies.

The blond Pict stood smaller than the other men. His spear did not pierce his opponent with the savage force of the black-haired Pict. The guard wrested the spear from his abdomen and quickly turned it upon his assailant. The muscular Pict who had brought the wine pounced on the guard, stabbing him in his kidney with a dagger. Both the guards tumbled to the ground.

The blond and black-haired Picts rushed at me as the third wiped the blood from his blade.

"Clodius! Thank God you're alive!"

"Olaf!"

Olaf grinned. "We have to hurry. More Picts could be here at any time."

Fritigern cut away the ropes binding me to the tree. My hands fell free. My palms and fingers tingled. I rubbed my wrists to restore blood's flow.

Eutychus squeezed my left arm and lifted me up. "Can you walk?" he asked.

My hip throbbed painfully, but joy overcame my suffering and fatigue. "I can run if I have to."

"Good. Follow me."

Eutychus rushed off in the same direction Olaf and Fritigern had first approached from. I hobbled after him, the stiffness in my legs loosening with each succeeding step until eventually, I could keep pace with his loping stride. Olaf and Fritigern ran beside me, carrying their bloody spears. We traversed a shallow gully then came to a limestone outcropping at the base of the rocky hills. St. Antony's lay just over one mile away. Instead of heading toward the monastery, Eutychus led us through a stand of oaks toward boulders stacked high against the wall of a limestone crag. I followed him into a crevice behind a massive slab of fallen rock. It opened to a small cavity, not quite tall enough to stand in. Inside the shelter, Eutychus struck flint and steel. Sparks ignited a tallow candle. The refuge fitted the four of us. Pallets and small jars littered the cramped interior.

"We're safe here," Eutychus said.

"Thank you! I thought I was dead!"

Fritigern lifted his hand to his mouth. "Shhh. Keep your voice down. The Picts are everywhere."

"How? How did you find me?"

"Dumb luck," Eutychus said.

"God's grace," Fritigern said.

Eutychus shrugged. "Whatever. When we arrived at Coria, Sunno said you had left an hour earlier to return to St. Antony's with Prior Tomas. What in the world possessed you to join him? Where is he?"

"I don't know. I hoped you might know. I fear he's dead."

Eutychus shook his head. "We haven't seen him. We decided to chase after the two of you."

"I saw you first," Olaf said, "being hauled on a pole by two Picts."

"We followed them to their camp," Eutychus said.

"I thought you were more warriors."

Olaf's face beamed. "It was Eutychus's idea. Before we left the monastery, we mixed dried woad with piss, painted our bodies, and spiked our hair. The Picts can't tell us from their own."

Eutychus smiled. "I remember enough of their language to pass as one of them. When we saw that you were tied with only two guards, I had the idea of using the wine to get close enough to attack them. We returned to the monastery to retrieve the wine. You know the rest."

Fritigern sneered. "Mutter's going to be furious when he finds out we stole the wine."

"You stole it?"

Eutychus chuckled. "We didn't have time to ask permission, and I didn't want to risk his refusal."

"So, Abbot Mutter is still in charge?"

"Who else would be?" Fritigern asked.

I hesitated, unsure of how much to say. Just a few moments earlier I'd been certain of my impending death. God had abandoned me to the Picts, and my quest had been lost. Now I had been saved by Christ's blood and the three masquerading companions gawking at me. I drew a deep breath to steady my nerves. I decided on being honest for a change.

"It's why the prior and I went to Coria. The bishop gave us his edict removing Mutter from office and temporarily placing Tomas in charge. The prior planned to abandon the monastery so the monks could flee to the city."

"Jesus!" Eutychus said, then immediately looked apologetic. He crossed himself. "Sorry, but why didn't you tell me?"

"I tried to but … well … we got into a fight."

"What were you fighting about?" Fritigern asked.

I glanced at Fritigern and Eutychus. Fritigern wore his curious, busybody face. Even beneath the blue paint, I could tell Eutychus blushed. I shook my head. "It's not important. I went to Prior Tomas because I thought he could help me prove Mutter had killed Adalbert."

"Christ Almighty!" This time Fritigern burst out with the Lord's name. He also crossed himself. "Lord forgive me. Mutter? Are you sure?"

"Tomas agreed with me, and Bishop Bonifatius. It's how Tomas got the edict. But it doesn't matter anymore. If Tomas is dead, the bishop's order is lost. There's nothing else we can do."

"You can explain it to Lucius. He'll listen to you," Fritigern said.

"Lucius? Why should he?"

Fritigern blushed. He wrung his fingers. "Adalbert was our … our friend … more than a friend." He cleared his throat. "When he died, Lucius and I swore to each other that we would find the murderer." He glanced at Eutychus, then bowed his head. "It's why I've been following you, and Lucius has kept an eye on Eutychus. We thought you two had some hand in it."

The memory of digging Adalbert's grave and spending a long night of prayer in the church flashed through my head. I should have been angry, but Fritigern's words struck me as humorous. I laughed.

Fritigern frowned. "What's so funny?"

"Just a guess. Did you exchange your oath in the balneary the night we buried Adalbert?"

Fritigern puffed his chest. "What of it?"

I shook my head and gazed at the stone ceiling. "I can't believe how stupid I've been."

Eutychus snickered. "Wiser words have never been spoken."

I exhaled slowly and stared at him through the corners of my eyes. "Thanks."

"You're welcome," Eutychus said. "But what do we do now?"

My companions looked at me with expectant eyes. I had no idea what to say. The pain in my rear distracted me. I lifted my robe over my sore hip. Blood continued to ooze from the wound. It felt worse than it looked. The spear had lodged in the meaty portion of my buttocks, the wound ragged, but shallow.

Fritigern flinched, his lip curling with a painful spasm. He reached to his shoulder and pulled forward, craning his neck to see his back. A red stripe oozed down his shoulder blade.

I tapped his furry kneecap. "We've both been bloodied."

He released his shoulder and smiled. "Does that make us blood brothers?"

I cocked my head and shrugged. "Trust me. Blood relatives aren't all that special. It makes us more than blood brothers." I extended my right hand. "It makes us friends."

His smile widened. He reached for my hand. We shook.

Eutychus whistled. "If you two lovebirds are finished, we need a plan."

I squeezed Fritigern's hand and released. "Do you think we can get back into St. Antony's? We can go to Lucius. If he believes me, maybe he can persuade the others."

Eutychus grabbed a clay jar. "We can get back, but you'll

need to strip naked."

"What?"

"You can't walk about the forest in your habit. It's time for you to join the Picts."

Chapter XXVII

I trotted beneath the drab sky, through undergrowth shadowed by the forest canopy, soft fern fronds brushing against my naked calves and tickling my thighs and free-swinging genitalia. I experienced an odd mixture of embarrassment, fear, freedom, and excitement.

My companions had lavishly decorated my bare limbs, back, and chest with spiral lines, fanged animal faces, all-seeing eyeballs, lightning bolts, and handprints. I could not inspect my face, but the smelly paste dried upon my cheeks and forehead suggested I looked every bit a fierce Pict warrior. The blood seeping from my hip and drooling down my thigh enhanced my illusion of fearsomeness, a warrior bloodied and battle tested. At any instant, the real thing might see through my disguise, fall upon me from the trees, or rise from the ground and sever my blue head, but for the duration of these surreal emotions, I was invincible.

We made an odd-looking war party. Olaf looked more a girlish blue nymph than a soldier. Fritigern's hairiness cracked and peeled his paint to the point where he had more black fur than blue paint covering his skin. These defects had been invisible to my terror-stricken eyes and the inebriated brains of my guards. But soberer, more discerning Picts might surprise us with catastrophic results. Of my companions, only Eutychus truly looked the part of a Pict warrior. He had a well-developed physique, and a lean, narrow-eyed ferocity about his face that had I not known him would have terrified me. I hoped my disguise equaled his, but the lack of muscular definition to my chest and arms left me with no illusion of matching his magnificent deception.

We stopped and crouched as soon as the monastery's outer wall came into our view. I scanned the brush and trees ahead for any sign of an enemy lurking in ambush. Eutychus slowly rose until he stood straight, then signaled for us to follow him. We skirted the top of the graveyard, keeping to the concealment of the trees and tall grass, then scaled the corner of the compound's wall.

When we landed on the ground, Michael sprang from the concealment of the church's wall ten paces in front of us, his pitchfork leveled at our chests, his hairy brow inclined over his only good eye. "Stop there, or I'll run you through!"

Eutychus raised his spear and lunged forward one step. "Aahhh!" he screamed.

Michael parried with his pitchfork.

Eutychus said, "I don't speak your language. Do you speak Pict?"

Michael's pitchfork drooped, matching his lower lip. "Eutychus? Is that you?"

"If not, you'd be dead by now."

Michael's mouth opened wider, his gaze stopping at my crotch. "What in God's name are you doing?"

"Looking for Brother Lucius," Eutychus said.

"Clodius? Fritigern? Olaf? Have you all gone mad?"

"We need to see Lucius," I said. "Where is he?"

"He's in the church, but you can't go in there dressed, or rather undressed like that. Those you don't kill with fear will die from shock."

"Clodius needs to go to the infirmary," Fritigern said. "Could you fetch Finnian and Lucius to join us there?"

Michael's gaze shifted to my bleeding hip. He nodded. "I'll get them." He turned to leave.

"Wait, Michael," I said. "Don't tell anyone else we're here."

"But the abbot—"

"Especially don't tell the abbot."

"Huh?"

"I'll explain in the infirmary. Promise you won't tell him."

His eyelids narrowed to a suspicious stare. "What is this about?"

"Meet us at the infirmary. I'll tell you everything."

Michael's mouth twisted with doubt, but he nodded. He trotted toward the church's front door.

We crossed the compound without encountering anyone else. A muffled, droning sound drifted across the yard from the church's windows, the brothers maintaining their prayer vigil. Brother Bremen sat on a stool in the front gate watching the trail. He did not move as we dashed behind him into the main house. Was he asleep? It did not bode well for St. Antony's security.

Michael, Lucius, and Finnian entered a few moments after we settled in the infirmary.

"My Lord!" Finnian said, his eyeballs as large as apples.

Lucius's mouth dropped open. "Fritigern? What are you doing here?"

"We need your help."

"But you should be safe in Coria."

I said, "Everyone should be there."

Finnian stepped toward me, his massive jaw jutting outward. "Up on the bench. Let me look at your leg."

"It can wait. You need to listen."

"I can listen while I mend your wound. Don't argue with me."

I complied, lying on my side. Finnian reached for a pitcher, then poured water washing my wound. "It needs stitches."

"Okay but listen. It's about the abbot."

"The abbot?" Finnian backed away; his bushy brown eyebrows arched.

"Bishop Bonifatius has suspended Abbot Mutter's authority. He's appointed Prior Tomas as the temporary abbot."

"What's this?" Finnian said.

"That's outrageous!" Michael exploded. "He has no right!"

Lucius remained calm. "He does, actually, but why in the world would he do so? Where is this order? Where is Prior Tomas?"

I paused to collect my thoughts. The baffled and angry eyes staring at me did not encourage me. "It's about

Adalbert. Cassius and Fabian killed him. He discovered a library of heretical books hidden in a cave. Mutter wanted him silenced to keep the secret."

Michael stabbed his finger at me. "That's nonsense! Abbot Mutter would never harm anyone!"

Lucius turned pale. "Adalbert told me some stories he'd heard about hidden treasure. He never said anything about books."

Finnian showed no emotion, his stare firmly fixed on me. "By heretical books, do you mean Pelagius's library?"

I jolted upright. "How did you know?"

Finnian remained calm. "Never mind that. What's Tomas's role in this?"

"He and I went to the bishop. Tomas told the bishop everything and obtained the order removing the abbot from office until he can stand trial. We were bringing it back here when Picts ambushed us. They captured me. They must have killed Tomas."

Finnian drew a deep breath. He gazed at the ceiling, then glanced at the other two monks. "Michael, Lucius, a word with you." He pointed to the far corner of the room. The three men huddled outside our hearing.

Eutychus shrugged. "Do you think they believe you?"

"I don't know. How does Finnian know about the books? Unless—"

Michael broke from the huddle and rushed out the door. Finnian and Lucius walked toward us.

My heart raced.

Finnian stepped to his tool cabinet. He pulled out a drawer and withdrew a knife.

Lucius sidled next to Fritigern and wrapped an arm around Fritigern's shoulder. He whispered something into his ear.

I jerked my head at Eutychus. He gazed on oblivious to the danger. Olaf stood sheepishly at his side, sporting a modest grin.

Finnian eyed me through narrowed lids. He stepped to the

table at the head of my bench. He lifted a ball of twine, measured several hand spans, then cut the string. He laid the knife on the table.

My racing heart slowed.

"This will hurt," Finnian said. He threaded the twine through the eye of a finger-length needle.

Abbot Mutter burst through the open doorway, followed by Michael.

I jumped off the bench and backed away from Finnian. Eutychus leaped to my side and leveled his spear at the monks.

"Wait!" Finnian said. "We haven't betrayed you!"

Abbot Mutter stepped forward. "Lower your spear, Eutychus. No one will harm you."

I said, "Is that what you told Adalbert before you killed him?"

Mutter staggered backward. His eyes drooped. His lips sagged. He bumped into a stool and melted to the seat. "I'm no threat to you, boys. Keep your spear if you like but listen for a moment. Can you do that?"

The tension etching Eutychus's muscles eased. My racing heart stopped drumming in my ears.

Mutter spoke with sobering steadiness. "I did not kill Brother Adalbert. Nor did I instruct anyone else to do so. Adalbert did not find any secret because the books were no secret to him or to any of my brothers."

I jabbed my thumb at my breast. "But I saw Cassius and Fabian hiding the books."

"We all know about them," Finnian said. "Only their location is kept secret."

Lucius and Michael nodded. Lucius said, "The library's existence is only withheld from the novices. The final vow we take to join the order is to protect the books with our lives, and to never tell anyone outside our order about them."

"It's why we had to call the abbot," Finnian said. "He's the only person allowed to break our silence to the uninitiated."

My knees felt weak and almost folded. "But the prior … he said it's heresy … he said it's secret."

"Half-truths at best," Mutter said. "I don't know what has motivated him, but I'm afraid Tomas has led you down a path of lies, Clodius."

"But the bishop—his edict—why would he remove you?"

Mutter glared at me. "Did you see the order? Read it?"

"No. Tomas had it in his satchel. But he went to the bishop. We nearly lost our lives to get there."

Mutter folded his hands in his lap and nodded sympathetically. "I don't doubt your bravery or your good intentions. Whatever Tomas carried in that satchel, I promise you, it was not an order for my removal. Bishop Bonifatius is also a Pelagian, as was Bishop Ivus. He is united in our reverence for the books."

My head swam with confusion. I reached for the edge of a table to steady myself.

"What about Adalbert and Lazarus?" Eutychus said.

Mutter arched his eyebrows and placed his palms on his knees. "That's something I can't answer. Poor Brother Lazarus was close to the prior. Whatever Tomas has been up to, it would not surprise me if it involved Lazarus. But why it would cost him his life, I have no idea. How Adalbert's death connects to this, if it does at all, is a complete mystery. I'd dearly love to question our prior on those subjects, but it seems he's already standing before God's judgment seat and paying for his sins. Perhaps we'll never know the answers."

I gasped. "But … but … how did Cassius and Fabian know where to find Lazarus's body?"

"Prefect Linus sent word that a shepherd boy had found a monk's body in the hills. Only one of us was unaccounted for. I sent Cassius and Fabian to bring Lazarus home."

Mutter arose from the stool. He walked toward me. He placed his hand on my shoulder. "You've made a mistake, Clodius, but don't judge yourself too harshly. I have to share some of the blame with you."

Mutter removed his hand from my shoulder. He glanced

at Finnian and Lucius. "Perhaps I've failed all of you. I've known Tomas longer than any of you. He carries a weakness … a burden that I've ignored in favor of his many strengths. He arrived at St. Antony's soon after the Ninth Legion departed Eboracum, returning to Rome. Emperor Honorius recalled all the Roman soldiers to defend Italy from massive barbarian invasions. Tomas tried to disguise it, but I knew he was a deserter. I didn't judge him because he was hardly alone in his crime. Many soldiers abandoned the empire they had never seen for the homes and lives they had established in Britannia."

Mutter released a deep sigh. "Later, as I came to know Tomas better, I realized his desertion did not sprout from his divided loyalties. The British legions had enjoyed peace for over one hundred years. They spent more time gardening than guarding. The road returning to Rome would be crowded with enemies. The Roman soldiers would have to fight as soon as they landed on the continent and then all the way across Gaul. If they survived that ordeal, their reward would be to die fighting to save Italy. Emperor Honorius's recall was an almost certain death sentence. That's what troubled Tomas. You see … he is a coward."

Mutter stepped back and turned to Finnian. "I think many of us sensed his weakness, but it hardly seemed significant. We have no enemies, no reason to fear, at least not until the Picts began raiding. Even then, we lived in Coria's protective shadow. The danger seemed remote at best." He paused. He lowered his head and sighed. "At least it seemed remote to me. Tomas worried incessantly. He asked on several occasions for permission to leave and join another order on the continent. I refused him and told him to pray on it. I had confidence the Lord would aid him in conquering his fear. He appeared to accept my decision. I heard no more about it until a few nights ago. My decision to remain at St. Antony's infuriated him. In retrospect, maybe I should have let him go."

The abbot folded his sleeved arms across his chest. He

cocked his white-haired head. "Now, what do we do about you four?"

Lucius squeezed Fritigern's shoulder. "They won't tell anyone about the books. Will you, boys?"

"Of course not," Fritigern said.

Olaf shook his head, his eyes wide and fearful.

Eutychus lowered his chin to his chest. He shrugged. "No."

How I had been so horribly mistaken? I covered my face and hung my head in shame. I could not see them, but I felt them—everyone's stares—their condemnation heating my skin like scorching flames. Damn me! I had bought into Tomas's lies, accused the abbot of murder, misled my friends, risked my wretched life, and safely guided the prior through whatever twisted, evil game he played. I felt the naughty child again, caught with my hands stealing wares from a merchant's wagon. But this time, I deserved all the blame.

Hell's gates creaked as they opened for my accursed soul.

"Clodius?" Mutter said.

I swallowed the little pride I had left. "I'll never tell anyone."

Mutter smiled. "Thank you, but it's not just keeping the secret that has me at a loss. I'm looking at four disobedient novices, unspeakable parts dangling in plain view, painted like heathen savages, ready to fight rather than trust in God's protection or my orders. What am I to do with you? An ascetic, contemplative, peaceful lifestyle hardly appears your calling."

Mutter pointed at my bloody hip. "Clodius, Brother Finnian will stitch your wound. The rest of you boys go to the dormitory. Clean yourselves and for heaven's sake put on some clothes. When the Picts leave, we'll decide what to do about you. In the meantime, you can join us in prayer."

"Yes, sir," I murmured, my words echoed by the others.

Everyone left except for Finnian, who wiped his hand across his brow, then leaned into me with his needle and thread. "This is going to hurt," he said with a hint of pleasure.

He was right.

After he completed his sewing, he told me to lie still. He said he'd return later to check on me.

Alone in the large infirmary, my insides boiled with guilt and confusion. I could not believe that I had been so wrong and so easily deceived by the prior. Nor did I understand Tomas's motives for lying. The answer had to be in Coria. A coward would not have risked that journey unless his life absolutely depended on it. He was terrified of staying at St. Antony's, but once we had reached the safety of Coria, why then turn around and risk his life a second time? Not to save the lives of the monks. He had wanted to meet with Bishop Bonifatius. The prior had returned from the bishop with something in his satchel worth risking his life. Only the bishop could provide the answer.

Bare feet patted on the stone floor. "Clodius, are you awake?"

I raised my head. Eutychus stood naked near my feet. He still wore his blue paint.

"What are you doing? If Finnian catches you, we'll be in even more trouble."

My friend smirked. "I doubt that's possible. You've made pretty sure of that."

My shame resurfaced, my bowels roiling. "I'm sorry. I'll tell Mutter this was all my fault. None of you are to blame."

Eutychus tilted his head and smiled. "Don't worry about me. The abbot is right. I don't fit in here. Never have. My future waits for me in Coria. I just came to say goodbye."

His decision did not surprise me. It made perfect sense to my addled brain. He loved Julia. He could save her from her cruel father and the Picts more surely than any of my foolish fantasies had ever played. I couldn't do anything to fix the awful mess I had made of things, but I could make sure my best friend rescued the love of his life.

"I'm coming with you."

Chapter XXVIII

I left a note on Finnian's table asking Abbot Mutter to forgive us, but to especially forgive Fritigern and Olaf. Through no fault on their part, I had led them astray. Me. Blame me. No one else. Falling on my sword is what the Romans called it. The consequences of my mistakes were mine to bear alone. Fritigern and Olaf desired to join the monks and to take their vows. Hopefully, my confession would placate Mutter. It was the best I could do for them.

Eutychus and I departed the infirmary in secret. Our route led us to the rear of the balneary where we halted, confronted by Olaf, Fritigern, and Lucius. The novices still wore their paint.

Lucius caught my arm. "Where do you think that you two are going?"

Eutychus glanced at me then answered, "We're leaving. We'll try to reach Coria."

"Good," Lucius said. "Fritigern is going with you."

"And me," Olaf said.

"I don't want to go," Fritigern said.

Lucius grasped Fritigern's shoulders. The men stood face-to-face, inches apart. "We've already discussed this," Lucius said. "You agreed to go when Bremen told you. Your return shocked me. This time don't let me down. Go to the city and stay there. It's the safest place."

Fritigern shook off Lucius's pudgy hands, crossed his hairy arms, and frowned. He remained silent.

I said, "If we make it there, Eutychus and I are not returning."

Lucius arched his brown eyebrows. "Oh? I'm disappointed to hear that, but it makes no difference. You will be safer in the city. After the Picts leave, Fritigern and Olaf can return here if they choose to, assuming there's anything of St. Antony's still standing."

Eutychus shrugged. "We're wasting time. If you want to come, I can't stop you, but there'll be no turning back. We reach Coria or die trying."

"Make it the former," Lucius said. He turned to Fritigern and hugged him.

Fritigern's back remained stiff, but his eyes turned red and glistened.

Lucius stepped back. "Now go. I'll have greater peace knowing you are safe in the city."

Eutychus, Olaf, and I left the misty-eyed cantor. Fritigern held back. He leaped at Lucius. They exchanged a more emphatic embrace, then Fritigern raced to join us.

We scaled over and jumped from the compound wall, then dashed into the pine forest's depths. We cut through the trees, avoiding the dirt trail, and emerged at the forest's edge bordering the grassland and the old road. From there, we followed the edge of the tree line running north toward the town and stayed clear of the road.

A wind blew from the north and swept the sky clear of clouds. A bright blue band stretched across the horizon before us. We trotted up a rising slope that ended at a bluff overlooking miles of trees to the north. I halted to catch my breath. A peculiar black pillar rose into the sky from the point where the Roman highway vanished on the horizon.

Coria burned.

Eutychus saw it too. "Julia!"

"Julia? Who's Julia?" Olaf asked.

I waited for Eutychus to explain, but he just stared at the distant column of smoke. Then, he burst into a sprint.

"Eutychus's girl," I said. "She lives in the city."

Fritigern's jaw dropped. "Eutychus has a girlfriend? How did I miss that?"

"You weren't the only one," Olaf said. "What do we do now? The city is under attack."

My gaze remained fixed on Eutychus. "We follow Eutychus."

Fritigern stabbed his finger toward the burning city. "He's crazy. He'll be killed. We should go back."

"Coria or die trying," Olaf said. He tilted his head toward

Eutychus's route and raised his eyebrows.

I nodded.

We sprang forward after our friend.

"Hey! Wait for me!" Fritigern yelled.

Half-a-mile later we'd almost caught up to Eutychus. We gasped for air.

"Oothelvulf!"

The cheer came from the road on our left. In our foolish haste, we had blindly passed a disorganized band of Picts marching on the road toward the city. The man at the head of the group hoisted his spear skyward, jerking his arm up and down. "Oothelvulf!" he yelled again.

Eutychus stopped ahead of us and lifted his spear high above his head. "Oothelvulf!" he shouted.

The entire band of warriors raised their weapons. "Oothelvulf!"

We ran onward, the Pict warriors paying us no more attention.

I huffed and puffed beside Eutychus. "What did they say?"

"I have no idea," he said.

"Then how did you know how to answer?"

Breathing through his mouth, he spoke in choppy spurts. "It's some sort of—greeting—maybe some chieftain's name—we heard Picts yelling it yesterday on the road." He slowed and inhaled. "If you get into a fix, just raise your hands and start screaming Oothelvulf. The Picts will leave you alone."

After another hour of steady jogging, we reached the north edge of the woods overlooking the River Tyne and the bridge crossing to Coria. We stopped, our dread overwhelming.

Smoke and flames rose from every corner of the city. The main gate had been battered down. Soldiers' bodies littered the entrance. In many places timbers had been laid by the Picts to span the flooded ditches, allowing them to reach the low walls that encompassed the town. With only one hundred men-at-arms, it would have been impossible for Prefect Linus to defend the walls. The city's defenders had been totally overrun. Somewhere within the burning buildings, I prayed that Julia hid in safety. If not …

Eutychus threw his hands skyward, brandishing his spear. "Oothelvulf!" he screamed and rushed forward.

I threw my hands up, yelled "Oothelvulf," and charged after him. Olaf and Fritigern copied me. If Eutychus were to die, he would not die alone.

We crossed the cleared fields to the bridge without encountering any Picts. The fighting and pillaging looked to have moved entirely within the city's walls. At the bridge, I glimpsed Sunno's massive hulk, lying face up, three arrows sprouting from his chest, a spear lodged in his belly. Four dead Picts lay near him. He had not died without a fight.

I stopped and yanked the spear from Sunno's gut. I yelled, "Oothelvulf," and sprinted toward the battered gate.

Whizzing flying insects whisked by my ear. An arrow buried into the bridge's decking with a thud. I whirled to my right. Two men-at-arms stood behind a shoulder-high wall, drawing back their bows.

"Stop! We're Britons!" I shouted.

A second volley of arrows flew toward us. I dived to the ground. An arrow whished over my head. I didn't know if the archers heard my cry, or merely decided they'd done enough. They disappeared behind the wall, their heads bobbing over the edge as they fled east.

"Clodius …"

I searched for the voice. Olaf lay on his back, an arrow planted in his chest. I scrambled to his side. Beneath his sternum an arrow protruded, buried to its fletching. Blood radiated from his back, pooling on the bridge's planks.

"Dear God, no!"

Eutychus and Fritigern came running from behind me.

Fritigern wheezed, his chest heaving. "The town watchmen shot at us. They must have thought we …" Fritigern gasped. "Oh my God. What do we do? We have to find help."

Eutychus knelt at Olaf's side. "We need to carry him to shelter. We're too exposed here,"

"It doesn't … matter," I said.

"He'll be safer if—"

"He's … dead," I said.

Eutychus and Fritigern froze. After a few heartbeats, Eutychus's lower lip wrinkled. He began to sob. Fritigern wrapped his arm around Eutychus's shoulder and consoled him.

Of the three of us, I expected that either Fritigern or I might show the greatest remorse. Eutychus had always seemed annoyed by Olaf's adulation. But his pretended disdain had masked a true affection.

"Julia," I said. "We must find her."

Eutychus jerked straight. His hand flashed across his face, wiping away his tears. He spun and shot through the gate into the city.

Fritigern and I followed, leaving Olaf's corpse lying near Sunno's.

Inside the city, the Picts had slaughtered men, women, and children indiscriminately. Slashed bodies lay on the streets and hung out windows. I saw few dead Picts. I hesitated for an instant at a burning insula where a young woman lay sprawled on her back over the threshold of the shattered front door. He clothes had been ripped from her body and her legs spread wide for an obvious evil purpose. Her neck had been slit from ear to ear. Hopefully, Eutychus had not seen her. I turned away and raced down the street after him.

The flood waters had receded. Drying clothes and blankets still hung from windows and balconies, painting a colorful, disconcerting background to the Picts' butchery. We ran into the smoke-filled forum. The air reeked of rancid, burning flesh. A few Pict warriors pillaged buildings. They ransacked homes and businesses without any sign of organization. Shattered barrels of Bremen's beer littered the street. Two drunken warriors sat with legs sprawled next to a barrel with its lid pried off. They smelled like they had bathed in the ale. We did not stop to examine the destruction, and none of the blue heathens paid us any attention. Their looting resembled a frenzied competition, every man for himself.

From the west came clanging steel and screams. I chased after Eutychus, who raced toward the basilica, Fritigern's heavy footsteps slapping the pavement behind me.

The church burned. Four priests lay dead on the steps in front of the open front door. A few armed townsfolk fought with the Picts in scattered groups. Eutychus dashed past the church, ran another block, then turned down an alleyway. He made a second sharp turn into a canyon-like lane. I followed him around the corner. A man's angry shout split the air. Iron clanged. A glint of light flashed from a blade. Julia's father brandished an ax in one hand and a meat cleaver in his other. Three Picts had him cornered. His foes held swords and javelins. Julia cringed behind her father, trapped at the dead end of a three-story brick wall.

Her father's face changed from desperation to utter despair. He counted three more Picts, not realizing we had arrived to help him. Eutychus, Fritigern, and I charged forward. Before we could reach the warriors, one reared back and threw his javelin into the fuller's belly.

The big, bearded man gagged and spewed blood.

I rammed my spear into one Pict's back, but too high for a killing thrust, my intentions deadlier than my aim. Fritigern threw his body into another Pict, tackling him to the ground. Eutychus leaped at the throat of the third whose eyes popped wide with confused terror. The man tumbled backward, knocking his head on the cobblestones.

The warrior I had wounded spun around to face me. The sounds of Eutychus and Fritigern fighting their foes surrounded me. I focused on my wounded opponent. He had a banded tail of black hair rising from his crown and hanging down his back. Blue paint covered his face. He jabbed at me with his spear. His other arm hung limp, his left hand holding a dagger. My spear had ripped a hole beneath his scapula. A flow of blood coursed down his left side, spurting with each beat of his heart.

Julia screamed. Her father folded and fell on his face. Driven by either insanity or grief, Julia seized her father's ax and came charging toward the wounded Pict. She swung sideways, catching him squarely in the ribs. He crumbled to the ground. Julia reared back with the ax ready to aim at me.

"Stop!" I shouted. I caught the ax's handle as she swung it down. The blade stopped inches above my crown.

Julia froze. She released the ax and backed away; her eyes wide with fear.

Eutychus rushed beside me. The Pict he had been wrestling lay dead. "Julia!"

She stumbled backward, her face drained of blood, her jaw hanging, her green eyes batting away tears. Color rushed to her cheeks. She raised her arms and jumped into his. "Eutychus! My God, I thought I'd never see you!"

They gripped each other in a desperate embrace. Their joy instantly infected me, and I felt an intrusive outsider, watching without permission as they hugged and kissed in ecstatic bliss.

"A little help?" Fritigern's voice strained.

I turned from the lovers. Fritigern had the last Pict wrapped up on his back, pinned except for the man's left hand holding a dagger, slowly inching toward Fritigern's neck. The blade pierced Fritigern's skin, raising a trickle of blood. In panic, I grabbed at a sword dropped by a Pict. I wildly stabbed it in the man's side. The Pict's body went limp. He dropped the dagger.

Fritigern pushed the corpse off him. "A close call. Thanks."

"I owe you," I said, then inspected the heavy blade I held. A serpent's body had been hammered into the iron. The sword's tip and edges dripped fresh crimson blood toward the hilt.

I had just killed two men. The feeling differed from my boyish fantasies. No cheering crowds, no flower petals thrown by adoring women fluttering to my hair. Just blood, gore, and dead men lying where, but for chance, my body might have lain. The urgency ended; my emotions caught up with my survival instincts. My hands and knees trembled.

Fritigern pushed up from the cobblestones. He must have noticed my shaking because he wrapped his arms around me and squeezed. "You did what you had to, Clodius. It was them or us."

"What are we doing … Olaf … I almost got you killed."

Fritigern released his hug. He held me at arm's length. His big brown eyes, gazing from beneath his furry black eyebrows, held steady. He looked straight into my heart. "It's what brothers—friends do." His gaze shifted to the lovers still lost in their embrace. "That's what it means to be a family."

My family had been a father I could not remember, a mother who didn't know my name, and two blood brothers who would have happily traded my life for a cheap meal. Yet, Fritigern, who I had fought with and mocked, had saved my life from bandits, left the man he most cared for, and risked his life to save Eutychus's lover. He made me ashamed of my conceit.

Fritigern squeezed my arm. "Forgive me. I'm sorry I ever doubted you and Eutychus."

I embraced him a second time.

"Clodius, you're beginning to worry me." Eutychus and Julia hugged cheek to cheek, their eyes watery and my friend's mouth slanted in a sarcastic grin. "Maybe we should try to get out of here."

I stepped back and wiped my eyes. I pointed my new sword out the alley. "We should go the same way we came."

My companions nodded, then followed me to the intersection.

Up and down the street, Picts ran in and out of buildings, their arms loaded with bolts of cloth, open chests, and bags stuffed to spilling. They looted whatever their gaze landed upon. Shouts of fighting had grown sporadic and distant. A woman's scream echoed up the street, bouncing along the brick walls. I glanced at Julia, remembering why we had come.

"We can't risk the streets with Julia," Eutychus said. He held a spear in one hand, his other arm wrapped around Julia's waist.

I scanned the road. "Agreed. I don't think yelling Oothelvulf will be enough to protect her."

Eutychus's eyes bloomed red and jittered. His lips wrinkled. His spear hand trembled. Something I'd never seen before. He behaved bravely and often rashly with his own life, but with Julia … "We need to hide her."

Fritigern shook his head. "We can't. The whole city's in flames. Walls are collapsing. There's nowhere safe to hide."

I glanced about the street. The basilica's bell tower caught my attention. "We need a higher vantage point. Maybe we can find an escape route."

"St. Alban's," Julia said.

"The church is on fire," Eutychus said.

"The tower is made of stone," I said. "If the stairs are intact the tower will give us the best view of the city."

Eutychus looked at Julia, then nodded.

"I'll lead," I said, then paused. "Carry Julia on your shoulder. If we run into any Picts, she needs to look like booty, not a bride. Fritigern, you protect our rear."

Eutychus kissed Julia, bent, and hoisted her over his left shoulder.

We stepped from the alley into the street. Three Picts poured out from a burning building and into our path. One lugged an amphora of wine at his chest. One carried a chest overflowing with silver cups and plates. The third, a massive brute with spiked black hair, hauled a young red-haired woman outside. She screamed and struggled to escape, but his hand locked upon her wrist like a vise. He laughed as she thrashed her free hand at his muscular arms and chest.

"Oothelvulf!" I shouted, brandishing my sword above my head.

"Oothelvulf!" the Picts responded.

The warrior fighting with the redhead stared at Julia on Eutychus's shoulder. He snarled, then spun the poor girl to the pavement at Eutychus's feet. He pointed at her, spoke some gibberish that did not sound like Oothelvulf, then jabbed his finger at Julia.

We froze. I prayed that Eutychus could understand what the Pict had said and that Fritigern would not do anything rash.

The big Pict took a step toward Eutychus. His face flushed red and angry. He yelled more gibberish, his spittle landing on my friend's composed face.

Eutychus calmly lowered Julia to the ground next to the redhead. He motioned for Fritigern and me to step back. He then turned to the irate giant, growled some Pict gibberish, and leveled his spear at the man's stomach.

If Eutychus wanted to save Julia, he would have to kill a taller and stronger warrior in single combat.

Chapter XXIX

The sun hung low in the west, long shadows cast on the cobblestones by crumbling walls, black smoke billowing from the Picts' destruction. A cold gust of wind blew up my back. My legs shivered. My heart shuddered. But my eyes locked on the leering Pict standing opposite Eutychus.

The huge warrior lifted his weapon. He snarled, swished his spearhead, slapped Eutychus's, then feigned a thrust.

I had a sword in my hand. I wanted to slash at the challenger, but his two companions had swords, too. They set down their loot and watched Fritigern and me closely. If we interfered, we'd be dead before we could help.

Eutychus crouched forward, spreading his feet wide, staggering his left foot in the lead. He held his spear shaft at an upward angle, left hand forward, pointing the tip at the Pict's chest. He wagged the blade left and right, waiting for an opportunity to lunge. His much larger opponent showed no fear. The Pict lowered his spear and circled to his right. My friend mirrored his movement.

The monastery's curriculum did not include spear fighting. The warrior badly outmatched Eutychus. I feared the worst, looking for some way to intervene. The giant Pict stumbled slightly, his lead foot tripping upon a curbstone. He briefly lost his balance but gave Eutychus no chance to strike. My heart leaped when the giant stumbled a second time. The neck of the amphora his companion carried had been broken open. Purple stained the man's lips and chin.

The Pict lunged forward. Eutychus parried the thrust and jumped backward, beyond the reach of the spear.

The drunken Pict regained his balance. He resumed his slow circling to his right. He lunged a second time, charging with clumsy steps. Eutychus ducked to his left and sidestepped to avoid the thrust. His spear's tip caught the Pict's right arm, slashing a crimson trail on his forearm, but not deep enough for serious injury. The giant roared. He quickly adjusted his stance to face his enemy.

Eutychus tapped the man's spearhead with his own and spoke some Pictish babble. His lips spread wide with a taunting sneer.

The Pict growled and lunged again. This time Eutychus stood his ground. He caught the Pict's spear shaft with his own. He pushed outward so that the giant's iron tip shot harmlessly over his right shoulder. Eutychus swung the butt of his spear upward between the man's spread legs. It landed in the big Pict's pelvis, crushing his dangling parts.

The man howled. He dropped his spear, melted to the ground, curled his body, and clutched his groin.

Eutychus showed no mercy. He reversed his spear and plunged its head into the Pict's exposed throat. Blood spurted outward, spraying my friend's face and chest.

The other two Picts glared at Eutychus. They raised their swords to strike him down. I swung mine at one, catching his hand where he grasped the hilt. His fingers exploded red. Fritigern rushed the second man with his spear. The Pict veered away and planted his sword's tip into Fritigern's stomach.

I swung my blade again at shoulder level and caught my opponent full in his neck. Blood sprayed my arm. He dropped to the ground.

Eutychus jerked his spear from the dead giant. He reared back and threw, hitting Fritigern's opponent in his chest. The iron tip protruded from the man's back. The Pict's knees buckled. He tumbled to the street.

Fritigern stood motionless for a heartbeat, the Pict's sword jutting horizontally from his belly. His legs folded. He crashed to the stones.

I jumped over the Picts' corpses and knelt beside Fritigern, rolling him to sit upright. Eutychus rushed to his other side. The sword had planted deeply.

Eutychus's worried eyes confirmed my fears. Fritigern would die. We could not save him. I gently lay his head on the stones.

Fritigern coughed blood. He gritted his teeth. "Is there …

anything … you want me … to tell Olaf?"

"Don't say that," I said. "We'll find some help."

Fritigern's lips flickered a grin. "Tell Lucius … tell him I remembered … remembered him …"

"I will," Eutychus said. "I'll never forget you."

Fritigern's face contorted with a painful spasm. "Do me a favor."

"Anything," Eutychus said.

"Name your first son after me." Fritigern gurgled and smiled, bloody sputum leaking from his mouth. The tension in his features relaxed. His lifeless eyes stared skyward.

Eutychus and I stared at Fritigern's corpse. I didn't know how long we knelt. The gusting wind shot icy arrows into my hunched back.

Eutychus lifted his gaze. "We're not going to make it, are we?"

Our deaths seemed inevitable. "We can't give up."

"If I die, promise me you'll take care of Julia."

The image of Julia in my arms flashed through my head. The romance of my fantasies had faded. The picture no longer enticed me. It made me sad. I turned toward her. She sat beside the giant's former captive. The other woman's face leaned into Julia's shoulder; her sobbing muffled by the folds of Julia's dress.

I inclined my head toward the girls. "We have two lives depending on us now."

Eutychus's lips stretched flat, his jaw tense. He drew a sharp breath. "You're right. There's no time to think about dying." He stood and went to Julia, placing his hand on her shoulder. "We need to keep moving."

I followed him and offered my hand to the other girl. She trembled, leaned back from Julia's shoulder, and hid her face in her hands.

"It's all right," I said. "We're not Picts. We're Britons."

She pulled one hand away from her face. She had glistening, sky blue eyes. Freckles sprinkled across the bridge of her nose. She brushed the tears from her cheeks. A hopeful smile cracked her lips. She accepted my hand, her touch cool and soft. I held steady as she pulled up from the curbstone. What had possibly displeased the big Pict about her? She was quite lovely.

"Come on," Eutychus said. "We still need to find a way out of here."

"What's your name?"

Her voice squeaked, barely audible, still choked with emotion. "Bethany."

"Is there anyone else in the house?"

She lowered her gaze. "My mother and father are dead."

"Forgive me, but we must go. If you come with us, it's best I carry you on my shoulder. There may be more warriors."

She jerked a nod.

I lifted her onto my shoulder. She weighed no more than a feather. "We must hurry. We're heading to the church." I hustled after Eutychus, who carried Julia on his shoulder toward the basilica's limestone steps. We scrambled up to the base of the bell tower. A fire raged within the main building but had not yet reached the tower's stairs.

I lowered Bethany to the ground. "Eutychus, stay here with the girls. Only one of us should go up."

Eutychus's lips parted as if to protest, but before he could lower Julia and speak, I had turned and leaped up the stairs, taking two or three steps with each bound. At the tower's top, the open arched windows revealed the full extent of the devastation. The entire city had been put to the torch. Shattered bottles, dropped plunder, and dead bodies littered the roads. Beyond the city's wall to the west, a long trail of wagons, pushcarts, Picts, and their prisoners stretched along the Roman road heading westward away from Coria. The Picts had filled their bellies and wagons. They were returning home.

I whirled to check the roads east and south. Nothing moved. No sign of ongoing battle.

I ran down the stairs to share the news. Only Julia and

Bethany awaited, clutching each other's hands.

"Where's Eutychus?"

Julia's voice cracked. "He went into the church. Someone cried for help."

"Dear God, what now?" I said.

Smoke billowed from the adjacent archway leading into the sanctuary. The walls were made of brick and mortar, but wood paneling, carpets, and huge buttress beams provided plenty of fuel for a fire. The conflagration looked risky enough for anyone entering, but the risk would grow even greater once the brick began to crack and crumble from the intense heat. Once the walls began to crumble, the central dome would come crashing down. Anyone caught inside would be smashed.

"I'll find him. Stay put until we return," I said.

I dashed into the basilica. Black smoke stung my eyes, skin, and nostrils. I choked from the fumes. My vision blurred. Fiery streamers blazed from the bottom to the top of lacquered wall paneling. Hanging tapestries burned and ripped. The rugs that had covered the floor had turned to charred embers.

"Clodius! Here! Help me!"

On the altar dais, Bishop Bonifatius lay on his back. Black robes blanketed his corpulent body. A massive, charred timber pinned him across his legs. Eutychus knelt beside the bishop. I jumped over burning debris and joined my friend.

Eutychus gagged. Roaring flames surrounded us. He pointed at the huge timber. "He's been blinded by the fire. Help me lift the beam!"

We squatted at the top of the beam and lifted. Grunting and straining until my legs burned from the effort, I collapsed exhausted. The timber would not budge.

"It's no use," I said. "It's too heavy."

The walls groaned.

My gaze shot to the dome. "The building's ready to collapse. We have to leave him."

Eutychus glanced at the dome. He nodded. He crawled to the bishop's bloody, soot-smeared face. "I'm sorry, Bishop. We can't save you. The walls will fall at any minute."

Bonifatius coughed. His voice cracked, weak and raspy. "Save yourselves. My body is crushed. But hear my confession so I may die clean of sin."

"I can't. I'm only a novice," Eutychus said. He squeezed his eyes shut, slapped his forehead with the heel of his hand, and pursed his lips. His eyes shot open, looking straight at me. He waved for me to join him. "But Father Clodius can hear your confession."

I stepped back and shook my head. Impersonating a priest was a terrible sin.

Eutychus balled his fist and leveled it at me. "Quickly! He must confess before he dies!"

"But I can't—I mustn't!"

Eutychus sprang at me, grabbed my wrist, and dragged me to Bonifatius's side. "There's no time for niceties now, *Father*. You must hear his *confession*."

My face became heated. I glared at my friend and struggled to free my wrist from his grasp. He released my arm and stretched his hands flat, raising them to his shoulders. His eyes pleaded. He winked.

Ahhh … Bonifatius wanted a confessor. I had a few questions. "Eutychus, go back to Julia. I'll come when he's finished."

My friend nodded and ran off, leaping over a blazing panel and disappearing into the smoke.

I leaned toward Bonifatius's ear. "I will hear your confession."

The bishop spat blood from his cracked lips. "Forgive me, Father. I'm a glutton. I've betrayed the church's trust. I've sold indulgences, preferences, and church offices."

I scratched my nose, pausing to think. "Gluttony is more harmful to you than to anyone else. Your gout is your penance. But as for simony, sins sowed in the kingdom of God must be weeded. Tell me their names and I will pray for absolution."

"Ethelred … Marcus Atilius … Tomas." He gagged. "And others."

"By Tomas you mean Prior Tomas of St. Antony's?"

"Yes, Father."

"And what did you sell him?"

He wheezed and choked. His lips barely moved with a whisper. "My authority for his transfer … for … his installation as prior or abbot … anywhere in Christendom."

"And the price? Quickly, you must speak before you die or be damned."

"One hundred denarii."

The walls groaned louder.

A final breath wheezed from Bonifatius's lips.

Bricks popped. Crumbling mortar rained from the dome.

"God forgive you, Bishop." I placed my forefingers on his forehead, then tapped his sternum, left breast and right, making the sign of the cross. "In the name of the Father, Son, and Holy Ghost."

Stones crashed to the floor at my right. The dome was collapsing.

I jumped over Bonifatius's corpse and sprinted into a cloud of dust and smoke.

At the tower, the bottom floor was vacant, the air choking with debris thrown by the crumbling bricks. I raced through the open archway. Its supporting columns wobbled. A cloud of dust encircled me, scratching my eyes, fouling my breath. I stumbled in the direction I guessed led outside, my feet probing for the steps, trying to avoid tripping on fallen stones and dead bodies. I coughed and gagged. Eutychus called from somewhere distant. I wiped my eyes, blinded by the grit clinging to my face and swirling in the air.

Footsteps clattered toward me. Someone grabbed my arm and yanked me away, forcing me to run blind. The stones beneath my feet shook and grumbled. A great roar deafened me. A violent gust of flying debris sprayed across my back. The hand of my savior kept pulling me.

At last, the air cleared. My breathing became easier. We stopped. A wet cloth wiped over my face. I blinked away tears, washing away the blinding grime.

Bethany's blue eyes greeted mine. "A moment later and you wouldn't have made it."

I glanced over my shoulder. Where St. Alban's had stood, a gray mushroom cloud blossomed into the sky. "Thank you for saving me."

Her full lips spread into a gracious smile. "It is I who must thank you."

A delicious chill coursed down my spine. My toes tingled.

My naked blue companion came running with Julia beside him. "What did Bonifatius say?"

"Not now. Let's get out of here. The Picts are heading west. The roads east and south are clear."

Eutychus scoffed. "I can't go back to St. Antony's. Never."

Julia tugged at his elbow. "I have a cousin in Segedunum. He's a fisherman. He can help us."

"East then. Hurry!" I said.

The sun hung low behind us, the cloudless sky to our front turning dark blue. Our shadowy forms bounced before us as we ran down the street, through the forum, and toward the eastern gate. The devastation looked the same in all directions. I'd seen so many corpses I'd grown calloused. No longer sons and daughters, mothers and fathers, the bodies had become lifeless lumps to hurdle. Except for the dead, the streets were deserted. The Picts had been thorough. They had left nothing valuable or living behind.

My mind should have been focused on our escape, avoiding another encounter with the Picts or at least mourning the losses of Fritigern and Olaf. But no … I could not keep my thoughts or my eyes off the newest member of our troupe. Her hair, a fierier red than Julia's and cut shorter, swirled about her creamy neck in a fascinating way. I longed to comb my fingers through it, to caress the curves of her nape, to draw her pink lips to mine.

Bethany caught me watching her as she ran at my side. A smile creased her lips. Her eyes glimmered with a token of adventure.

We stood on a cliff overlooking the eastern seas, my arms wrapped around her, her red curls swirling about my neck. Her warm body pressed into mine, shielding my skin from a chilly ocean breeze, her heart thudding upon my chest. I lowered my lips, and she raised hers and—

"Ouch!"

Pain shot up my leg from my big toe. I stumbled, nearly falling face first on the uneven cobblestones. Swinging my arms wildly, I regained my balance and resumed my trot, though with a slight limp to lessen the throbbing pain from my stubbed toe.

The street opened to a small plaza. My pace slowed to a walk. I stopped. At the square's southeast corner, a fountain gushed water from broken pipes jutting vertically from its limestone basin. At the spilling water's edge, a one-armed man lay on his back. His chest had four stab wounds. Astor, his horse, had gashes ripped by swords and spears across her neck, back, and legs. She was still harnessed to a wagon, its wheels shattered. The bones and sinews of her knees protruded from her ripped hide. Matted hair and blood covered her pasterns and cannons. Four ragged crimson trails extended from her raw knees to the wagon's bed like lines painted poorly with a frayed brush. Her head lay across the veteran's lap, his arms folded over her chestnut mane. They lay frozen, united in death. The man must have fallen first, then the hamstrung mare had dragged the broken wagon to her master and died in his caress.

"Come on, Clodius! We can't stop!" Eutychus shouted.

His call jarred me from my distraction. I raced after my comrades. When I caught up with them something inside me had changed.

We reached the east gate. Its iron-reinforced oak beams had been reduced to smoldering embers and twisted metal. The road to Segedunum lay open ahead of us.

I turned to Eutychus. "It's two days from here if you follow the river."

Eutychus panted. "You? Don't you mean we? Two days if *we* follow the river."

The sight of the old soldier and his horse had spoken, even louder than what I had mistaken as God's whisper. The decayed Roman Empire crumbled around me, its last vestiges lying butchered on a forgotten street, in a forgotten town, on a forgotten island. My homeland would be overrun by the Picts, the Scots, the Saxons, the Danes, the names didn't matter. And yet, in that devastation, I had not seen death and futility, I had seen loyalty—love. I had seen family—a bond between a man and his horse, two novices who had given their lives for the sake of another, a bond between me and the men who had been my true father and brothers. I could not abandon them—not when I had any means to atone for my mistakes.

"I can't leave. Not yet," I said. "I have to return to St. Antony's."

"Are you crazy? Why? What did the bishop tell you?"

"Nothing," I lied. "It's not that. The abbot must be told that Coria has been destroyed, that Bishop Bonifatius is dead. There's no reason for the monks to remain at St. Antony's. They have to move and move quickly before the Picts return."

He eyed me through narrowed lids. "They'll figure that out for themselves soon enough. They don't need you to tell them."

"How can you be sure? I don't know when the Picts will return. Our brothers can escape now if I don't desert them. It's the least I can do. I owe them."

"And when you've delivered the message? What then?"

"I'll come to Segedunum."

Eutychus frowned at me. "I don't like splitting up."

I stepped toward him and grasped his upper arm. "You're my friend. I'll never forget that again. It's your job to protect Julia and Bethany. Take the road east. Go to Segedunum. I'll find you."

Chapter XXX

As the sun set behind the western hills and darkness enveloped me, my loping stride slowed, hampered by the diminished light and my fatigue. The grass bordering the pitted road leading to the south had been trampled flat by the flood of refugees and Pict warriors, leaving a wet carpet of long blades and green straw, easy to follow and a cushion for my feet. Abandoned fire pits littered the fields. I ran past fly-infested heaps of charred corpses. The ungodly smell of burned hair and flesh soured my nostrils. But I saw no one alive, or any sign that the Picts remained. Even if I should happen across warriors, I had confidence that my disguise and sword would conceal my identity. I'd just yell Oothelvulf and run onward.

Eutychus did not know the truth. I regretted having lied. Bonifatius's confession had cleared up one mystery for me. One hundred denarii the bishop had said. A large sum. Far more than any monk could have ever saved, even if he had perfidiously jettisoned his vow of poverty. Nor could Tomas have stolen the coins from the monastery treasury. Nebridius, the almoner, kept a careful tally of every receipt and disbursement. The abbot never permitted the accumulation of a large treasury. He had faith in God, not money. The notion of saving for a rainy day was tantamount to blasphemy in his mind.

There could be only one source for Tomas's payment to the bishop—Adalbert's buried treasure. My initial instincts were correct. Adalbert had found his hidden Roman wealth. Two caves held treasure, one with books, one with gold and silver coins. Somehow Tomas had discovered Adalbert's secret. Probably Lazarus. Tomas rewarded him for his espionage with a knife to the gut. Maybe Tomas wanted to ensure the secrecy, or maybe Lazarus had helped himself to some of the coins. That explained his taste in pastries. Whether Tomas had murdered Adalbert, or Lazarus had acted the assassin for the prior, I did not know, but Tomas's motive was now clear. Abbot Mutter had denied him permission to leave the monastery. He could have left without the abbot's authority, but he would have become an outcast. No other holy order would have accepted him, and certainly not with the rank he had worked decades at St. Antony's to achieve. And too, the Romans had a long memory for deserters, but even they would not question the good faith of a high-ranking prelate. Tomas's only alternative was to go to the bishop, who'd been happy to oblige him with the necessary papers for a price. Lazarus's news of Adalbert's treasure must have seemed a godsend to the prior.

What about me, the gullible know-it-all, so ready to believe the worst about his abbot? For some reason, Tomas had not yet received the bishop's written authorization to leave St. Antony's. Maybe he hadn't paid the full price, or maybe he had made payment, and it took time for Bonifatius to prepare the documents. Whatever the reason, he had to meet with the bishop in Coria before he could flee. But I played right into his plot. The Picts' arrival had spoiled his plans. Too much a coward to risk the journey to Coria alone, Tomas found a ready-made dupe. I walked into his office and became his guide and guardian.

The fact that Tomas had been willing to risk the return journey south, even with me as his protector, had only one explanation. He'd never intended to return to the monastery to depose the abbot. He'd used me to guide him to within an easy distance of whatever remained of Adalbert's treasure. With the money and the bishop's letter of authorization, he could go anywhere in Christendom he desired, become the leader of any holy order that he chose. When the Picts had ambushed us and wounded me, I had thought Tomas had his knife ready to fight the Picts. What a fool I'd been! He'd planned to plunge the dagger into my back. The Picts' ambush had saved my life.

I no longer operated under any delusion that my ambitions had been divinely inspired. I'd proved my lack of spiritual acuity too many times. What my ears had read as

God's whisper had been Fritigern's and Lucius's verbal pact. I'd been too quick to find fault with the abbot and an easy target for Tomas's deception. Even if Tomas's tale had been true, and I had rescued my holy brothers from Abbot Mutter's suicidal mandate, the result would have been that we'd all lie dead in the burning city or be tied and marching to a life of slavery among heathens. Whatever God's will might be, I was the last person in Britannia who could discern it.

No, Tomas had proved me a fool. He was responsible for Adalbert's death and, but for my dumb luck, would have murdered me. I had falsely accused Abbot Mutter, and the architect of my sin still ran free.

I had to stop him.

Prior Tomas still lived. There'd been no sign of him where I had been held prisoner. My friends had not seen any sign of him when they found me. The prior never had any intention of returning to St. Antony's. I'd find him hiding in a cave, Bonifatius's letter of transfer in his bag, reveling in Adalbert's gold, biding his time until the Picts left, readying for his escape south. I had a good idea of where. It was miles away and in the wrong direction for Julia and Bethany. They had to reach Segedunum and safety. Eutychus had proved he could manage without me. His future lay with Julia. If he had any idea of what I planned to do, he would have insisted upon coming with me, and I could not accept that responsibility.

And what about Adalbert's treasure? Though I would have preferred to run away from the Picts and start a new life—a life with Bethany—my selfish desire could not overcome my desire for redemption. Adalbert's treasure could pay for the monks to escape to the continent. After the horrible things I had said and done, if I could present the money to Abbot Mutter, it might buy peace for my tortured conscience.

Dusk turned to darkness. Countless stars sparkled in the heavens above me. The air grew colder as I left the forest and climbed into the hills. My sweat dried. I shivered. A gnawing emptiness hit my stomach. The last thing I had eaten had been a handful of bread torn from a barley loaf at the monastery that morning. My bloody hip ached, my muscles felt weak, fatigue dizzied my vision. I stumbled and almost fell but regained my balance. I slowed to a more cautious pace.

Precisely where I'd find Tomas, I couldn't be certain. Lazarus's body was my best clue. I doubted that Tomas had randomly selected the location to murder him. It had to be close to the site of Adalbert's treasure, and if so, Tomas would be nearby. The last time I had searched the area, the light of a waning moon had lit my path. This time, with only starlight to guide me, many features of the rugged landscape looked different. The face of the limestone crag was bald and gray. The boulders littering the landscape seemed bigger, the pits broader and deeper.

The ground shifted, loose rocks rolling under my feet. I climbed through egg-shaped boulders, ascended a gravel-covered slope, then came upon the ledge where once I had seen Coria's torchlights but nothing now except the black top of a forest canopy stretching to the star-filled sky.

Somewhere in that vast landscape Eutychus, Julia, and Bethany would be hiding, huddling together in the darkness to combat the night's chill. Hopefully, Eutychus had shed his war paint and donned some clothing. I didn't like the idea of Bethany cuddling and studying his body.

Now what a silly notion. Here I was, searching through fields, fir trees, limestone, and lichen, entering the valley of the shadow of death, searching for a murderer, blood-thirsty heathens lurking in ambush behind every rock, and how a blue-eyed, freckle-faced girl might be comparing my manhood to my well-equipped friend worried me more than my safety. Was I jealous? Of what? Eutychus and Julia were bound to one another. Their happiness thrilled me. My teasing fantasies had landed upon a new target. The smooth touch of her skin, the graceful, cheerful lilt of her voice, her freckles, the way her curls draped down her neck and shoulders…

Bethany.

Was she thinking of me? The stocky, funny-looking boy, wearing nothing but blue paint, whose awkward company had been forced upon her by the tragic loss of her home and family.

My sin was beyond depravity. The poor child deserved compassion, not my sordid lust. I tried to think of her as a sister, and then as an angel. No matter what I tried, my thoughts kept returning to her soft skin, her shapely curves. Hopefully, she had not lost more than her family to the blue giant. The Pict may have deflowered my pretty rose before our random encounter. If so, her scars would need time to mend. She'd be grieving, healing, searching for new life and hope. I'd been a fool to think that she could care for me. As soon as they reached Segedunum, she'd find a man with a safe home and stable life who could feed and protect her. She'd never be interested in a washed-out novice with no family and no future.

Down the side of a ledge, slag descended steeply before me. I recalled the spot of my tumble days earlier. Turning my face to the hillside, lowering my hands to the rocks, I stepped cautiously, keeping my feet perpendicular to the slope. Rocks slid and rolled down the hill around me, but I controlled my slow descent. I managed to reach the base of the slope without duplicating my fall.

The round rock where Lazarus had rested lay twenty paces in front of me, the edge of the forest, dark and looming, at my left. The chirring of crickets filled the air, and a wolf howled far in the distance. The night seemed vast and empty. My planning stopped here. I had no idea where to look next. Tomas could be just behind me, counting coins in the depths of some cavern, or he could be ten miles away. If my gut instincts lied, he might even be dead, his body sprouting Pict spears in some forgotten corner of the woods.

Hunger, fatigue, and depression weakened me. I could

add one more folly to my ever-expanding library of failures. My half-cooked notion that I'd find Tomas doing a raucous jig around a bonfire, throwing gold coins into the air, worshipping some newly minted golden calf like a naughty Israelite was absurd. Instead of cuddling next to Bethany's warm body, I wandered about the wilderness, naked and alone, chasing one more foolish dream of grandeur conjured by my childish notions of purpose. Life's reality was not the simple and sweet victory parade of my reveries. Both good and evil died and triumphed. Sometimes it wasn't easy to tell the difference.

Exhaustion overwhelmed me. My head sagged and shoulders slumped. I dragged my feet to Lazarus's rock. The sword in my right hand fell with a thud. My knees folded. I curled my body to fight the chill. Sleep welcomed me.

Chapter XXXI

I awoke to dawn's orange streamers and someone kicking the soles of my feet.

Three Pict warriors looked down at me with emotionless stares.

I jumped up, instantly awake. I searched for my sword. One of the Picts held it, inspecting the blood and scroll work on the blade. He had an elongated, ferret-like nose and beady black eyes. He showed the sword to his companion on his right, who had an unkempt bush of black hair tied with a fox tail and stone amulets. The biggest of the three men smirked at my display of alarm, his smile wrinkling an ash gray scar than ran from his chin to his left ear. He had a snake painted on his right side from his shoulder to his ankle. None showed any hostility toward me. Why should they? Who but a Pict would be sleeping in the middle of nowhere wearing nothing but blue paint? They stood relaxed; the butts of their spears planted in the earth. They were the same men who had ambushed and captured me, the same scouts I had first seen outside St. Antony's main gate.

Ferret-face gripped the blade of my sword and extended it, handle first. He spoke a few words of his native gibberish. I had no idea what he had said. I grasped the blade, raised it above my head, and shouted the only word I could think of, "Oothelvulf!"

The Picts replied with the same cheer but showed little enthusiasm. They exchanged words, then the scar-faced Snake-man directed more gibberish at me.

I didn't pretend to understand him. I lifted my palms up and shrugged, hoping the gesture would be universal. To enhance my ruse, I mumbled meaningless syllables filled with oval-mouthed vowels and soft consonants.

The Picts looked at each other with dismay. They shook their heads. To my immense relief, they appeared to accept me as one of their kind, just some backward oaf from a distant corner of Caledonia who spoke a different dialect. I surprised myself, mustering a commiserating chuckle and a big smile to demonstrate my eagerness to join their merry blue band.

Snake-man pointed to the ground at his right. Ferret-face walked to where he pointed. He knelt and fingered the weeds and loose rocks. Lifting a stone to his nose, he sniffed like a canine. He tossed the rock to the ground and spoke, his words ending with a staccato of, "Ha-ha-ha-ha-ha." The other two grunted what sounded like assents. The big man gestured at me with his hand. He wanted me to go with them. I nodded and grunted, then followed Ferret-face up a rocky path.

The men halted to jabber from time to time, looking as if they were conferring on the trail's signs. After a few minutes, I came to understand the hierarchy of the group. Snake-man, the largest and oldest, led the team. Ferret-face was the tracker. Foxy, the youngest, held the lowest rank if you excluded me. Although I would have been ecstatic to escape their company, I hoped that at least they tracked something tasty and large enough to make a generous meal for four. The morning's excitement had exacerbated my hunger. I could have eaten an entire wild boar.

Our hunt continued, carrying us deeper into the hills. Ferret-face always assumed the lead, with Foxy behind him, then me and the big Pict following at my heels. Though he showed no overt suspicions, I sensed that Snake-man kept a close eye on me. It might have been just my nerves, but I tried to appear at ease. Despite my best efforts at demonstrating kinship, Snake-man never let me wander far.

By mid-morning, the hillside terrain became familiar. I had been this way before, though it was difficult to remember exactly when.

Ferret-face stopped to examine a tree's bark. He called Snake-man forward. He pointed at a chevron notched in the bark then at another a dozen paces in a different direction than we had been tracking. He laughed with his annoying ha-ha-ha-ha-ha, made even more obnoxious by my realization that he laughed at me—not the me running alongside him, the naked, blue, and perspiring me, but the me who had wandered lost in the woods and so cleverly left a trail of markings that even a one-eyed child could follow.

Snake-man knelt beside Ferret-face, scratched the back of his head, then exchanged whispers with his tracker. Ferret-face punctuated the conversation with another of his annoying laughs. Snake-man looked at Foxy and me, spoke a few syllables, and pointed in the direction of the next marked tree.

Ferret-face walked toward the tree and stopped after a dozen steps. He turned to his right. He knelt and poked his finger into the imprint of a sandal pressed into soft mud. He spoke some gibberish followed by his irksome laugh. He lifted his gaze, then pointed up a nearby slope. He raced onward ahead of us, disappearing over a ledge.

I'd been straining my brain trying to remember when I had made the marks and where I had been going. Dread overwhelmed me. We neared Abbot Mutter's cave.

After a long pause, Ferret-face's head reappeared at the rim of the ledge. He waved for us to join him. We climbed the slope. At the top, even my untrained eyes recognized the path, repeatedly trod by Cassius and Fabian, and twice by me. We followed the route to the leaning rocks. Ferret-face ducked into the boulders then seconds later re-emerged with an excited grin. He held the charred remains of a monk's torch. My companions scurried into the cave, the big man pushing me ahead of him impatiently. I feigned confusion and hoped he could not see my apprehension.

Foxy found and struck the flint and steel. The torch blazed. Ferret-face led us deeper into the cave. My head raced with ideas on how I might distract the Picts from what I knew awaited. Every scheme I conjured ended with my impaled body. Outnumbered and unable to communicate, I had no choice but to continue my ruse.

We rounded the corner, and the Picts halted. A linen shroud covered the books beneath. Foxy excitedly lifted the covering. Ferret-face tilted his head and sneered. He spat a single syllable Pict obscenity.

Rows of books lay neatly stacked. Foxy lifted one of the heavy volumes, flipped open the cover, and scrutinized a page. He tossed the book back to the stacks with another Pict vulgarity.

Snake-man pushed past me and began his own investigation, opening one book after another, discarding each with a frustrated grunt. They had no clue what they had found. I played along, pretending to be completely disinterested, then pointed toward the cave's entrance, hoping they would agree the books were worthless and we should move on. After several more attempts, I made my intentions known, and Snake-man nodded.

I turned to leave just as the big man took hold of the Ferret-face's torch, and to my horror, poked the flame into the stacked volumes. Flames jumped from book to book until the big chamber became bright with a roaring fire.

Mutter would have a heart attack. I blamed myself. Not only had I led the Picts to the abbot's treasure with my childish navigation skills, but I had also been among the arsonists when they had torched the abbot's prize. I could do nothing but watch.

Smoke billowed from the books, making the air inside the cave foul and poisonous. Ferret-face wrinkled his nose. The smoke burned my eyes. I blindly groped forward, hacking and coughing until I stumbled from the cave's entrance. I found a rock to perch my rear upon until my lungs and eyes cleared.

The Picts joined me outside the cave. When he stopped coughing, Ferret-face said something he punctuated with a tepid, "Ha-ha-ha-ha-ha." He walked along the ledge then pointed down the slope. The discovery of the books did not end their hunt. He shielded his eyes with his hand, peered about the landscape, then hopped over the ledge and descended the steep slope. I drew a deep breath and followed with the other two Picts.

The tracker retraced our steps back to the spot where my

tree marks intersected with their original trail. He pointed to his right, and we resumed the hunt for whatever they had been originally pursuing.

By midday, the sun hung above us, bright and punishing in a cloudless sky. We stopped in the shade of a copse of oak trees adjacent to a small, spring-fed stream that had etched a serpentine gully down a slope. The cold, clean water refreshed me. Snake-man withdrew several flakes of a dried white fish from a pouch slung over his shoulder and passed the food among us. The salty meat did not fill me, but it stopped the hunger pains knotting my guts.

The short rest allowed me to focus on my escape. My best hope would be to wait until night, then to sneak away while the others slept. My confidence in my navigation skills had grown to the point where I believed I could outrun the Picts even if they should awaken and chase after me. This time there wouldn't be any marked trees for them to follow.

My senses registered someone studying me. Snake-man's gaze was glued to me, or rather to my hip, where Brother Finnian had stitched my spear wound. He tilted his head to one side and scrunched his eyebrows in a studious pose. His head jerked when he noticed that I looked back at him. He lifted his chin and pointed at my wound and spoke.

I could not translate his words but understood his question. I lifted my sword, tapped the blade's tip, then thrust it upward to communicate a knife had stabbed me. Inventing my own language, I spouted, "Ollo tapas moalaki."

He frowned and shook his head.

I lifted my sword, "ollo," pointed the tip to my hip, "tapas," then tapped the wound, "moalaki."

A knowing grin sparked on his lips. "Wasu," he said, pointing at my blade. "Wasu."

I tapped a weathered stone with my sword. "Wasu," I said.

He nodded vigorously. "Wasu."

It had long since dawned on me that Oothelvulf was the name of the Picts' reigning druid or chieftain. I grasped the middle of my blade, then pressed it to my forehead. "Wasu Oothelvulf."

He lifted his spear. "Pila Oothelvulf."

And now we smiled, one big happy heathen family, he of Oothelvulf's spearmen, and me of Oothelvulf's swordsmen.

I had no idea how much longer I could maintain my charade. Sooner or later, we were bound to come upon more Picts and eventually they would figure out I was a fraud. It constantly worried me. Eutychus had done a persuasive job of painting my body and thank God I had not been circumcised. If all this had happened a year later, I would have taken my vows to join the monks. More than my scalp would have been tonsured. That's a feature I could never disguise with just blue paint.

Although Snake-man's scrutiny of me seemed to ease, I grew ever more conscious of Foxy's fascination for my sword. He eyed it with a lusty avarice that worried me. I had no sheath, so I had to carry it in my hand. When we stopped to rest, drink, or eat, my hand seldom left it. Unsure how Picts defined ownership, I had no intention of allowing Foxy to make any claim to it. Despite my concern, I became tired and careless as the day dragged on. I leaned the sword against a fallen tree so I could use my hands and lower my face to the brook to drink. When I stood, the sword was gone. I whirled around.

Ten paces away, Foxy swished the blade in a mock sword fight.

"Hey!" I shouted and clapped twice, then stretched my palms demanding the sword's return.

Foxy froze. His gaze darted from me to Snake-man. The big leader frowned at him, pointed at me, and spoke some gibberish, hopefully not telling Foxy to use the blade on me.

The Pict grunted unhappily, stomped toward me, then thrust the sword at me, handle first. I grabbed my sword and nodded.

A trilling bird-like noise came from beyond the trees. Ferret-face had left us. Snake-man popped up from his repose and charged off after the sound. He returned and signaled for us to follow. Foxy and I chased after him through the trees, over the gully, and across a slope to the base of a rock pile taller than my height. Ferret-face lay prone, peeking over the top of the pile. He signaled for us to keep low as we approached. I fell to my knees and crawled beside him.

We were on the south side of the limestone hills where they gave way to a boggy lowland, the ground made level by years of silt carried from the hills' many streams. The sun hung high in the sky, the shadows of a few bruised clouds drifting across the flatland. At least four hundred paces beyond us, and separated from us by a wider ravine, a lone figure wearing a reddish-brown robe hiked through tall grass, heading away from our position. At this distance, I could not identify the man, but I had a guess. Tomas had escaped when the Picts wounded and captured me. I'd been unconscious, but after they had deposited me with the guards at their camp, they must have returned to the ambush site and begun tracking Tomas. He would have had a five- or six-hour head start, but I knew from experience that the prior traveled slowly and left a trail easy to follow.

Snake-man tapped my shoulder and pointed to a thick stand of yew trees growing out of the ravine to our right, about two hundred paces from our position. The ravine opened broader to a hollow peppered with rocks and the big trees' tangled roots. He flattened his hand and jabbed it twice at the yew trees. He wanted Ferret-face and me to cross the ravine at the yew trees, circle around the stranger, then cut off his escape in that direction. He popped his fist against his chest, pointed at Foxy, then at a saddled ridgeline to our left. I nodded. He and Foxy would approach our victim from the other direction.

Ferret-face crawled back from his perch, then sprang at a trot toward the yew trees. I followed close behind. I could easily have slain the man, but explaining his absence to the remaining two might prove difficult, especially with a vocabulary of only a few words. Hoping for a better opportunity to escape, I lowered my sword and chased after my blue comrade.

When we reached the yew trees, they provided cover, but their tangled roots presented a greater challenge to crossing the ravine than had appeared from a distance. The thick roots twisted and buckled, diving into the earth and springing back out in a tangled arboreal frenzy designed by demons to snatch at an ankle and throw the traveler into the ground. I tripped twice in the crossing. It required the utmost restraint to seal my lips and not curse in my native Latin, which would have unfrocked me with disastrous results. I mimicked the curses I'd heard in the cave.

We finally reached the opposite bank of the ravine. Looking over the bank's rim, Ferret-face whispered, his words followed by his ubiquitous ha-ha-ha-ha-ha. I gathered that he liked our chances of catching our prey. I pointed my sword forward and jabbed into the air. He nodded and crawled over the ravine's rim with me at his rear.

As we drew near, our target's sunburned tonsure contrasted brightly with his black hair. Prior Tomas ambled across the grassy plain, leaning noticeably to his right side. His arms flailed skyward. He broke into a run. To my left, Foxy and Snake-man burst over the crest of a shallow rise, howling at the top of their lungs in the Pict fashion. All surprise lost, my ferret-faced ally and I sprang to our feet and joined in the screaming pursuit.

Though a grassy plain, hidden rocks broke the turf, making our running far more difficult than expected. Ferret-face sprinted ahead of me, leaped a stone outcropping, bellowed ha-ha-ha-ha-ha, then flopped face forward into the dirt having tripped on a second, better-concealed slab of sandstone. His painful groan made me more cautious, slowing my pace and shortening my stride.

The concealed hazards in the field proved no less arduous for Tomas. He ran with faltering steps, tripping and falling multiple times. With each heaving breath, I closed on him. After running a considerable distance, I could hear his choppy breathing and flagging footsteps. He looked over his shoulder, his mouth gaped, his eyes wide and desperate.

Foxy caught him first, bounding at Tomas's flapping robe and tackling him at his waist.

The prior hit the ground hard, his loud, high-pitched shriek blasting the air. "Mercy! Please have mercy!"

I arrived next and pressed my sword's tip into the red wool covering his heaving chest. Ferret-face and Snake-man ran up almost at the same instant. They thrust their spear tips inches above the prior's terrified eyes.

We had caught our prey, but I had no idea what my companions intended to do with Tomas. What concerned me, even more, was that he did not carry anything in his hands or on his shoulders. Whatever burden may have caused him to list to his right when we first spotted him he had jettisoned somewhere along the route of our pursuit.

The Picts did not seem to recognize the disparity. They shouted gibberish at Tomas, accented with Ferret-face's annoying laughter. They rolled Tomas to his stomach and tied his hands behind his back. All the while the prior blubbered for mercy. His pleas died when he realized that he would not be executed. Though he looked at me many times, his panicked eyes showed no signs of recognition. Even if he had any reason to think that I might still be alive, the Clodius he knew wore a habit. I had become quite comfortable in my blue skin and fierce nudity. I must confess, I even experienced an unholy glee as I brandished my blade about the prior's trembling face.

Snake-man hoisted Tomas to his feet and shoved him before us toward the north, opposite to the direction the prior had been traveling. Although he might have been on the wrong side of a good age for slavery, the prior had provided a fair demonstration of his health and vigor. He would be worth something to the slavers. His capture had also pacified whatever lingering suspicions my pendulous companions might have harbored against me. Now one of their band, we exchanged congratulations even though I could only communicate through sign language. Nonetheless, I did not kid myself. My odd dialect would be exposed soon enough, whenever we reached the main Pict camp to dispose of our captive. My new friends would discover that they had not one, but two prisoners to sell.

I had to find a way to escape, and now Tomas's capture complicated my plans. While happy to steal away during the night, leaving the prior to the living hell of enslavement, I regretted the absence of his baggage. The whole purpose of his nefarious conduct had been to steal Adalbert's treasure and buy the bishop's endorsement of his transfer and rank. So what happened to the treasure?

Our route took us near to the stand of yew trees Ferret-face and I had crossed and back to the broader portion of the ravine. We skirted the base of the limestone hills, heading east toward the Roman highway. Before we reached the road, the sun descended below the horizon, and Snake-man decided that we would camp for the night next to a small rocky stream.

Foxy tied Tomas to the trunk of an oak tree and remained on guard while the rest of us gathered wood and started a fire. The big Pict distributed more dried fish without offering any to our captive. I swallowed the salty morsels, then brushed away dead leaves and twigs around me to fashion some semblance of a bed. I lay on my side, curling my knees, ready to sleep.

Someone jabbed my chest with the blunt end of a spear. Snake-man towered above me, glaring. He pointed at Tomas, then waved his hands about his head in a display of frustration. My confusion gave way to excitement. The big brute was annoyed because I had not been doing my share of guard duty. I did not want to appear too eager, so instead of enthusiastically accepting the assignment, I growled at him and curled up again on the cold ground. My disrespect earned me a second, much harder jab to my chest. Playing the role of a disgruntled and tired foot soldier, I grumbled, cursed in my augmented vocabulary with appropriate poignancy, then wrestled to my feet.

My acting proved to be convincing. Within minutes of my assuming the night watch, the three Picts rested deep in sonorous nocturnal bliss. I made three rather noisy circuits around our campsite, cracking dead wood, tossing stones, and hacking at thorny bushes with my sword. An occasion grumble or stuttered snore sounded, but a modest amount of noise was unlikely to rouse the warriors from their slumber. Time to attempt my escape.

Although I had killed two men in Coria, I had no confidence in my skill as a swordsman or my ability to kill the Picts even as they slept. I could certainly have murdered one, but I had no idea what kind of commotion I would arouse in my victim. How do you kill someone without making a sound? It must be possible, but not a lesson taught by the monks. Tomas might help. The two of us could kill two sleepers, then take our chances with the groggy third. However, the notion of arming the prior gave me shivers. He would just as gladly turn the blade against me. My best option seemed to be to free Tomas and for us to run. With a head start, we could place a safe distance between ourselves and our enemies before they awoke.

Tomas sat upright, lashed to the tree, his chin drooped to his chest, his breathing shallow, his hands tied behind his back. Crouching, I slip my cupped hand over his mouth. His head jerked up, and his eyes flared open.

I whispered into his ear, "Shhh. Keep quiet. I'll cut you free.".

His lids narrowed, deep furrows crossing his forehead as he stared at me with frightened, disbelieving eyes. He jerked a nod.

I lowered my hand from his mouth. "It's me, Clodius. Don't make a sound." I sawed the ropes binding him to the tree with my sword, then cut the bonds at his wrists. With my help, he rolled to his knees and gained his feet. We scurried into the darkness as quietly as stalking felines. Forty paces beyond the smoldering fire, we broke into a run.

"Clodius! How is it possible?"

"I'll tell you when we have the time. Keep running. The road's not far ahead. We can make it back to the monastery before dawn."

Tomas slowed. "St. Antony's? Is it still standing? Then I'm not too late."

I had just saved the man's life, and already he lied. He didn't know I had discovered his deception. I pretended ignorance. "The Picts haven't attacked it yet. There's still time to save our brothers with the bishop's order."

"B-but, I don't have it. I tossed it down a pit. We'll have to retrieve it."

"What?"

"When the Picts chased me, I passed a pit. I tossed my bag into it."

I stopped and bent double, grabbing my knees, taking deep breaths. "I can get us back to the bog. Are you sure you can find it?"

"Positive."

A new scheme hatched in my head. "Okay. It's this way," I said, pointing toward the southwest. "Come on."

I was taking a terrible risk.

I had to know the truth.

Chapter XXXII

Starlight illuminated the broken terrain grayish beneath a darker, clear sky. The prior and I walked through the night, halting if we happened upon fresh water to drink, or when we became tangled among invisible roots or vines. My legs stung from my ankles to my hips from the combination of nettles, scratching branches, and thorn bushes we blundered into. The ache of my ragged hip wound throbbed like repeated punches with every step.

Traveling beside a hypocrite who had lied, used me, and proved me a fool, did not sit well. A savage anger burned in my gut. Nor did I consider that he had probably killed Adalbert and Lazarus a trivial matter. I did not know for sure. He had deceived me to obtain his precious endorsement from the bishop, but I could only speculate as to the source of his money, and still did not know what role Lazarus's death played in this business.

Different plans to coax the truth out of him unfolded as we hurried along. Torture seemed an obvious candidate, but I didn't have the stomach for it. The prior had said that he'd thrown his bag into a pit. That image jelled in my head as we arrived at the ravine sprouting the tangled yew tree roots.

"This is where we first spotted you. You stood about two hundred paces in that direction when you began to run."

"Excellent, Clodius. It can't be far. Help me look."

The dark night concealed us as we climbed up the side of the ravine and onto the plain. Tomas whispered his count as he strode into the lowland. When he reached two hundred, he stopped and scanned the ground. "It must be here. Fan out. It's a big hole. You can't miss it."

Time crawled as we searched in vain. A gray streak split the darkness of the eastern horizon, followed by dawn's orange and pink fingers expanding across the brightening sky. If they weren't awake already, my blue buddies would most certainly be rising with the sunlight. The lost and lonesome warrior who spoke a nonsensical dialect turned out to be someone different than he pretended. They would not see the humor in it. Our clumsy nocturnal escape had undoubtedly left a trail that Ferret-face could follow. I scanned the northern horizon. The Picts would be upon us soon.

"Here!" Tomas shouted. "Here it is!"

I raced to him. He pointed down a four-foot-wide pit. I leaned over the dark hole. It might have been dug as some ancient hunter's trap, or it might have been washed out with years of rain. Whatever its origin, it looked deep and inhospitable.

"A perfect viper's den," I said.

"You'll have to go down, Clodius. My old legs are already beyond exhaustion."

I reached to the ground, grabbed a pebble, and dropped it into the hole. A brief silence preceded tapping as the stone bounced along descending rocks. Near the top of the pit, a rope-like root jutted from the dirt wall and drooped, disappearing into the shadows. Rocks and small crevices were visible a few feet down, scattered across portions of the hole's walls.

"I may not be able to climb out," I said.

"Don't be a coward. Here, hand me your sword." He reached toward my blade.

I jerked it away from him. "If there are any snakes down there, I'll need it."

He lowered his hand. The edges of his mouth curled into a grin. "Then down you go."

I had no idea what might lie in wait in the darkness. I drew a deep breath and dropped my painful buttocks to the ground, my legs dangling over the edge. "Keep a good lookout. The Picts will not be far behind us."

Tomas glanced about nervously. "Then hurry."

I shifted my weight left and right, scooting my sore rump to the edge. My right foot found a crevice for support. I slid over the side, clutching my sword with my right hand, my left grabbing gnarled roots tangled about the pit's opening. I found a second foothold and shifted my grip to the thick, rope-like root drooped over the edge. Faint light glinted from my blade, reflecting rocks at the pit's bottom in the dull flash. I lowered myself, searching with my foot for support. I found a toehold. I released the root.

"Aah!" I yelled, feigning a fall. My feet hit bottom. I squatted low, concealing myself in the depth's darkness.

"Clodius! Are you all right?" Tomas's dark silhouette blocked the dim gray circle of light at the pit's opening. "I can't see a thing! Are you injured?"

"I-I'm okay. A little bruised, but okay."

"Good. Now be quick. Look for my satchel."

I felt about the floor near my body, then crawled on my knees, groping in the darkness for the feel of leather, praying I would not touch anything alive. After a few nervous breaths, my hand closed around a broad leather strap. I lifted the heavy bag. Rustling coins clinked within.

I drew a deep breath while scanning the walls and hole above me. Several stone outcroppings would provide me secure footing to climb out. I would be able to reach the thick root at the hole's surface without much difficulty. I swallowed hard, readying for the most important performance of my life.

Beady eyes rose and shimmered inches from my face. A thick, shadowy rope wavered. A slender tongue glistened and vanished.

My hand shot forward. I grabbed the serpent below its head. Armored muscle writhed and squirmed. The snake wrapped around my arm. Its coils squeezed ferociously.

I reared back and hammered down, once, twice, three times, smashing the snake's head to the rocky floor.

The thick scaly rope went limp and released its grip. I tossed the corpse into a dark corner.

"What was that?"

I glanced at the prior's silhouette. I had planned to fake a venomous encounter. God had supplied the real thing. I didn't care for his sense of humor.

I screamed, "Yiiiiih!"

"Clodius! What happened?"

"I found your bag, but something bit my leg."

"Dear Lord! Hurry! Climb out!"

"My leg! It's on fire! I can't stand!"

"Don't panic! I'll find a branch to lower as a ladder. Quick! Throw me the satchel to lighten your load!"

I gripped the satchel's shoulder strap and spun it with my arm like a slinger. I hurled it upward as hard as I could toss it to make certain it would land far beyond the pit's entrance. It landed with a heavy thump, clinking coins scattering.

"The branch, Prior. Push down a branch!"

My unholy companion did not reply.

"Prior Tomas, did you find a branch? Hurry! It's dark … I'm afraid …"

The sound of spilled coins being gathered and sacked drifted down the hole.

"Prior Tomas?"

More gathering of coins, slapping leather, followed by a heaving grunt.

"Prior Tomas, are you there?" I tested the footing on the pit's walls.

"Yes, I'm here … but I'm afraid it's time for me to leave you, Clodius."

"What?" I placed my right foot in the first foothold.

"I do regret abandoning you. I could have never made it this far without you."

"You can't leave me here! You owe me your life!"

"I thank you, Clodius, but I cannot return the favor."

"You're leaving me to die? How can you? What about your faith?" I waited. Silence. I reached for the dangling root. My leg muscles flexed as I prepared to launch upward.

Feet scuffled outside the hole. "I'm sorry, Clodius. I truly am, but God has bigger plans than we can see. It's taken days for me to understand."

I relaxed, waiting for him to continue.

"Brother Adalbert's wanderings were a constant worry.

Imagine the scandals his secret trips to the town's taverns might bring upon St. Antony's. I sent Lazarus to watch him. God answered my prayers when Lazarus reported that Adalbert had found a treasure. I've repeatedly asked for permission to leave St. Antony's, but the abbot is a jealous and selfish man. He couldn't bear to let me go. I went over his head to the bishop, but the black-hearted fiend wanted one hundred silver pieces, an impossible sum, that is until God intervened, and Adalbert found his treasure. I told Lazarus to bring the treasure, but the demented fool made a worse thief than a spy. Adalbert discovered him in the act. They fought. Lazarus killed him. He dumped the corpse in the lake and left the money where Adalbert had found it."

"And Lazarus?"

"I told Lazarus to retrieve one hundred denarii for the bishop, but the greedy dolt kept a few coins for himself. Someone spotted him eating pastries in town. His foolishness risked everything while I waited for Bishop Bonifatius to make good his pledge. I sent Lazarus out to retrieve the remainder of the treasure and followed him. He led me to the cave. On his return to the monastery, I ambushed him. He killed Adalbert. A life for a life. God's justice."

"So, the stories about the books and Mutter's heresy were just a lie. You used me."

"I'm truly in your debt. Rest assured, I'll say prayers for your soul every day. When I reach Jerusalem, I'll burn a candle for you at Christ's holy sepulchral. Goodbye, Clodius. God bless you."

Footsteps crushed grass stalks and grew fainter with distance. I clenched my sword with my teeth, scrambled up the root and footholds, then bounded out of the pit's opening like a snake springing from its lair.

Tomas walked away at a swift pace; his shoulders tilted to the right from the weight of his bag.

"Ha-ha-ha-ha-ha!"

The laughter sent chills down my spine. Three distant blue figures bounced through the grassland, speeding in my direction.

Tomas whirled around. His eyes shot wide. His hand flew to his satchel. He withdrew a dagger. He pointed the blade at me.

I jerked the sword from my mouth, lifting it over my head, and charged at him.

Tomas's jaw dropped, panic in his eyes. He flung the blade at me. It sliced skin near my brow, passing over my ear. He spun and fled. I sprang after him. By his third step, I caught up to him. I pulled down with my sword, smashing its flat side against his skull. His legs crumpled. He collapsed with a semi-conscious moan.

With no time to relish the victory, I slashed his shoulder strap, grabbed the bag of coins, secured it under my arm, and ran for my life.

Chapter XXXIII

Things had not gone according to my hastily conceived plan. I had secured Adalbert's treasure and Tomas's confession, but my fantasy had ended with me marching the crestfallen villain at the end of a leash through the monastery's gate. Bremen would cheer. Mutter would forgive. Even Bethany's inviting lips had somehow found their way into my daydreams, though the means of her arrival at the triumph remained fuzzy at best.

The Picts' arrival had necessitated rash improvisation. I had hoped they might be satisfied with Prior Tomas's recapture. They could sell him or sacrifice him to their heart's contentment. I did not care. I sprinted away, glancing behind. Tomas staggered to his feet, stumbled, and dropped dead with Ferret-face's spear planted into the back of his neck. There'd be no parade or trial for the evil prior.

The thin-faced Pict hesitated only long enough to jerk his bloody spear from Tomas's corpse. He chased after Foxy and Snake-man, who had not even stopped to watch Tomas die. They wanted me!

The boggy grassland I raced through concealed all sorts of stickers, pointy twigs, and sharp-edged stones that cut and bruised my blistered feet. Sheer terror blunted the pain and spurred my heart. My fatigued arms and legs ached. The wound in my hip throbbed. The weight of my sword and the prior's satchel slowed me.

I jettisoned my sword. I had no illusions about my skill as a fighter. If the Picts caught me, they would kill me. Tomas's bag I clasped tightly. I could not deliver the murderer to the monastery, but the blood money might still purchase a small measure of redemption. A few minutes later, a victorious cheer split the air. Foxy held the sword triumphantly above his head.

"You're welcome," I said. "Now it can slow you down."

I jumped over the edge of a rocky ravine, splashing into a muddy pool. The cool water felt good on my feet and legs, but I had no time for refreshment. I scrambled over the top of a dead, gray log, then shot over the far bank and back into the boggy grassland. Ahead lay the base of the rugged hills and the fringe of a pine forest. The Roman highway lay somewhere to my right, beyond my sight, the fastest path back to the monastery and my best chance to escape. I veered in that direction.

The sun rose higher. Its heat added to my stress, sweat covering my body. My lungs burned, my sides ached, my feet bled, my hip throbbed, but I could never stop, not until my tortured heart drummed its last beat.

My stride faltered. Three shrieking beasts chased behind me. I'd made fools of them and robbed them of their prize. What horrors had they planned for me if they caught me? Fear reenergized my blood. My feet grew lighter.

Trees flashed past me, streams under me, an endless blue ceiling rolling above my head. Time became meaningless. A vast distance lay before me. My only hope to reach the safety of the ramshackle monastery somewhere beyond the next hill, the next tree, the next stream. I ran and kept running. Another step seemed impossible.

The blur of my surroundings and my fatigue jumbled my thoughts. My mother's demented cackle fell upon me. Rubicus sneered at me. He laughed. His voice echoed, "I told you so." A burly tradesman grabbed my wrist and yanked me from the bed of his wagon, berating me for thievery. My dreary cell smelled of piss and mildew. Lucius chanted a hymn. Cassius and Fabian glowered at me for interrupting their work. Julia smiled at me. A candle burned. Eutychus punched me in the face. An arrow jutted from Olaf's chest. Fritigern's dead eyes stared into space. Bonifatius's chest fell with his last breath. Bremen slaved in a dank iron pit. Mutter's disappointed eyes glared at me in his office. Bethany's blue eyes glowed invitingly.

Keep running.

My pace slackened; there was no reserve left in my legs. My life drained, my breath failed, my consciousness blurring with no place to hide, no clever disguise to don, no intoxicating blood of Christ, no slithering snake to save, only the pounding of my heart, the pouring of my sweat.

Ha-ha-ha-ha-ha!

God laughed at me. God or Tomas? No, he was dead, or did I dream that, too?

Find the murderer. I had done my bit. I'd found two. Lazarus had killed Adalbert, and Tomas did the foul deed to his accomplice. I had not just found the killer; I had executed him. Me! The naïve novice, the faithless friend, the coy confessor, the feckless flame. Me! The blue streak, the balls' knee, the books' burner. Me!

Run, Clodius! Run!

Eutychus smiled. He laughed. He jumped from white stones, splashing water in my eyes. Julia floated there, too, gleaming in white silk, the sun's rays bouncing from the lake's ripples, glimmering on her flawless skin.

My feet hit flat stones, cold and hard, weeds poking from cracked seams, water puddled in divots, bushes sprouting from curbs. Bethany reached for me, extending her arms, stretching with her fingers. Her eyes beckoned me onward. Her winged body flew before me, just beyond my grasp, a wispy spirit caught in a retreating gale. I chased her.

Ha-ha-ha-ha-ha!

Laugh at me. But don't catch me. No, no, no, no. I couldn't be caught.

Coughing behind me. Gagging and gasps. Close but fading. Far or near? Echoing in my head. Threatening. Terrifying.

Run, Clodius! Run!

One foot after another. The road's stones passed beneath me. Instinct alone drove me onward. Why was I running? Some danger. Naked men with spears?

I stumbled on a rutted dirt track. My leg muscles cramped. My lungs burned. I gasped for air. Drowning. God help me! Help me!

A wall, a gate, someone brandishing a broom—no a

pitchfork.

I dived headlong. My face scraped loose rocks and dirt. I lay flat, unable to move. A gate slammed.

Darkness took me.

Chapter XXXIV

I awoke to the underside of clay tiles and oak beams above me. I lay on a bed, my feet wrapped in bandages and throbbing with pain. A clean linen sheet covered my legs and abdomen. The side of my head felt tight, stretched like a drum. I reached to my scalp and fingered a long row of stitches sealing a wound.

"Ah, you're awake at last." Brother Finnian's blue eyes smiled at me. "Afraid you'll have a nasty scar there. Must have been quite a fight."

I dropped my hand to my side. The image in my mind remained hazy, then the pit, my sword, and the prior's terrified face came into focus. "Not really. More a near miss. Tomas threw a knife at me."

"The prior? Blessed Mother of God, whatever for?"

"It's a long story."

"Brother Bremen said three of those blue devils chased you. From his description, they were just as exhausted as you."

"Is the abbot here?"

"In his office. I'll fetch him. You've given him one more nasty shock. You have an amazing capacity for finding trouble, Clodius."

"You have no idea."

Finnian left, and I spent a few moments examining my arms and hands. Every movement generated dull, aching pain. Shallow cuts and scabs marked where sharp thorns and branches had lacerated my skin.

Abbot Mutter appeared at the door. The wrinkles on his long, drawn face had multiplied and deepened, his mouth dourer than I had ever seen. He stepped to my side and patted my arm weakly. His gray, bloodshot eyes glistened. Dark rims shadowed his sunken, bony eye sockets. "You look a fright, my son, but I am glad to see you. I thought you and Eutychus might have gone for good."

"Have you seen him?"

"No. I thought you might tell me where to find him."

"I'm not sure. We split up at Coria. They … he went to Segedunum."

"Then we must pray for him. There's been no word from the coast."

"Coria has been destroyed."

"Yes, I know. Brother Nebridius led a team to bury the dead." He sighed. "There'll be no rebuilding this time. The town burned to the ground. The Picts left no one alive."

"They'll be back, Father. You must leave for Eboracum before they return."

"Must I? What makes you so sure."

"The only reason they didn't destroy the monastery is that they looted Coria. They couldn't carry anything more. Next time, there will be nothing to distract them from St. Antony's. You must leave. You can use the money I brought."

Finnian delivered a stool. The abbot's bones creaked as he sat. "I wondered about the bag of coins. Who do they belong to?"

"They're yours, Father."

He stroked his chin and chuckled. "Odd. I don't remember misplacing such a large purse."

"Adalbert found it. It's why Tomas killed him. Tomas stole the money. Bishop Bonifatius sold him a letter authorizing his transfer to another monastery."

"And the prior? Where is he now?"

"Dead. Killed by the same Picts who chased me."

"Poor Tomas."

My throat tightened. "Olaf and Fritigern, too. They died in Coria."

The abbot's eyes watered. "Dear God, the bloodshed never stops."

I closed my eyelids to gather my thoughts. "There's more bad news."

The abbot's wiry white eyebrows arched. "More?"

"Your library has been destroyed. The Picts found it and

burned every book."

His lips flattened, he shut his eyes and rubbed his forehead. "Yes, I know about that already" He lowered his hand. "Cassius and Fabian discovered the loss yesterday."

"I'm sorry, Father. I feel responsible."

Mutter smiled. "Oh, don't spank yourself. It's no one's fault but mine. My foolish pride caught up with me, but God is just."

"God didn't apply the torch."

"Perhaps not by his hand, but most certainly by his instrument. I was so certain our prayers and our faith would save us, but not so certain that I dared to risk my precious books. It's God's little jest. We remained quite safe at St. Antony's. The library I hid is lost for all time. If I had been true to my faith, the books would still be in my library."

"God spared you, Father. Books can be rewritten. The dead are dead."

"Yes, books can be rewritten, and someday no doubt they will be, to be followed by more book burnings and bloodshed. That's the tragedy of it." He shifted his head and stared out the infirmary window toward the garden. "I suppose you were shocked to discover that your abbot harbored heretical manuscripts."

"No, Abbot. I didn't ..." I stopped myself from saying "didn't think badly of you," remembering that I'd accused him of murder.

He grinned. "I didn't know Arius, but Pelagius was my mentor and a good friend. He didn't set out to foment heresy, you know. To the contrary, I've never met a more saintly or wiser man. He lived a pauper's life despite the wealth of his station. The plight of the poor broke his heart. He gave away everything that came to him. I've tried to model my life after him, but sadly, I'm a poor copy of his perfection."

The abbot stood and walked to the window, then drew in a deep breath and smiled. "Pelagius was deeply troubled by what he saw in so-called Christian cities. The poor were neglected, even oppressed by the wealthy who saw their riches as a form of God-given privilege. The Lord's mercy was treated as a quick and easy way to indulge in sin because no one can be perfect. Right? We're all sinners, every one of us. So, go ahead and sin. It's all right. Your sins are forgiven. God can expect no better of us."

He turned back. "Pelagius taught inherent good resided in all of us. With God's help, we could achieve Christ's perfection—not just in the hereafter—but here—now—leaving no excuse for our chronic sin. For that belief, they branded him a heretic."

The abbot rubbed the back of his neck. He glanced at the ceiling, then fixed his sad gaze on mine. "I don't have Ambrose's wisdom, Augustine's wit, or Jerome's knowledge of the scriptures, but what I do know is that by destroying Pelagius's books, they destroyed the only record of his reasoning. I think it's better to have a dangerous route marked and illuminated. If you hide the road, it becomes a trap for the unwary traveler. By destroying Pelagius's writings, they have ensured that someday someone will wander down the same path. The controversy will live anew. That's why the bishop and I decided to preserve his books and those of other heretics that we came by."

He lowered his gaze to the floor. "Sadly, my lack of faith has doomed us to repeat the mistakes of our past. God has punished me for my hubris."

The abbot looked defeated. His depression worried me. Did God really patiently wait for some small sin to creep into our lives, some excuse to slap us down and destroy our dreams after a lifetime of good deeds?

"Pardon, Father, I'm just a novice, but I think you have misunderstood God's will."

The abbot's eyebrows shot upward. "What? What did you say?"

"Our job is to love people, not books. Maybe God wanted to remind us of that. God hasn't punished you. He has liberated you. It's time to leave this place, Father. God is calling you to go to the south to be with his people."

The abbot blankly stared at me for what seemed a long time but may have been just seconds. It had been incredibly presumptuous of me—the same person who had thought God wanted me to depose the abbot—to suggest that he had misunderstood God's will. If the last week of my life had taught me anything, it was that I was not on the same page as God.

"Thank you, Clodius." The abbot smiled. He reached to my scalp and combed his fingers across the crown of my head. "Thank you, son." He turned and left the room.

Chapter XXXV

After one week, I could stand without pain shooting from my bandaged feet up through my legs. After nine days, I could walk, though my soles were as cracked and brittle as sun-bleached cowhide. On the tenth day after I'd escaped death, I stepped outside St. Antony's main gate wearing a belted wool tunic, woolen trousers, and carrying a knapsack slung across my back.

The monks had stacked their wagon high with robes, furnishings, sacred ornaments, caged chickens, and a few provisions they had rescued from Coria's ruins. They readied to journey south. We exchanged warm and sometimes tearful farewells. I reserved my longest and final embrace for Abbot Mutter, the man I would miss the most.

"Where will you go?" the abbot asked.

"Eutychus went to Segedunum. I'll start there."

"According to the last news we received from the coast, sea raiders in longboats have sacked the city. You may not find much left when you arrive."

"Eutychus is pretty resourceful. I'm sure he survived. I'll find him."

"You would have made a fine monk, Clodius. Maybe even been abbot someday."

I grinned and marveled at the abbot's graciousness. I had disobeyed him, accused him of murder and heresy, and watched as his life's work had been torched. I couldn't imagine how he could see any good in me. "That would take a real miracle," I said.

"God be with you, my son. We'll miss you. If things do not go well for you, come back to us. We'll be near Eboracum."

"Thank you. I'll remember that. Goodbye, Father."

Bremen steered Castratus and the wagon out of the compound. A ragged line of russet-robed men and a floppy-eared dog followed in the wheels' dust. The last man in the line, Gunther I think, disappeared beyond the trail's gradient.

A gust of wind kicked up a plume of dust. The gate creaked at its rusty hinges. The church's limestone walls glowed with brilliant sunlight. The villa's saffron finish shined with renewed life. Laughter echoed. My hairy friend splashed water in the balneary. Olaf smiled, his adoring blue eyes gleaming. Adalbert's spirit lifted from his grave and floated skyward.

My heart warmed. I drew a deep breath, swelling my chest.

I'd spent many days reflecting as I healed in the infirmary. Triumphs, failures, tragedies, joys, I weighed them all. But of all my adventures, what I treasured most were three words carried to my ears on a night's gentle breeze. Find the murderer. God did not whisper them. God used Fritigern's mouth and tongue to speak. I obeyed.

I pulled the gate shut and turned to the sloping dirt trail. The past lay behind me, my future to the east. Her name was Bethany.

AUTHOR'S NOTES

Coria, located on the River Tyne (modern-day Corbridge), was established in the second century A.D. as a Roman fort, approximately two-and-a-half miles south of Hadrian's Wall. The army unit stationed there departed in the third century, but the town thrived, becoming an important commercial center at the intersection of two Roman highways, Dere Street, leading south to Eboracum (York), and Stanegate, which ran east-west connecting Luguvalium (Carlisle) and Coria, where it may have changed to an unpaved trail leading to the mouth of the Tyne (Wallsend). The Roman names for these roads have been forgotten. The town thrived into the fifth century A.D. but collapsed at some date following Rome's abandonment of Britannia, which began about 402 A.D. and was completed by 411 A.D.

We do not know exactly what happened to Coria when the Romans left. Current thought is that the city was simply abandoned. The excavation of the present site dates to before the First World War. Very little is known about the large civilian settlement that must have sprawled the length of the roads and crowded the riverbanks and surrounding fields. However, archaeology in other nearby cities and forts such as Vindolanda, Chester, and Birdoswald has revealed that populations remained in towns and thrived for years after the Romans' departure.

The Romans built Coria's fort on a steep rise just north of the Tyne. Roman development included fountains, aqueducts, paved streets, sewers, public baths, and large granaries. There are unusual features such as undulating streets caused by successive development and subsidence. The Tyne occasionally floods with heavy rains. Maintenance of the sewers and streets ended with the Romans' exit. Plugged sewers and potholed streets could have caused localized flooding of parts of the town inside the wall and swamping of any structures near the river and the low-lying fields.

Southwest of Coria are limestone hills known today as the Pennines. During Late Antiquity, they would have been a rugged, wooded wilderness laced with streams and hiding crags and "pots" (Yorkshire for caves).

The monastery, St. Antony's, is fictional. Saint Antony, or Antony, was a hermit who lived in Egypt during the third century. He is sometimes called the father of all monks. In the fifth century, monasteries had little continuity, most living by their own rules and following their own brands of asceticism. Many centuries later, the Jesuit, Franciscan, and Benedictine orders established greater uniformity.

The basilica, St. Alban's, is also fictional. By tradition, Saint Alban was martyred outside the Roman town of Verulam (St. Alban's) in 209 A.D. There is no evidence of a church on the excavation site of Corbridge. In Vindolanda archaeologists discovered the remains of a Christian church and signs that Christians destroyed pagan temples in the late fourth century A.D. The fort at Coria once included a basilica, a large, fully enclosed structure for military assemblies that in my fantasy the early church has converted to a church and the seat of the first locally elected bishop.

Pelagius was a British monk. He traveled to and studied in Rome, Carthage, and Jerusalem, counting St. Augustine and St. Jerome among his acquaintances. Unfortunately for him, they condemned his theology because he rejected St. Augustine's doctrine of original sin (among other things) and instead held that it was possible for sanctified humans to live a sinless life. In 411 A.D., a synod in Carthage declared him a heretic. In 418 A.D., Pope Zosimus condemned and excommunicated Pelagius and his disciple Celestius. Little of what he wrote has survived.

Arius was an ascetic, born in North Africa in the third century A.D. He taught a theology based on Jesus Christ being like, but not the equal of God the Father, thus undermining the orthodox doctrine of the Holy Trinity. Arianism thrived throughout the Roman Empire but later encountered violent rejection. In 325 A.D., Arius was exiled.

When the Roman army departed Britannia, a dark age commenced for the northern islands. Very little of what followed is known except that the British Isles were overrun by Scots, Picts, Saxons, Danes, Jutes, and other tribes. Over many decades Roman culture, government, and religion were virtually, if not totally, extinguished. Our earliest recorded "history" of that era comes from the Venerable Bede writing in the eighth century A.D. The Christian church did not reestablish a secure foothold in the British Isles until the mid-sixth century A.D.

The Picts were a loose confederation of many different tribes who lived in Scotland, which the Romans called Caledonia. Their language is extinct. The word "Pict" is derived from the Latin word *Picti* meaning painted people.

Where possible, I've used Roman names for all locations. In some instances, I've used anachronistic terms (e.g., River Tyne for Fluvius Vedra) that may be more helpful to the reader.

All other characters in *Foul Pray* are fictional. The events take place in 419 A.D.

Acknowledgments

I wish to thank the many people who have assisted me in bringing Clodius's adventure to a conclusion. Members of critique groups over many years have provided encouragement and comments. They are an invaluable resource. I also wish to thank my editor, Susan Mary Malone, and my publisher, ACD Books.

About the author

Mark Harwell's stories have appeared in *The Copperfield Review*, *Mystery Weekly*, *Hair-Raising Tales of Horror* (Limitless Ink Publishing 2016), and *Out of Many One* (HWG Press 2017). He has won (Houston Writer's Guild) and received honorable mention in (86th Annual *Writer's Digest*, *AHMM*, Houston Writer's Guild) writing contests. He is a graduate of Rice University and the University of Texas School of Law. He lives in Lago Vista, Texas with his wife and a variety of wild and domesticated critters.